A LARK
OVER
NEW YORK

By

Bill Harrod

ISBN-13: 9798510183962

To my dear wife Sylvia and our family who must be tired of hearing the phrase, 'the book'.
I would also like to mention our dear friends Seamus and Mary Holden, who from the start have shown great interest in my book.
Finally, my friend Peter Boyce, who was good enough to give up his time to read and report back his opinions.

CONTENTS

PART 1

THE MEETING

Chapter 1

Norfolk, England, 1836

The sun shone brightly in its big fenland sky, shedding an artist's light over the Norfolk landscape. *Unusual for March,* Frances Cartner thought as she made her way to Renton. Now, aged sixteen, she was on her way to her first job interview for the position of personal maid to Mrs Hannah Hayward, the wife of the farm bailiff, James Hayward.

Frances lived with her Aunt Polly in the village of North Fenham, situated about three miles north of Renton. She had lived with her aunt since the age of six; following the sudden death of Uncle Walter. He had been the tenant of the White Swan Inn in North Fenham until his death from pneumonia at the age of forty-two. Following his death, the Lynn Brewery offered the tenancy to Aunt Polly, which she turned down and she was rehoused in a rented cottage, one of many owned by the brewery.

Now ten years on, Frances was making her way to Renton House

Farm. Until now, there had been no need for her to seek work. But, despite Aunt Polly's thriftiness, the money left by Uncle Walter had gradually dwindled and they now needed extra income to get by on. Frances was uneasy about leaving her aunt, for only a month ago, Aunt Polly had suffered a bad attack of the ague, a common ailment among fenland people. Most sufferers would 'doctor' themselves with poppy tea, an infusion made from the seeds of poppies grown commercially in parts of Norfolk and used in the manufacture of laudanum; but this attack had been so severe Aunt Polly had to call on the expertise of Doctor Dobson.

Full of apprehension, she broke into song, a subconscious reaction to her nervousness. She had a tuneful voice, on which many people had commented; nobody more so than Zachary Tomes, the choirmaster at St Mary's Church. He constantly attempted to recruit her into *his* choir. Ever possessive of the choir, he referred to it as *'my flock within a flock'*. Aunt Polly, had also put pressure on her niece, believing anything to do with the church should come first and foremost. Frances finally succumbed and reluctantly became a choir member. This morning, the music she had subconsciously chosen was appropriately the hymn, *'O God, Our Help in Ages Past, Our Hope for Years to come'*. On finishing, she released a long sigh from deep within at the thought of the impending interview. This was completely new to her as she and her aunt had done everything together; she knew that should the interview prove successful, she would be leaving the care and protection of her Aunt Polly for the very first time.

*

Dan Swain stopped at the end of yet another long furrow and mopped the sweat from his brow. It was the March ploughing, and he was getting the land ready for the seed sowing and the harrowing-in. He preferred the cool and overcast weather for his ploughing; this unseasonal weather made the ploughing hot work. Turning his pair of horses, he was distracted by the beauty of a young girl walking up the lane on the other side of the low-layered hedge. The sight of another human being, especially one so pretty, offered him a welcome distraction from the monotony of his ploughing.

'What brings you to Renton House this fine day?' he called to her; his team half-turned.

'And what makes you think it is any business of yours?' she called back in defiance of this nosey stranger, acting braver than she ever thought she could be.

The young ploughman was immediately struck by the girl's beauty and her spiritedness intrigued him. Her long black hair hung in tight curls and he liked the way she gently swung her head in a rather teasing fashion. The sun glinting off her hair caused it to take on a bluish lustre, which reminded him of the windblown feathers on a crow's back. A strange comparison, he thought, but true, nonetheless. Her eyes, a deep shade of brown, were almost as black as her hair, reminding him of the gypsy girls he had seen at the annual Durnham horse fair; he stood transfixed. After a brief silence, she answered him.

'I'm Frances Cartner – going to see the missus about the job as personal maid,' she shouted, surprising herself at this sudden disclosure of her business to a stranger.

'Oh, are you now?' he teased. For a moment neither spoke. He drank in the beauty of the young girl before him. She thought he was mocking her and wished she had been less forthcoming with her information. His pair of horses shifted legs impatiently, causing the trace chains to jingle noisily, jolting Dan back to reality.

'Must get on, can't have these two stiffen up on me; there's lots more to do before the light goes,' he shouted above all the clatter as he resumed turning the pair of heavy horses in readiness for the next furrow.

'Oh, by the way, I'm Dan Swain, pleased to have made your acquaintance Miss Cartner, good luck up at the house,' he called rather breathlessly above the noise. Making a clicking sound and a call of, 'Come on my beauties,' he continued back down the field.

Dan Swain was nineteen and had worked at Renton House Farm for the last six years. His father Philip, who also worked at the farm had secured Dan the job on leaving school at thirteen.

During his ploughing, Dan found his mind preoccupied by his recent meeting with the beautiful girl. After a while, he even began to doubt if he had seen her at all. Maybe it was an apparition brought on by the monotony of the ploughing. Hadn't old Ted Fuller, whose daughter was married to a sailor out of Lynn, told him a tale of mariners on long sea voyages, claiming to have seen mermaids? *'Boo-ful crea'toores thay were, with upper bodies 'f women and lower bodies 'f fish,'* was the way Ted had described them in his broad Norfolk accent.

One of Dan's horses stumbled, quickly shifting his concentration to the job in hand. Despite his strength he struggled for a moment to maintain his precision with the plough. With the plough once more under control, his mind returned to the young girl. He hoped she would get the job at the farm, allowing him to see her more often, the thought of which pleased him immensely. *Frances... Frances Cartner,* he mused, and the plough seemed lighter in his arms. He hoped Mrs Hayward would take as kindly to Frances as he had. *Surely, no one could find her disagreeable,* he thought, trying to pre-empt the outcome in Frances's favour. With good conditions and no distraction Dan, and his pair of shire horses, Noble, the bay gelding and Silver, the dappled grey mare, could plough all day without seeing anything but the swirling gulls and the rumps of his horses. Today was different, the beautiful young girl had been a distraction, which he could not and did not want to blank from his mind.

Today his ploughing was not getting his undivided attention.

Frances continued her way to the farmhouse, her meeting with the forward young ploughman still on her mind. For the first time in her life, she had met a boy with whom she had not been instantly dismissive. As a girl, she had always found boys irritatingly overconfident and barely tolerated them when she had the misfortune to find herself in their company. On reflection, the only boy she had ever found interesting, was a boy named Robert Hart with whom she had gone to school. He was two years older than she and he had been the school's cleverest pupil. Rev. Boothferry, recognising his talent and not wanting it to go to waste had managed to get Robert a job at the *'Big Hall'*. His Lordship had sponsored him to attend the newly established Cirencester Agricultural College in Gloucestershire, to study modern agricultural techniques, which His Lordship was promoting. Frances's interest in Robert Hart had only been an admiration of his academic ability. Her poor opinion of boys was the result of the time spent with her widowed aunt in a male-free environment. Her meeting today with this young ploughman, although brief, had left a feeling within her, the likes of which she had not experienced before, and she struggled to understand why.

Try as she may she could not rid her mind of her meeting with the pleasant ploughman, Dan… She sought to recall his surname… Swain… Dan Swain. She remembered his parting good wishes, hardly audible over the jingling noise of the wheeling horses. In her reverie, she pictured his dark intense features. She even remembered his strong sinewy arms flexing as he manoeuvred the heavy plough into position. Why had her meeting with this stranger affected her this way? How could someone she had never met until a short while ago, have this effect on her? Where was her dismissive attitude towards boys now? Frances had the answer to all these questions. She realised Dan Swain was no boy, he was a young man, and she was no longer a child.

*

Renton House Farm; made of red brick and flint with a pantile roof was smart, as farms go. A small cottage situated alongside the main house, was not of the same impressive construction. Being of black clapboard with a slate roof, it was typical of many other cottages in the area; built to house the farm workers. This one being slightly larger and its proximity to the main house suggested it was probably an important worker who lived there. As Frances passed the cottage, she read the wooden plaque on the gate. With letters burnt into the wood in scrawled writing, it read 'Renton House Cottage' and the thought crossed her mind that the name was both repetitive and unoriginal.

Her earlier apprehension quickly returned, ridding her mind of an alternative name for the cottage and certainly, any thoughts of the young ploughman. She reached the cobbled farmyard where two young lads were going about their work; at least one was. He was trundling a large, overloaded wheelbarrow on a zigzag course across the cobbled yard, shedding its superfluous load in its wake. As if in protest, the wheelbarrow threatened to tip all its contents at each turn of the wheel. The other lad was leaning on a large tined fork at the stable entrance, obviously taking an unauthorised break from his task of mucking out the stables. As Frances made her way across the cobbles towards the side door to the farmhouse, the youth at the stable doorway called mockingly, 'Like a carry over the muck, Your Ladyship?'

Frances ignored his impish remark, hoping to discourage any further mockery from the young upstart. He made her feel like a trespasser as she nervously crossed the yard towards the farmhouse. In defiance of the youth's sarcasm, she hitched up her skirt and hopped confidently over the trail of manure. Passing the farmhouse window, she caught a glimpse of someone rushing past in the direction of the door. She was about to knock, when it swung open and a young woman yelled – almost in Frances's face, 'Get on with your work, Fred Gill, or you'll have the master to answer to.' Her threat had the desired effect, as the said Fred Gill quickly turned and scurried back inside the stables. 'And you be sure to clear all the mess up after you, Dave Binney, I've told you before about trying to fill the barrow too full,' she scolded noisily. This had the opposite effect on young Binney as the shock caused him to lose control of the recalcitrant wheelbarrow. It wobbled for the last time, before coming to rest on its side, tipping all the contents onto the yard.

'Now see what you've done, you clod,' the girl chided. 'You'll never learn; now you've more work to do,' she added, holding back a smile, and feeling mildly pleased she had been responsible for his calamity. She shifted her gaze to the young girl standing in front of her. 'Sorry about that – teach him a lesson,' she said, releasing her suppressed smile on Frances. She wrung her hands in her rough apron, wiping away imaginary dirt and offered her right hand, saying, 'I'm Sally Groves and you must be Frances Cartner, come on in, the mistress is expecting you.' She ushered Frances through the kitchen and into a room at the front of the house. 'Frances Cartner, Mrs Hayward,' Sally announced.

'Come in, come in,' a voice said, rather impatiently. Hannah Hayward sat in a wing-backed chair, on the opposite side of the room, facing the window, overlooking open fields.

'Quickly, don't be afraid, we haven't got all day,' she ordered impatiently. Frances, already filled with apprehension, doubted whether she would impress the mistress of Renton House.

What little confidence she had arrived with, seemed to be rapidly diminishing.

'Now, let me see you, girl. Come around here and don't be afraid. I won't bite you.'

Frances hurried round to stand to the side of Hannah Hayward's chair. 'Come closer to the window where I can see you better. I'm getting a crick in my neck trying to talk to you over my shoulder. We'll have a little chat and get to know one another,' she suggested warmly. Hannah Hayward fitted the mental picture Frances had of a farmer's wife. Robust, plump and of ruddy complexion. She wondered why one so strong looking would ever need assistance from a slip of a girl like herself. Frances detected a hint of warmth in Mrs Hayward's voice, which made her feel slightly more comfortable about the impending questioning, notwithstanding the uncontrollable knocking of her knees.

'Pull up that chair over there and let's have our chat,' Hannah

Hayward said, indicating towards an oak dining chair in the corner of the room.

Frances carried the heavy chair laboriously over and placed it down opposite Mrs Hayward. Once seated, she squeezed her legs tightly together to control the trembling. Hannah Hayward waited until she thought Frances was comfortable before she continued the interview. 'Now Frances, on first impressions, I find your appearance most pleasing,' she continued, reassuringly. 'I understand from your letter, you are sixteen years old and you have lived with your widowed aunt, Mrs Polly Wragby, since the death of your uncle, some ten years ago.'

'Yes ma'am,' Frances replied nervously.

'And this is your first job of work? I was hoping you might have arrived with a bit more experience at sixteen years of age. I can see from your written reply you have a pleasant hand and well-schooled, maybe too well-schooled for this employment,' Hannah Hayward suggested, causing Frances's hopes of success to plummet.

'Oh no ma'am, not at all. If my grammar and my writing please you, it is because my good aunt saw to it that I attended school regularly. She had several books which she encouraged me to read but there aren't many jobs about these parts, and I wouldn't want to leave my dear aunt completely on her own, while I sought more lucrative work further afield,' Frances replied rather proudly. 'At least, if I should be successful in my interview, I would be less than three miles away from her if she should need me in an emergency,' she added.

'And over the years, has she taught you good housekeeping skills?' Mrs Hayward continued.

'I am pleased to say, Aunt Polly saw to it that I was well skilled in many aspects of cooking but of the simple kind; nothing fancy,' Frances replied.

As her confidence grew Frances hoped she did not appear too presuming.

'We are simple folk here, so I think the need for elaborate fare we will leave for the table over at Holkham.' Frances was relieved at Hannah Hayward's response and her confidence continued to grow.

'Well Frances, I'm not one to dither over a decision. Once I have made up my mind, which is usually quickly, I am not likely to change it. I will tell you, you are the third girl I have interviewed for the vacancy and without mentioning any names, the other two were nothing but flibbertigibbets, unsuitable even as scullery maids. I had pretty much made my decision early in our discussion. Mind you, you will have to keep your beautiful hair stuffed well up inside your mobcap when you are cooking a rabbit pie. Wouldn't want the rabbits to turn to hares,' and she laughed at her own play on words.

'Now you will be wondering what the job entails, are you not?' She posed the question and without giving Frances time to reply, she continued. 'In your new position you will be my personal maid. This will give you seniority over Sally Groves. I have already explained this to her, and she fully understands. Sally is a hard-working girl who is not likely to give you any trouble. She keeps the two boys about their business as you probably noticed on first meeting her. You will also have seniority over the boys until they are of age at which time, they will be treated the same as the other men working at the farm,' she explained. 'On Sundays you will be free to spend the day as you wish, with the only proviso being you attend church on a regular basis. You can attend All Saints in Renton in the company of Mr Hayward and I or you may want to attend St Mary's in North Fenham with your aunt,' Mrs Hayward declared.

'With due respect to yourself and Mr Hayward, ma'am, I would prefer to accompany my aunt to church in North Fenham, as in the past it has been our normal practice to attend Saint Mary's for both matins and evensong, another reason being, I sing in the choir there. I would like to use my free day to visit my Aunt Polly and this arrangement would give me the opportunity,' Frances explained, hoping Mrs Hayward would approve.

'It seems a perfect arrangement, although I would expect you to forego evensong during the dark months of winter, to allow you time for the return journey to Renton House,' her mistress stated. This disappointed Frances as it would curtail the time spent with her aunt.

'As a member of the choir, ma'am, the choirmaster Mr Tomes would expect me to attend evensong and I could leave immediately after the service for my return to Renton. I'm not afraid of the dark and I shall carry a lantern to light my way,' Frances countered.

'Well my dear, I understand your reasoning and so be it.' Quickly changing the subject, she added, 'You will be wondering about your terms; well you will receive three shillings and six pence a week and all board found. I'm sure it sounds favourable. I doubt if any other girl in similar employment will receive better terms anywhere about these parts.'

'I find the terms most generous and I am grateful to you, and I hope you find me suitable to your requirements, ma'am,' Frances replied, still deliberately choosing her words.

'That's settled then, Frances. You will start next Monday, nine o'clock sharp,' she instructed.

Although Frances was pleased with the outcome of the interview, nevertheless, her thoughts soon returned to the separation from Aunt Polly and her misgivings returned.

'When you make the journey from North Fenham next Monday, make your way with your belongings to the Cromer crossroads. There, Ted Fuller will pick you up with the brake at eight thirty, but be sure you are prompt, as Ted has other work to do and he'll be under orders not to hang around,' her new employer warned.

'Thank you, Mrs Hayward, I'm grateful to you and promise I will try my best to be of great service,' Frances said, bubbling inside with elation at the way the interview had gone.

'See yourself out, girl; Sally will be busy about the place somewhere… I hope,' she added, with a little chuckle.

'Good morning Mrs Hayward, and thanks again,' Frances said as she turned on her heel and headed for the door.

'Oh, one more thing before you go, you will meet Mr Hayward on Monday, as he is over at the Big Hall on farm business,' Mrs Hayward called after her.

The 'Big Hall', to which Mrs Hayward had alluded, was Holkham Hall, the country home of Thomas William Coke, MP for Norfolk, until 1832. He owned the land her husband James farmed. Renton House Farm was one of the many farms on the ex-MP's estate. On all his farms, Coke had introduced revolutionary agricultural practices by way of crop rotation and selective stockbreeding, thereby improving crop yields and creating healthier strains of stock. At Renton House, James Hayward farmed a mixed farm of 380 acres, producing arable crops and rearing sheep and cattle. Coke's four-crop rotational system of wheat, turnips, barley, and clover was proving successful in other parts of the country too. In addition, Parliament referred to this as 'The Norfolk System'.

*

After leaving the farmhouse Frances heard singing coming from the direction of the cowshed and making her way across the yard, she peeped tentatively in through the open door. There she saw Sally Groves sitting on a three-legged stool with her right ear pushed up against the belly of a reddish-brown cow. With her head turned toward the open door, she sang tunefully as she pulled rhythmically on the teats of the cow's laden udder. She stopped abruptly at the sight of Frances standing in the doorway.

'Oh! Hello,' she said. 'I bet you think I'm mad, but I always sings to 'em, I'm sure it makes 'em give up the milk better. How did it go with the mistress?' Sally continued nosily, hardly stopping for breath. Frances smiled at Sally's idea the cows would respond favourably to her serenading them.

'It went well – got the job!' Frances replied, unable to hide the mixture of elation and relief in her voice. 'Start next Monday. Nine o'clock sharp,' she said, almost parodying Mrs Hayward's insistence.

'Good for you,' Sally replied, for she too had taken a liking to the new girl and looked forward to her company. 'It'll make a change having another female my own age around,' she said. 'I'll look forward to working with you, Frances, and I'm sure we will become friends.'

This morning Frances hadn't a care in the world and bidding Sally good day, Frances crossed the yard and set off for home, leaving Dave Binney clearing the last of the muck from the earlier spillage. She retraced her steps back down the lane, which earlier had brought her to Renton House Farm and on approaching the field where the ploughman was working, she noticed the progress Dan Swain had made. She was so pleased with her achievement she wanted to share the news with everyone she met and decided to wait for the young ploughman to complete yet another furrow.

Looking between the two horses, Dan Swain caught sight of the young girl for the second time. When he saw her peering over the hedge towards him, he could not complete the furrow quickly enough and urged the horses into further effort. Bringing his charges to a halt, he lashed the reins to the hedge, and he turned to Frances.

'How did it go, Miss Cartner?'

'Start next Monday!' she exclaimed, excitedly, and pleased he remembered her name.

'I'm so pleased for you, miss,' he said genuinely, at the same time feeling a sudden rush of pleasure inside at the thought of possibly seeing her more often.

'You can call me Frances seeing as I will be working here,' she said, hoping in doing so she did not appear too free.

'And I'm Dan,' he reminded her.

With their introductions completed, Frances and Dan said goodbye for the second time, and she set off once more in the direction of North Fenham leaving Dan to complete his ploughing amidst the raucous squawking of the gulls.

Ted Fuller, who was the oldest of James Hayward's employees, had taught Dan his ploughing skills. James Hayward, realising Ted was getting on in years, had instructed him to teach Dan the skills of ploughing in readiness for Ted's retirement. Firstly, Ted had taught him the skill of harrowing being of the opinion this was a greater skill than ploughing, in as much as the harrow had no handles with which to steer. This required a greater understanding between the handler and his horses. Good harrowing skills were necessary to ensure the all-important covering of the seeds. Old Ted believed that Dan with this skill mastered, would take naturally to ploughing.

The following year Ted's rheumatism had become too much for him and Dan, at the age of eighteen, had taken over as ploughman. Although he found his work mundane, Dan appreciated the freedom of thought his job allowed. Unhindered, his mind could run riot with all manner of notions. One thought constantly running through his mind while ploughing, was one he had nursed since childhood, of going to America to make his fortune. Dan like other Renton children whose parents could afford it, had attended a dame school set up by one of the women of the village named Catherine Mullen. Some women running dame schools were only child-minders, allowing the village mothers to work full time on the land. Catherine Mullen's school gave the children a good grounding in the three Rs. She and her husband had arrived in the village with a band of Irish travellers about twenty years ago. The story was that she had eloped with the footman to Liverpool. Her father had struck her off without a penny and the pair had worked their way across country to avoid detection. Her accent, much more refined than that of her husband, indicated she was well educated for a traveller. The rest of the travellers had moved on, but the young fugitives had decided to settle in the village.

She also taught her class about America and of people making their fortunes in the land across the Atlantic Ocean. She talked to her pupils about equality and human rights. Dan still remembered his teacher telling them, *'Everyone is equal and if you put your mind to something, and you want it badly enough, nothing is impossible in America.'* Whether this made any sense to the rest of his classmates, Dan would never know, but one thing he was sure of, he would never forget his teacher's words. She had also expressed that in her opinion, the chances of success for ordinary working-class people would be greater in America than here in England. Dan remembered his teacher's words. *'America is a young country, free of class distinction, unlike England.'* These were radical views for her time, but Mrs Mullen was no ordinary woman and her views on America would stay in Dan's mind.

Over the years, the idea had become more urgent. He often thought of Mrs Mullen and he dreamed of the time when he would own his own land and home; free of the tied system to which his parents and all the other farm workers resigned themselves. Dan lived with his parents in one of the many tied cottages, which were part of the 'Big Hall' estate. His father, who worked as a general labourer was responsible for the maintenance of all the fences and hedgerows. He was also responsible for the maintenance of the ditches: all-important to fenland farming.

*

As Frances walked home, bittersweet thoughts went through her mind. On the one hand, she was delighted in the way her meeting with Mrs Hayward had gone but on the other hand, she was feeling pangs of remorse at the idea of leaving her dear aunt with whom she had spent ten happy years. She would dearly have stayed at home and worked after Aunt Polly, but Frances knew she would have to become the breadwinner to supplement her aunt's income. On reaching home, Frances ran up the path to the little cottage and dashed inside shouting, 'I got it, Aunt Polly – I got it!'

'Well done, Frances, now come and sit down while I put the kettle on, then you can tell me all about it over a nice cup of tea,' her old aunt said, adding, 'I'm so proud of you.' Frances continued her conversation while her aunt went about her tea making.

'I'm to receive three shillings and sixpence per week and all my board,' she disclosed, feeling she had done so well for herself and

Aunt Polly. 'I'm to start at nine o'clock this coming Monday. Mrs Hayward was kind enough to say these starting arrangements were to be with your approval, but I told her you would leave it to Mrs Hayward to decide. So, Monday it is,' Frances related excitedly.

'She seems a kindly person, Frances, am I right in thinking?' Aunt Polly asked, adding, 'They are handsome terms indeed for one so young.'

'She gave me the impression she was a person who will be firm but fair. If I work hard and keep myself right by her, I think I'll be happy at Renton House Farm,' Frances replied proudly. The lid of the kettle rattled telling Aunt Polly it was boiled. With the water on the tea leaves, Aunt Polly returned to the table carrying a tray on which were two china cups and saucers with a blue forget-me-not design, a milk jug, and a pot of economically brewed tea.

Other than the two china cups and saucers, nothing else matched. She placed the tray on the table and sat opposite her niece.

'I thought this called for the best china,' she said proudly, as she poured the tea. 'The best china' she so proudly displayed, amounted to the two cups and saucers, which she had extravagantly bought from a second-hand shop in Durnham early in her married life and she had treasured them ever since.

'Now tell me all about it, right from the beginning while we have our tea,' she said, expectantly. Frances excitedly related the events of the morning, deliberately omitting any mention of her meeting with the young ploughman, deciding it more prudent to keep such news for a more appropriate time.

Chapter 2

Monday morning arrived, and Frances set off once more for Renton House Farm knowing this time she would be staying with the Haywards and she would only see her aunt on Sundays. She had packed her few belongings into a leather valise the night before in readiness. She turned to her aunt and hugging her tightly, she kissed her on the cheek.

'Be sure to get word to me if ever you need me. If there is anything amiss, Aunt Polly, let me know right away and I will be back as soon as possible, it is not far from Renton.'

'Now you run along, Frances, or you'll miss your lift. You know me, I'll be fine, apart from the aches and pains all us fenland people suffer as we get older there's not much wrong with me,' she said reassuringly. Although Frances knew it was imperative that she became the breadwinner, it was with reluctance she bade her dear aunt goodbye. Picking up the valise, she set off for her rendezvous with Ted Fuller at the Cromer crossroads. She took a backward look towards the cottage and with tears in her eyes, she waved to Aunt Polly standing at the garden gate.

Ted arrived on time with the farm cart as arranged. 'Miss Cartner?' he enquired of the young girl standing at the crossroads.

'I am and you'll be Mr Fuller,' Frances replied respectfully.

'Oh, jist call me 'ed, tha's waa everyone round here calls me. Mind you, oi doon know waa they call me ahoind moi baack,' he said, with a chuckle in his voice.

'Ted, you may call me Frances, and thank you for coming to meet me. Although I haven't much baggage, this valise would probably have weighed heavily by the time I reached Renton House Farm on foot. It contains the Bible my dear aunt gave me, which alone is a sizeable volume,' she added as she climbed up alongside.

'*Well, me and owl' Dollie 'are, heft' sef' yow tha' discomfor', Frances,*' he said, feeling rather pleased with himself, '*and we hef' got clemen' wather for thur joorney,*' Ted continued in his broad accent.

'It will give Dan Swain a chance to get all his ploughing completed,' she replied.

'*Oh! You'v me' Dan, hev' yow?*'

'Yes, we met last Wednesday when I was at the farm for my interview. He was ploughing the field next to the lane leading to the farm house,' she explained.

'*He ois a good lad, ois Dan, 'ook 'o workin' 'hose horses like a duck 'o 'wa'er. Hev oi any criticism o'fim? Oolly, he doesn' tairke a drop of good ale, seen as him bairn abs'inant and all tha'. Bu' tha' does no' mairk a lesser man o' fim. Dan doesn' hang abou',*' he said with a glint in his eye, and the chuckle returned.

The cart trundled along the lane at a leisurely pace, Ted not asking too much of Dolly, remembering what a great servant she had been to him when they were both ploughing the fields together. He thought both had earned the right to take things more easily.

They eventually reached the farmyard where the old mare brought herself to a halt. Ted climbed down and gave Frances a hand to dismount from the cart. Thanking Ted for the transport, she bid him good day. As they alighted from the cart, Sally Groves joined them. 'Hello again, Frances,' Sally said. 'Come this way, Mrs Hayward has told me to show you to your room.'

Sally led the way into the house and up the oak staircase, chatting away as they climbed the stairs. 'You're to be in the room next to me. Bit small but big enough if you know what I mean, especially when we have to keep 'em tidy. Here we are,' she said, breathlessly, having continued her conversation even as they climbed the two long flights of stairs to the topmost part of the farmhouse.

'This will be fine,' Frances said as Sally stepped aside allowing Frances her first peep of her new 'home'. 'Mrs Hayward said to tell you, once you've got your things unpacked, you're to present yourself in the parlour where you're to meet her and the master,' Sally said rather officiously, which brought a wry smile to Frances's face.

'Thank you Sally,' Frances said, adding, 'please let Mrs Hayward know I will be down as quickly as possible,' and with her mistress's instructions carried out, Sally turned and left Frances to do her unpacking.

With Sally gone, Frances took stock of her little room. On first appearance she soon realised it was not as cosy as the bedroom at Aunt Polly's. It was clean and adequate. A simple bed ran lengthwise under the small attic window. Frances inspected the bed. A flock mattress covered the slatted base; a course blanket and a patchwork counterpane in turn covered this. Frances thought the mix of colours and the contrasting designs of the swatches of fabric gave the counterpane a quaint attractiveness, brightening the dull room. She bounced up and down a couple of times on the bed to see how comfortable it was, only to quickly jump off again at the noise the loose wooden slats made as they rattled against the frame. As she smoothed the counterpane back to its original pristine condition, she wondered if anyone downstairs was aware of her brief impetuous action. Guilt came over her and she hoped she did not have too many restless nights.

The window was on the front of the house and overlooked a field that separated the farm from the village of Renton. In the foreground, Frances could see the red tiled roofs of the cottages in Renton village with the spire of All Saints church rising above. Peering into the middle distance, she could clearly make out the square tower of Saint Mary's church in North Fenham. This immediately brought Aunt Polly to mind. She wondered how her aunt had taken her departure and how she would cope in Frances's absence. As she viewed the panorama, she realised how close she was to her aunt, both emotionally and geographically. In the far distance, towering above the remnants of early morning mist, she could vaguely make out Durrell's wheat mill at Stanton, with its four large vanes barely visible against the skyline. It was a modern structure, built only two years ago. She could also see the lane, which led to the farmhouse, and she tried to make out the field where she had first met Dan Swain. Looking far to her right, the circling gulls betrayed Dan Swain's present position as he continued his ploughing and as Frances's thoughts were once more drawn to Dan Swain, they once again sparked that feeling inside her which she had felt last Wednesday. She felt a mysterious physical change taking place within her. Suddenly realising her employers awaited her downstairs, her thoughts returned to her new accommodation. A single chair occupied one corner of the little garret and a small chest of drawers stood opposite the window. On top of the chest was an earthenware washbowl and large water jug of simple design, both devoid of any decoration. A small soap dish completed the set, none of which matched. On the wall, above the chest hung a crude wooden cross, which Frances thought would be of comfort to her whenever she had to draw on her faith. Nothing covered the floorboards and the curtains at the window were basic. In fact, they looked as if, a long time ago, someone had made them out of flour sacking. It did not take her long to unpack her few belongings and having done so, she placed her hairbrush alongside the bowl and pulled on her apron. She placed the Bible her Aunt Polly had insisted she took with her, on the top of the chest of drawers far enough away from the washbowl to avoid any damage from water splashes. Taking the tablet of soap, which Aunt Polly had bought for her the previous Christmas, she sniffed it first before placing it on the soap dish. With the calming smell of lavender in her nostrils, she set off downstairs to the parlour. She hesitated briefly at the bottom of the stairs. Remembering the route from her previous visit, she proceeded and knocked on the parlour door.

'Come!' a resonant male voice called from within, contrasting sharply with her timorous knock. *Mr Hayward*, she thought, and the comforting perfume of lavender quickly evaporated as she nervously lifted the door latch. She entered the room and James Hayward beckoned her before him.

'And you must be Frances Cartner, and I, as I'm sure you realise, am Mr Hayward. I will keep this brief as I have more important things to deal with. Suffice to say, Mrs Hayward has told me about you, following your interview last Wednesday and whatever Mrs Hayward decides in the hiring of the female staff is fine by me. The same goes with the dismissals, but let's hope it won't come to that,' he stated, and leaving Frances pondering over his final ominous remark, he quickly bid his wife goodbye. James Hayward's brevity suited Frances. He was *so* brief, their meeting seemed to be over almost in seconds. Hannah Hayward took over Frances's induction to the job. 'Well Frances, let us make a start by talking you through what I shall expect of you. Sally gets the fires kindled soon as she rises and stacks enough peat at the side of the hearth to serve the day. It will be her place to see to all the scullery duties and she also helps with the milking.'

Frances sensed Mrs Hayward was waiting for a response and asked, 'And what about breakfast, ma'am?'

'Well, all the kitchen duties will be down to you, although I shall decide what is on the menu,' her mistress pointed out. 'I maintain a well-stocked kitchen garden, which is my pride and joy. This keeps us well provided with fresh vegetables such as carrots, onions, peas, beans, and potatoes. Anything we do not grow in the fields I try to grow in my garden. I also have a few fruit bushes too which, as long as I keep protected from the fenland winds, do reasonably well,' she said with an air of pride.

'Will I be able to help myself to the produce as and when I need to, ma'am?' Frances queried.

'Of course you can, girl, as long as you keep to my order of things. I keep a tidy garden and that's the way I like it,' she replied rather insistently.

'That's good, ma'am, as my aunt has taught me some nourishing recipes for fruit-filled suet puddings which I'm sure we will enjoy when the fruit is in season,' Frances said, hoping this appealed to her mistress's palate.

'I shall look forward to those, Frances, they sound delicious,' she said expectantly. 'You will be catering daily for all the people abiding under our roof,' she said, 'and extra meals at busy periods such as harvesting and threshing, when the men work from sunrise to sunset; when the good Lord gives us the weather to do so,' she added.

Chapter 3

March 1837

Frances's arrival at Renton House twelve months ago, had coincided with the lambing season; the busiest time of the year for shepherd Rupert Monk. Frances loved to hear the bleating of the new-born lambs as they called to the ewes and she marvelled at the way each ewe knew its own lambs. As Frances went about her work of baking for the household, she mused over her first year at Renton House.

On reflection, each month had brought its own special time in the farming calendar and she had enjoyed her first year at the farm. March had been a busy month for Dan Swain. He had been busy with the spring ploughing in readiness for the seed sowing in April.

June and July had been time for the haymaking and August had brought her first experience of harvest time and the gathering in of the cereal crops.

September arrived filling the air with the early smells of autumn and the trees made their contribution with a myriad of autumnal shades. On the farm everyone was busy with the threshing for which James Hayward had hired a threshing machine. A steam-driven traction engine had arrived at the farm towing the threshing machine. Smoke billowed from the steam engine's tall chimney. This had created great interest among the village children, who chased the convoy excitedly until it had come to a halt in the stack yard. Not everyone had welcomed the device with the same innocent enthusiasm shown by the village children, nor had they approved of these innovative methods of farming. Many farm labourers saw them as a threat to their livelihoods. Although no machines had been broken on James Hayward's farm, there had been murmurings of damage in the area and rumours of some machines being broken in other parts of Norfolk. This had prompted James Hayward to mount an all-night vigil on the hired machinery and he had posted two men to carry out this task until the work was completed, and the machinery removed from his land. With this precaution taken, the cereal harvest had gone off successfully and without incident.

Although it was a busy time, Frances enjoyed the excitement these busy periods brought, and the Haywards threw a party for all concerned on the completion of the harvesting and threshing. Everyone was in celebratory mood at this important time in the farm calendar and Mrs Hayward had found time away from her garden to give Frances an extra pair of hands in the kitchen. Everyone had enjoyed a meal of freshly baked bread, cheese, and apples. The men washed it down with tankards of Mrs Hayward's home-brewed ale. She also made her own ginger beer for which she was renowned, having won first prize at the village fete almost annually. Some cynics amongst the villagers believed her success was down to the judges currying favour with the bailiff's wife, but anyone who had sampled Hannah Hayward's concoction agreed there was none better.

Dan shared this opinion. As an abstainer, he always chose the non-alcoholic ginger beer, having signed 'the pledge' at a temperance meeting he had attended with his mother at the Methodist chapel when he was thirteen years old and not a drop of alcoholic drink had ever passed his lips.

Rupert Monk, was almost as adept on the fiddle as he was with his sheep shears and played throughout the proceedings, stopping only now and again for a swig of ale. Apart from singing all the local favourites, his wife Margie could give a good rendition of the ballads she learned from the itinerant Irish workers. These workers would stop only for two days' work during the busy seasons and then move on. People danced, and it was a joyful occasion, everyone had a great time. For the villagers, it was the highlight of their year. Frances had danced all night with Dan Swain and their friendship had blossomed. On retiring to her bed, sleep had not come easily, despite all her dancing. She could not get Dan Swain out of her head. She wondered what was happening to her and why. No matter how she tried, she could not rid her mind of him. Whatever it was, it made her feel good inside and she wanted the feeling to continue.

During October, Dan had been busy with the final ploughing of the year, followed by the autumn seed sowing of the winter wheat and despite a couple of days when there had been heavy frosts, he had been able to complete his task before the end of the month. Each year, ritualistically, stalks kept from the harvested corn were fashioned into corn 'dollies' and ploughed into the first furrow of the October ploughing, in the hope it would please the good Mother Earth whom, in return, would yield a further successful crop.

December came and the slaughtering of the Norfolk Red cattle, noted for their high-quality beef, had taken place. It was traditional at Renton House, for all of James Hayward's employees to receive a Christmas joint of beef, taken from one of the prime steers and as in years past, James Hayward's employees had sat down to a prime beef joint for their Christmas dinners.

By Christmas time, with Mrs Hayward's permission, Frances and Dan had begun 'walking out'.

'While you are living under my roof, and in the absence of your good aunt, I will deem it my duty to adopt your aunt's responsibility for your well-being,' she had reminded Frances. On Sundays Frances and Dan walked over to North Fenham to see her Aunt Polly and the three had attended matins and evensong at St Mary's together. Since the beginning of their courtship, Dan had ceased attending the Methodist Chapel at Renton. Each week he and Frances set off early and strolled slowly over to North Fenham. This way, they enjoyed more time together and Frances had company back to Renton House on those dark winter nights. Their pace quickened at the sound of the twin-peals of St Mary's church bells, knowing Aunt Polly would get anxious if they were not there on time, especially when Frances had to prepare herself for her place in the choir; no one dared be late for Zachary Tomes. During one of these Sunday morning strolls Dan had told Frances about his plans of emigrating to America.

'Why America of all places?' Frances asked him incredulously.

'It began when I was at school and my teacher talked of people making huge fortunes in America. I have always dreamt I would make something more of myself than a simple ploughman,' adding, 'I dream of owning my own place some day and I am more likely to achieve that in America than in this country,' Dan had revealed. Frances was uneasy about his ambition and the idea confused her. She was falling in love with Dan, if love was what this strange feeling inside her was all about and the idea of him going off to America bothered her tremendously. She had no doubt, had it not been for her aunt, she would have followed him to the end of the earth. The church bells rang out across the fens, prompting Frances to remember her role in the choir.

'Race you to Aunt Polly's,' she shouted, starting off immediately. On reaching the garden gate, she stepped aside holding the gate open for Dan who ran straight up to the front door.

'Told you I'd beat you,' he said triumphantly.

They both entered, panting heavily. 'I hope you have got breath left for the hymn singing, it's carol service today,' Aunt Polly reminded them, adding, 'it's always a good congregation the last Sunday before Christmas.'

'I love the Christmas service,' Frances said as she remembered Christmases past. 'Curate Robinson gives such a good sermon on the Lord's birth and I love the carols.'

'Well we'd better get a move on or we will miss this year's

account,' Aunt Polly reminded them.

The vicar, Reverend Boothferry, ministered over this parish and three others in the area, taking a stipend from each, thus boosting his income. He would have a young curate carrying out his duties in each of his parishes and here it was Curate Robinson who carried out Boothferry's duties.

*

Christmas passed and the New Year of 1838 began. As was the custom, the villagers celebrated 'Plough Monday', the first Monday after 'Twelfth Night'. The ploughmen of the area decorated a plough with flowers and ribbons and dragged it around the village and into the church for the blessing. The men of the village, with their faces blackened and dressed as women they performed Molly Dances. Nobody seemed to know of the origin of the ritual. This was of no consequence to the villagers of Renton, who always looked forward to the festival and as in years immemorial the people of the fenland villages, saw it as a happy distraction during the winter months.

As they went through the village, the ploughmen collected money, with which they bought ale from the Red Lion Inn, to be drunk between dances. As they pulled the plough through the village, they knocked on people's doors and if they received no donation, they had threatened to plough a furrow across the front of the villagers' cottages as an indication of their meanness. As usual, Rupert Monk had provided the musical accompaniment for the Molly Dancers. In addition, on Plough Monday, people told fenland tales while the ploughmen quaffed their ale. Frances remembered the *Dead Moon Tale*. The story went; because of the enormity of the fenland sky, the moon shone brighter over the fens than anywhere else on earth, and at night, the moon came down to earth to walk about the fens, and on one of the moon's earthly excursions she was caught and snared by the *'demons of the dark places'* who wanted to prevent her from shining a way for any unwary traveller, thus saving them from being lost in the bogs and sinking in the mud. Luckily, when the villages saw this, they managed to free her, and therefore the moon allegedly shines brightest across the Norfolk Fens. The seasons of a new year began once more in the farming community. Soon March had arrived again, and Frances had completed her first year at Renton House Farm.

Chapter 4

One Sunday morning in March 1838, Frances and Dan were once more on their way to North Fenham to attend church with Aunt Polly and this Sunday would turn out to be different from any other.

Dan surprised Frances when without any warning, he looked at her and said, 'Will you marry me, Frances? I love you so much and I want to spend my life with you and care for you. I cannot bear to be with you only on our Sunday walks to and from North Fenham. I need you much more.'

On hearing his words, Frances's heart began to pound; she was both disappointed and surprised at Dan's sudden proposal. She had hoped for a much more romantic approach from him. Despite his haste, or maybe because of it, Frances quickly replied, 'Of course, I will, I have loved you since the first time I saw you, Dan Swain, and I can't wait to be your wife.'

He drew her to him, and they locked in a passionate embrace. Again, a warm, mysterious, exciting feeling rose within her; the same intense feeling she had experienced on the first day they met, only this time she knew the meaning of its overwhelming power drawing her more physically towards him. An intense physical attraction had come over him and their feelings fused as their lips met.

*

On arriving at Aunt Polly's, Dan asked for Frances's hand in marriage. Frances knew this was a mere formality and threw her arms around her aunt's neck when she gave Dan her approval. 'Thank you so much Aunt Polly, I'm so happy,' Frances squealed excitedly.

'I'm delighted for you both, I have expected it for some time and I'm sure you and Dan will be happy together,' Aunt Polly said sincerely, and she turned to Dan and kissed him lightly on the cheek. The thought went through Frances's mind; would her aunt have been so sure if she knew of Dan's plans for America? For the time being, she preferred Aunt Polly remained ignorant of his plans.

*

Later, they walked hand in hand along the quiet country lane that took them back to Renton.

The frosty ground glistened in the light from the lantern and the moonlight added its own romantic ambience to the scene. Dan stopped and placed the lantern on the ground and turned to face Frances. Without exchanging a word, he took her in his strong arms and drew her towards him. Looking up into his face, she excitedly anticipated the moment when their lips would touch. She was not disappointed; Dan was so gentle for such a strong man. No movement was hurried, he took her slowly to him and the moment their lips touched, she knew the answer to all the questions she had asked herself the day she first met the young ploughman. She now knew what those strange early feelings had meant… it was love.

As they broke from their embrace, his right hand inadvertently brushed against her left breast. A searing thrill rushed through her body and she was no longer conscious of the chill March air. Oblivious to the cold, she hastily undid the buttons on her coat. As the coat fell open and with similar eagerness, she loosened the bodice of her dress. Dan placed his right hand on her left breast. He thrilled at the warmth of her body as he cupped his hand over her beautifully formed young breast. As he explored her beautiful body for the very first time, Frances was aware of his touch, sending sensuous tingling feelings throughout her body. Dan as if led by some animal instinct breathed in the smell of her body and kissed her neck.

'I've got to have you, Frances,' he said breathlessly, for the excitement of the moment seemed to be sucking the very air from his lungs.

'I must have you too,' she gasped as feelings were rising within her, which until now, had remained untapped. Just when she thought these feelings would consume her being. She suddenly became aware of something deeper down within her yelling, 'NO!' It took all of her resolve to fight off this urge and to suppress this rising, new emotion. Deep down she knew she wanted to commit herself completely to him, but this was not the time or the place; she wanted the first time to be perfect, not snatched hurriedly in a cold country lane. Becoming aware of the cold air on her exposed body, the excitement quickly dissipated as she regained control of her senses. She broke away from Dan, feeling angry for leading him on.

'Please Frances, I must have you now, I can't wait any longer,' he pleaded, for he had reached total arousal.

'No please, Dan, for my sake… not like this… not here, please,' she beseeched him. 'I am so sorry, please forgive me… please not before marriage and especially on the Lord's Day. It will happen but not before we marry, and when it does it will be perfect, I promise you,' she sobbed as she now struggled to fasten the buttons on her clothing which a short time ago she had undone so readily.

Dan accepted her reasoning and kissed her a little less passionately as he fought to suppress his feelings of arousal. Frances hurriedly made final adjustments to her clothing and the moment had passed. They made the rest of the journey back to Renton in a guilty silence.

*

It was April and Dolly the old mare had spread a shoe. Dan had brought her into the yard to be re-shod by Dick Hempsel, the farrier. Frances had received the news from Mrs Hayward, old Ted Fuller was to retire and would be going to live with his daughter in Lynn at the end of May.

When Frances saw Dan in the yard, she rushed out to tell him the news of Ted's impending retirement. 'You know what this means,

Frances?' Dan asked excitedly. 'It means we can get married,' he continued.

'How does our getting married have anything to do with Old Ted's retirement?' she asked, rather puzzled.

'Well, we can put in for Ted's cottage, but we would have to be married first,' he explained.

'Oh Dan, I cannot wait,' she replied and immediately led him into an impromptu jig around the farmyard with Dolly trotting behind them.

'Watch tha' yow two shay-brained buggers, I'm 'are to do a job yow know,' Dick scolded as he angrily grabbed Dolly's lead from Dan's hand and tethered her to the hitching post.

With Dolly settled, he got back to the idea of marriage flying around his brain.

'I'll see Mr Hayward tomorrow, soon as I turn up for work,' he promised her, adding: 'If he approves, we can set the date for our wedding.'

'Ted retiring at the end of May is perfect. It means we could have a late May wedding before the June haymaking,' she said hopefully. 'The barn will be empty, and we can ask if we can use it for the wedding celebrations.'

It was where Ted and his wife had lived following their marriage in 1788 and where they had raised their family of two sons and a daughter. He had lost touch with his eldest son. Rumour had it, the authorities transported him to Australia at the age of twenty-three for sheep stealing. His second son, on the other hand, was a successful bailiff on a farm in the Lincolnshire Wolds. The following morning Dan approached Mr Hayward to discuss the occupancy of Ted's cottage when it became vacant, explaining their plan to get married if their request was successful. James Hayward saw no problems with this arrangement, as he would not be replacing Ted when he retired. He had kept Ted on, doing odd jobs about the place in recognition of the service he had given James and James's father before him.

*

The reading of the banns took place on the first three Sundays in May and they were married on Saturday 26th May 1838 at St Mary's Church, North Fenham. The little church was full to overflowing as the people from the two villages of Renton and North Fenham crammed in to witness the ceremony, officiated over by the resident curate Harry Robinson. Sally Groves attended Frances as her bridesmaid and Tom Gibney was Dan's best man. Frances had worn the wedding dress Aunt Polly had kept folded safely in a linen sheet inside an old wooden chest. She had kept it all these years in the hope that someday a daughter of her own would wear it. This was not to be and now her niece whom she loved and regarded as the daughter she never had, was wearing it instead. Unlike most other married women of her time, Aunt Polly never had children. Five months into her first pregnancy, she had suffered a miscarriage when attempting to move a barrel of ale. She and her beloved Walter had prayed and prayed for a family of their own, but she never fell pregnant again.

After Aunt Polly had made one or two astute adjustments, the dress fitted her perfectly and with Frances's long black hair set against the ivory-coloured muslin wedding dress, she looked stunning. Mrs Hayward, on seeing the dress and thinking it a little low cut for at the neckline, had lent Frances an embroidered muslin pelerine to wear over the dress. It matched the dress beautifully, but Frances knew Mrs Hayward's real reason for the offer of the pelerine was she thought the neckline too low for a girl of eighteen to wear to church.

'It will be your 'something borrowed', also it's still only May and remember those winds coming of the North Sea can be cold,' Mrs Hayward reasoned, and Frances smiled to herself at her mock concern.

Frances had decided her headdress would be a simple matching bonnet, free of any adornment: no flowers, or feathers, not wanting to outdo poor Sally, who would be wearing her one and only cornflower-blue Sunday best dress.

Ted had worked his last day at the farm the previous weekend but had stayed on for the wedding and as a wedding present to the young couple, he had left his meagre furniture in place saying he would have no need for it at his daughter's place. For the newlyweds to move straight in on their wedding night, the Haywards had arranged for Ted to stay at the farmhouse in the room newly vacated by Frances and they had arranged for George Binney to take him to his daughter's the next day.

The church organist struck up with the opening bars of Mendelssohn's Wedding March, and Dan turned to see Frances walking slowly down the aisle on her father's arm. He had never seen Frances looking so beautiful and his mind quickly returned to the time he had proposed to her in the lane and of their aborted intimacy. His piety quickly caused him to remove the thought from his mind as he remembered he was in God's house. She looked radiant and he realised once again how much he loved her.

The ceremony over, everyone made their way to the big barn the Haywards had placed at their disposal. Frances was pleased at meeting her family again. Her brothers and sisters were growing, and she missed them all. Everyone had a great time, dancing and singing and drinking ale. Again, Rupert Monk and his wife Margie led the entertainment. With the drinking of more ale, the more ribald the innuendos came from their young friends to embarrass the newlyweds.

'Yow watch owl Ted in hidin' in tha' owl waardrobe of his. He in givin' yow thay foorniture for naathin, yow know,' teased Fred Gill, attempting to mimic Old Ted's accent.

She blushed at the idea of Old Ted hiding in the wardrobe. Even though she knew Fred was teasing them, she promised herself she would look inside the wardrobe on going to bed.

It had been a truly happy day, but they could not wait for it to be over and the last of the guests had finally dwindled away. Eventually, by the light of a single candle lodged securely in a pewter candleholder they climbed the stairs to the bed they would share for the first time. On entering the bedroom, they saw, as was the custom, the villagers had decorated the wedding bed with flowers and greenery to induce fertility. Dan placed the candle on the old chest of drawers by the window and quickly cleared the bed of the floral adornments. He walked across the bedroom and smiled as he watched his new bride slowly open the wardrobe door, remembering Fred Gill's teasing. She tentatively peeped inside. 'Look, Dan — empty,' and they broke out laughing.

Despite her haste on the day Dan had proposed on the road to Renton, a trembling entered her body. Frances was aware she was about to experience something of which she knew nothing. Still an inner compulsion drove her on. She closed the wardrobe door and still facing the wardrobe she coyly began to undress. She slowly eased the second strap of the last of her undergarments and let it fall to the floor. She turned to face her husband, revealing her naked beauty to him for the first time. Dan drank in the exquisite form standing tremulously before him. The candlelight seemed to lend itself to the mystery of this new experience as it cast dappled shadows across her beautifully formed body. The flickering light of the candle created an erotic sense of movement as if Frances was swaying evocatively while standing stock still.

'Please be gentle with me, Dan, I'm not sure about any of this and I do want it to be so good for you,' she pleaded.

'You know I would never hurt you deliberately and if at any time you are not happy, we will stop, I want it to be good for both of us. I would gain no pleasure from hurting you,' he reassured her. Frances turned, seeing her young husband's naked body for the first time. He had waited so long for this moment. Frances admired his strong muscular body and a strange tingling sensation returned to the tips of her breasts. A feeling of security crept over her now he was hers and only hers. The revelation of each other's bodies was a precious moment, never to be shared with others.

Drawing her towards him, they embraced, each naked body

moulding to the form of the other. The earlier feeling of security had crept over her slowly, but now a fast-moving tide of excitement was rushing through her entire being, the like of which she had never felt before. Frances enjoyed the warmth of Dan's body as he cradled her in his strong arms, comforting her against the ambient coldness of the bedroom.

'I feel so safe in your arms,' she told him.

'And you always will. I promise you,' he replied.

Her body trembled with excitement, which Dan in his naivety thought was the effect of the coldness of the room. Taking her in his arms, he placed her gently on the bed. Straddling her slowly, he took in the beauty of his new bride. His head hovered above her face as he looked into her beautiful eyes and stroking a cluster of black curls back behind her right ear, he slowly lowered his head until their mouths fused. Frances was aware of his sweet breath; a breath not sullied by stale alcohol or tobacco. She responded by slightly opening her lips. He again cupped her young, firm breast as he had done that time in the lane. The newlyweds reached the point which previously had been the limits of their lovemaking. Now they were about to tear down their self-imposed barrier forever, allowing their unfettered passion to consume them in their expression of love for one another. He moved between Frances's alabaster-pale thighs. Taking his body weight on one arm, he gazed down at her beautiful young body beneath him. The candlelight guttered, once more rippling her form with pale light, making it even more tantalising. Her body trembled uncontrollably, a mix of excitement and a fear of the unknown. She let out a gasp at Dan's first attempt at penetration. He retracted sympathetically, gently kissing her in his attempt to reassure her; hoping it would allay her fear. She breathed heavily in measured gasps. 'Are you, all right?' he asked.

'I'll be alright soon, I'm sure,' she reassured him, between gasps, adding, 'we have much to learn.' They lay together exploring the mystery of each other's body, gently stroking, caressing one another.

Frances calmed to Dan's gentle treatment. Once more, the aching returned, and her nipples again responded to Dan's touch.

'Try again, Dan, I want you desperately,' she said. For the second time Dan attempted penetration and this time after one more gasp from Frances, he slid slowly into her. All their pent-up emotions and suppressed feelings brought on by their self-imposed celibacy now flooded from them as they moved in a frenzied rhythm, venting their feelings for each other in their first real act of lovemaking.

It was over rather quickly but it had been long enough for them both to realise what a beautiful, but somewhat bewildering experience their first attempt at lovemaking had been. They both lay stretched out side-by-side, breathing heavily as they lay drinking in this newfound feeling of contentment.

'Was it good, Frances?' was all Dan asked.

'It was, my love. Thank you for your patience and gentleness,' she replied and she kissed him. 'Goodnight, God bless.' Sleep did not come readily and by morning, the marriage had been well and truly consummated.

Chapter 5

Early in their marriage, the topic of conversation was their emigrating to America. While Frances was not as keen on the idea as Dan was, she supported his plans wholeheartedly. She knew he was not acting impulsively for he had spelt it out to her from the early days of their meeting, and they thought of ways to save as much money as possible to pay for their passage. Dan had already made enquiries as to the cost of their passage and he thought it would be in the region of £5 each. Apart from their passage, they would need to buy all the cooking utensils and provisions for the journey across the Atlantic; enough provisions to last for at least a forty-day crossing. Possibly a longer duration if they should encounter bad weather. In addition, they would need suitable clothing to keep out the Atlantic wind and rain.

One morning in August, Frances was baking extra bread to feed the people doing the harvesting, when she had to quickly dash outside to the yard. Mrs Hayward who had been helping her in the kitchen followed her, wiping her floury hands on her apron as she tried to keep up with her maid.

'Are you alright, dearie?' she enquired of Frances who was retching violently onto the cobbled farmyard.

'I'm ever so sorry, ma'am,' Frances apologised. 'I do not know what came over me; never had a turn like that before,' she gasped, trying to regain her composure. 'Must have been something I've eaten,' she added.

'I don't think so,' Hannah Hayward replied, knowingly. 'When did you have your last 'show'?' she enquired. Frances, taken aback by her mistress's abruptness, hesitated; unused to a relative stranger confronting her on such a personal matter she answered her mistress out of a sense of duty.

'I don't know exactly but I have not 'seen' since we were married,' she said.

'There you are: I thought as much. I am sure you are with child, dearie,' she concluded, and she tapped the side of her nose, pleased with herself that she had been able to predict Frances's present condition.

What will I do now? Frances asked herself as thoughts of Dan came rushing through her mind. She knew this latest development seriously compromised his plans.

'Carry on as normal, in the first instance,' Mrs Hayward said, not being aware of Frances's real fears, adding, 'see out your pregnancy and after your confinement, bring your baby round to the farmhouse with you each day. It will be good to have a baby in the house again. We'll manage something between us, I am sure,' she said, confident she had reassured Frances about her present situation.

Both the Haywards' son and daughter were married and had successful careers in London and neither had produced a grandchild, so the idea of having Frances's baby around appealed to Hannah Hayward and she had become fond of Frances. Mrs Hayward's kind words did not placate the turmoil growing inside her. Frances had misgivings about being pregnant. She worried about how Dan would feel about it. She knew this did not fit in with Dan's plans for their future. A morbid fear built up inside her as to how Dan would take this latest news. She hoped he would not blame her for having to shelve their plans for going to America. Indeed, if she were honest about it, it would please her if the birth of their first child would end Dan's enthusiasm for America, as she would prefer to settle down, here in Norfolk and raise a family amongst all their friends and relatives. She knew she had little hope of that. Dan was obsessional about his scheme, and she loved him too much to try to influence him otherwise.

*

Their daughter was born on the morning of Saturday 16th February 1839. She had her mother's jet-black hair and her father's hazel eyes. Looking down at her baby cradled in her arms, Frances could not help but wonder what lay ahead of her in life and whether she would be happy and successful. The baby uttered a little cry, which soon developed into a full-blown bawl. 'I think she needs changing,' Frances said rather tentatively, never having changed a baby before. She removed the soiled nappy and began cleaning the baby who was lying across her lap. 'Oh, look Dan, she has a large birthmark here on the inside of her right thigh.'

'Supposed to be lucky, that is,' Dan Swain said, not convinced but he thought it would please Frances who continued with the baby's ablutions.

With the baby cleansed, Dan sat on the edge of the bed next to his wife and baby. He was so proud of Frances; he leaned over and kissed her on the lips.

'You are so clever,' he said to her, stroking Frances's forearm gently as he kissed their new-born baby on the head.

'Dan, I have something to ask you. It has bothered me since I fell pregnant and I need you to reassure me.' She thought carefully on how she would ask her question. The last thing she wanted was to influence him in any way.

'Please tell me; now the baby is here, do you still want us to make a fresh start in America?'

'Of course, Frances, this doesn't change anything. It will take a little longer than we planned now we have our baby; it makes me more determined to go ahead, for her sake as well as ours.'

Frances was not hearing what she wanted. The faint ray of hope she clung to, that Dan may change his mind and settle down, here in

Norfolk, now they were parents, had vanished forever. On the contrary, Frances realised Dan was more serious than ever about emigrating to America. They decided to call their daughter Jemima after Frances's grandmother and she was baptised at St Mary's. After her confinement, Frances had returned to work at the farm.

Dan carried their baby, in her cradle, round to the farmhouse each morning, and placed her in the corner of the kitchen where Frances could keep an eye on her. Mrs Hayward spoilt the baby whenever she was around, picking her up at every opportunity. Whenever Frances was baking, or doing work where her hands were messy, Mrs Hayward would be there. 'You carry on, my dear, I'll see to the little one; save you cleaning your hands till you are done,' she would say.

Although her mistress meant well, Frances was a little jealous of her attention and was pleased when Mrs Hayward was too busy tending her kitchen garden to be fussing over the baby. And overall, the system worked well.

Chapter 6

May 1839

One Sunday in May, almost to the date of their first wedding anniversary, Frances had swaddled Jemima in a woollen shawl and strapped her across her chest for the journey to Aunt Polly's. They reached the top of the gradually rising ground between Renton and North Fenham. Usually, a panoramic view unfolded before them, but today all that appeared above the mist-shrouded fens was the top of the square tower of St Mary's church. A feeling of unease came over Frances and she hung on tightly to Jemima.

'I don't like this mist, Dan; it has a strange atmosphere about it. I'll be glad when we reach Aunt Polly's and get indoors; it is eerie,' she said, with deep misgiving. Dan said nothing but thought the mist was no different from any other that settled over the fens.

They approached Aunt Polly's cottage and Frances noticed there was no smoke coming from the chimney.

'There *is* something wrong, Dan; I could sense it on the way over here. It's Aunt Polly,' and she hurried towards the cottage. On reaching the front gate, she noticed the curtains were still unopened and her heart slumped at the sight. They rushed to the front door, and when Dan tried it, he found it locked, confirming Frances's worst fears. She banged franticly at the door and called out, 'Aunt Polly!' several times, each time louder than the first. Jemima, disturbed by her mother's shouting, began to cry. On hearing Jemima crying and seeing Frances's distress, Dan charged the little cottage door with his broad shoulder and it yielded immediately like dry tinder. They rushed inside and found Aunt Polly lying at the foot of the stairs in a state of collapse. Dan squatted down next to Aunt Polly's prostrate body; her feet lying at the bottom of the stairs and her head towards the door. He turned her head to one side, put his ear next to her open mouth and listened for a breath. He placed two fingers on her neck feeling for a pulse but could find none.

'Oh, please Dan, tell me she isn't dead, please,' Frances cried.

'I am afraid so, Frances,' he replied and went to her side and cuddled her and Jemima to him, comfortingly. There was no sign of injury and he thought how peaceful she looked.

'Will you be all right, Frances? I will have to seek Dr. Dobson before he leaves for church.'

'You go ahead but please try to be as quick as you can,' Frances replied between her sobbing. The heaving of Frances's breast and the violence of her sobbing caused Jemima to carry on crying as if in sympathy. Dan soon returned with Dr. Dobson who on examining Aunt Polly immediately pronounced her dead.

'Has she ever complained to you of chest pains?'

'No, never,' Frances replied.

'Well I can tell you, I haven't attended her since she had that particularly bad attack of the ague some two years ago; by the colour of her lips, I am of the firm opinion she has suffered heart failure. With hindsight, I can conclude, the attack of the ague had probably left her with a weak heart, but I am afraid none of us was to know that fact until now. With no outward sign of injury, I also believe she collapsed where you see her, and she did not fall down the stairs. If I am correct in my assumption, it will be some consolation to you both to know she would not have suffered. It would have all happened quickly,' he said. 'Let us get her up to her bed, Dan,' he added.

Frances drew out the deep bottom drawer of a chest of four and placed her sleeping baby comfortably in amongst the clean linen.

'You'll be safe there, my darling,' she said.

Taking Aunt Polly's slight frame between them, Dan and Dr. Dobson carried her slowly up the stairs. They reached the bed and Frances, who had gone ahead of them, drew back the sheets and they respectfully placed Aunt Polly's body on the bed. Dr Dobson drew one hand over Aunt Polly's face and closed her eyes. *She looks as if she had dozed off to sleep,* Frances thought.

'I will leave you now, but you will have to inform the undertaker as soon as possible and you will have to lay your dear aunt's body out in readiness for him,' the doctor advised. 'I will let myself out,' he added and left them to attend to the task of preparing Aunt Polly's body for the undertaker.

Frances looked around the little bedroom, which she had shared with Aunt Polly for ten happy years. She remembered cuddling in to Aunt Polly, as they lay awake on stormy nights. Being comforted by her when easterly gale-force winds raging off the North Sea howled across the fens and whistled down the chimneystack like an angry banshee screaming at the little cottage that had the audacity to stand firm against its power. The gentle voice that had been such a comfort to Frances for so long, now silenced. Frances burst into tears and sobbed uncontrollably for several minutes. The doctor's words came back to her and she managed to compose herself sufficiently between less frequent sobs to advise Dan he would have to see Bob Turner, the joiner and undertaker.

With Dan gone, Frances bathed her aunt's body, dressed her in a clean nightgown and combed her grey hair. Strange as it seemed, Frances thought she looked much younger as she lay there, so at peace.

*

An overcast sky heralded the morning of Aunt Polly's funeral, but thankfully, the rain, so often prevalent across the fens on these sad occasions, had held off. Her funeral was a simple affair. Bob Turner had fashioned a plain coffin without adornment except for a small brass plaque which read: -

PAULINE WRAGBY
1779 – 1839

In the way of working-class people, the coffin was carried to the church by members of the deceased's family. Frances's father and her brothers, Anthony, and Peter, the two eldest of her siblings, along with Dan, carried out the role of pallbearers. It was a short journey from the little cottage to St Mary's Church and the cortège moved slowly in step with the doleful funeral knell of a single church bell. As usual on these sad occasions the whole village turned out and as the coffin reached the gathering outside the church, the male members doffed their hats in respect and the women bowed their heads solemnly. After the family members, led by Curate Robinson had passed, the whole gathering slowly followed the cortège, into the church. The organ which had been played so joyfully at Frances and Dan's wedding such a short time ago, now in stark contrast played sombre funeral music. The pallbearers placed the coffin on two trestles that had been set up in front of the altar in readiness. Frances and her mother and sisters took their places in the front pew and after the coffin had been placed on the trestles, Dan, her father, and brothers joined the rest of the family.

Curate Robinson began the service, but Frances's mind was elsewhere. Childlike, she tried to fathom out how the spirit of her aunt would enter the kingdom of heaven. She tried to concentrate on the curate's words…

'I am the resurrection and the life, sayeth the Lord. Those who believeth in me, even though they die, will live and everyone who liveth and believeth in me will never die…'

At that moment, the sun broke through the cloud, sending a dusty shaft of sunlight beaming through the stained-glass window which depicted Christ on the cross. The light illuminated the simple coffin with the diffused colours of the glass… *'The Lord gaveth and the Lord hath taken away, blessed be the name of the Lord,'* Curate Robinson continued…

This, thought Frances, was the answer to her ponderings of how the soul of her aunt would enter the Kingdom of Heaven. This, she thought, was God's way of guiding her aunt's soul to Heaven. He was lighting her path. Whether this was correct or not didn't matter, for it consoled her to think this *was* the case.

With the service completed, the coffin was raised again by the pallbearers; their task made effortless by her dear aunt's slight frame. Their feet shuffled in unison and led by Curate Robinson, the column of chief mourners retraced their steps back out of the church, as they proceeded to the newly prepared grave. Frances moved as if by instinct as she took her place at the side of her aunt's grave.

As the coffin was slowly lowered into the ground, she once more became vaguely aware of Curate Robinson's voice droning out the committal, *'We have entrusted our sister Pauline to God's mercy and we now commit her body to the ground: earth to earth, ashes to ashes, dust to dust…'* And with these words still ringing in Frances's ears, her Aunt Polly's body was laid to rest alongside her Uncle Walter. Frances took a small handful of soil and dropped it into the grave.

As Frances was about to leave the graveside, she was brought out of her surreal state by a young man of smart appearance who introduced himself as Jonathan Hope, a junior manager at the Lynn Brewery. He explained he had been sent to represent his employers and 'to offer their condolences to your good self and the rest of Mrs Wragby's family,' as he put it. Frances thanked him for taking the time to attend her late aunt's funeral, but she recognised the insincerity of this stranger's words as he fidgeted rather nervously in her presence. She didn't have to wait long to realise the reason for his edginess. Almost in the same breath he blurted out, 'I should inform you, the brewery now needs your late aunt's cottage for a young drayman who has recently married, and could you make it available for re-occupancy in two weeks' time,' he declared officiously, continuing to fidget as he forced his right index finger down his starched collar as if it was choking him. The urgency and delivery of the notice was both untimely and insensitive. It could have waited a day or two until after the funeral. She was aware they would have to remove her late aunt's furniture from the cottage and she and Dan had discussed this already. Indeed, next week a dealer was coming from Durnham to remove the pieces of furniture for which they had no use.

'My husband and I are aware of this and the cottage will be ready for repossession well before then. If you could arrange for someone to collect the keys from our address at Renton House Cottage, adjacent to the farmhouse, we will see they are available,' she said curtly, for she was seething at the indelicate way he had handled the matter. She left him and quickly caught up with Dan and the rest of her family.

*

Two days later, as arranged, Isaac Pound the dealer arrived at the cottage with his horse and cart to remove the unwanted furniture, giving Frances four shillings for the lot. The dealer slowly and deliberately dropped the silver coins into her open palm and a sense of guilt on taking the money stole over her. The clinking of the coins seemed to reverberate around the little empty room and Aunt Polly's bible readings came back to her. The vision of Judas's thirty pieces of silver for his betrayal of Jesus flashed through her mind.

'I reckon you got a good deal there, missus, although I say it myself. Not much profit in second-hand furniture these days; did you a favour getting rid of it for you; I'll let myself out.'

Frances didn't reply. She cared not what deal she had made. It was a task she hadn't looked forward to and she was glad it was over. With the dealer finally gone, the stark quietness of the empty cottage left her with little consolation. Now alone, she looked round the little downstairs room and the memories of the years spent with her dear aunt came rushing back. In the tiny downstairs she remembered her aunt teaching her how to cook, for hadn't her aunt fed many a weary traveller who passed their way in the days when Uncle Walter had been the landlord of the White Swan. She remembered being taught to knit and sew, acquiring all the domestic skills that would stand her in good stead for the future. Even as a little child when visiting her aunt, she had knelt on a chair next to her watching her baking and waiting in anticipation to lick the sweet mixture lining the almost empty bowl. Thinking back, Frances was convinced Aunt Polly deliberately left a little more than the scrapings in the bottom of the bowl for Frances's benefit. In this deep pensive mood, she could even smell the newly baked bread as she remembered her aunt lifting it from the little round oven at the side of the range. The same oven which was now stone cold as the grate stood empty of the cheering burning peat.

She climbed the stairs and entered the single bedroom. She could hear her aunt reading stories from the Bible and their reciting together the Lord's Prayer, before bidding each other *'goodnight, God bless'* then snuffing out the candle. She even recalled the pungent smell from the slowly extinguishing wick, strong in her nostrils. Back from her musing she left the room, closing the door slowly behind her. She reluctantly descended the stairs and as she passed through the downstairs room for the last time, she felt the little cottage was now bereft of its soul. She closed the old wooden door behind her and turned the large cast-iron key subconsciously in the lock for the last time. Turning, she made her way down the short path to the gate and closing the gate behind her she set off back to Renton.

As she reached the end of the lane she turned and took one last backward look. In her mind's eye she could see her Aunt Polly waving, as she had done three years ago, on the morning Frances had left for her interview with Mrs Hayward and she instinctively returned the gesture. During her walk back to Renton she cried unchecked for most of her journey home.

It was a red-eyed Frances who was greeted by her mistress when she reached the farmhouse. 'That's a thankless task out of the way, my dear, I can see it hasn't been easy for you; these things never are. You look upset, which is understandable. I tell you what, we'll have a nice cup of tea,' she said reassuringly.

'You are right. I *am* glad it's over. I'll put the kettle on; a cup of tea is what I need. How was Jemima?' Back in her own kitchen, Frances was already beginning to feel better.

'She has been as good as gold, as always. I don't think I've known a more contented baby. I don't know what's in that milk of yours, but once she had her fill, she settled straight away,' Mrs Hayward remarked. As they sat drinking their tea, Frances ran her forefinger subconsciously round the rim of the saucer. She remembered the two matching cups and saucers with the blue forget-me-not pattern which Aunt Polly had so lovingly kept for special occasions like birthdays and Christmas; it pleased her they had not been included in the things that had gone to the dealer that morning.

'Well another episode in your life is over, Frances,' Mrs Hayward said. A fact Frances knew only too well.

Chapter 7

Kenmare, Ireland

1849

Landscape artists viewing the scene before them in the Valley of Kenmare, County Kerry, in South West Ireland, would see a scene of tranquillity, clothed in differing shades of green, broken only by the silvery mountain cascades and crags that formed the Kerry landscape. But the artists' views in the Valley of Kenmare belied the truth. For the local people here in County Kerry saw no such scenes. No poetic moments for the artist to capture to canvas in vibrant colours – for in recent times, death had stalked the Valley of Kenmare. The only sign of life on the present Kerry landscape was the ragged shapes of three impoverished souls, a man, a woman, and a small boy, moving slowly away from a cabin which served as their home. The man was Michael Crowley and he carried on his outstretched forearms the coffin of his one-year-old daughter, Breda, who had died the previous day from 'famine fever'. His laboured pace – his body weakened through starvation was still too quick for his wife Mary and their four-year-old son Seamus, who struggled to keep up. Weakened from the lack of wholesome food, *they* viewed the treeless landscape in monochromatic shades of grey, through eyes clouded by the dark hues of death and desolation, so prevalent about these parts. The dead child's remains appeared to be nothing more than a rude bundle of sticks, for it was wrong to call it a coffin as it was barely fit for purpose. Michael had lashed together bits of wood he had salvaged from an old hurdle he had found washed up on the shore of the local estuary. Most wood about these parts was already long gone to make the coffins for the victims of last year's famine. Formal burials had ceased to be observed and the dead body was about to be interred in a shallow grave, which Michael in his weakened state had struggled to scrape out from the unyielding ground. No priest was in attendance; no last rites had been given. Father O'Brien's duties these days were permanently taken up in Kenmare. Rumour had it, shopkeepers were finding dead bodies huddled in their doorways on opening each morning. The poor were coming in from the rural areas in the hope they would find some sustenance or even gain admission to the workhouse; but that was a forlorn hope as the workhouse occupancy was already twice that for which it had been designed. The death rate from the famine had now reached such proportions the authorities were no longer able to cope. Now this year's crop of potatoes had also failed, compounding further the plight of these people who attempted to scratch a living from this impoverished land.

The land in this area of Ireland, as indeed in many other areas, was owned by a member of the English aristocracy. Lord Lansdowne, with his country seat at Bowood House in the county of Wiltshire, England, was the absentee landlord of this area of County Kerry.

The pitiful little cortège reached the prepared spot and Michael placed the deathly faggot into the hole in the ground. He scraped the small heap of useless earth onto the 'coffin' with a well-worn boot, spreading it across, rather than into the shallow hole; the deathly hush, unbroken by earth falling against the lid of a proper coffin; in a proper grave. Michael finished the 'grave' by carefully arranging stones he had gathered laboriously from the surrounding area, over the small patch of newly disturbed earth. Speaking in Gaelic, he uttered a short prayer, which translated into, *God accept the soul of our child into Heaven and her body into everlasting peace.* Gathering his wife and son to him, they slowly returned to the crude cottage that was barely a shelter. A fire burnt in the centre of the floor, fuelled by the remnants of the rescued hurdle. They huddled together in a vain attempt to keep warm.

'What are we to do, Michael? We can't go on like this,' Mary sobbed.

'Me belly hurts, Mammy,' young Seamus cried.

'Sure, tomorrow I shall make the journey into Kenmare, there's only one thing for it. We'll have to go with the rest of them and make the journey to America. We won't see the summer for sure if we stay here,' Michael said, forlornly.

'How are we to manage, Michael? Where is the money comin' from for such a venture? We have no relatives in America to send us money to pay for such a notion,' Mary stated, with despair in her hunger-weakened voice.

'I'm after hearing, that tomorrow Lansdowne's agent is collecting names of tenants and their families who want to take part in what they are after callin', *'an assisted passage scheme to America',* whatever that may mean but tomorrow I'll set off at the crack o' dawn to add our names to his list and get all the details. I want us to be among the first to take up the offer, 'tis our only chance now.'

The scheme Michael alluded to was devised by William Trench, Lord Lansdowne's agent. Recently, Trench had been summoned to Bowood to report on the problem of the famine and the effect it was having on the starving tenants and their issue. For some time, Trench had nursed an idea for solving the burgeoning problem of the destitute residents on Lord Lansdowne's large Kerry estate; a problem which had now reached embarrassing proportions. On his arrival at Bowood House, he put forward his idea of an assisted passage scheme to America, to Lord Lansdowne. Trench was convinced his scheme would alleviate the problem of the starving tenants and the embarrassing situation that existed in the overcrowded Kenmare

Union Workhouse. The plan had so impressed His Lordship that he adopted the scheme and placed at Trench's disposal the sum of 8,000 sovereigns for its immediate implementation.

Trench returned to Ireland and set about putting his scheme into practice. This was not an act of benevolence. Indeed, it was nothing more than a stopgap measure to alleviate an embarrassing situation which through gross mismanagement in previous year, had reached uncontrollable proportions. Trench knew, this was not the answer to Lansdowne's predicament, but he saw it as a temporary solution.

So, it was decided, two hundred paupers at a time, would be offered the opportunity to sail to a new life in America. The group were placed under the supervision of Eamon O'Shea, whose brief it was to shepherd the bedraggled group of emigrants on the sixty or so miles from Kenmare to Cobh and not to let them scatter until they were onboard ship. He was like a shepherd driving his human flock to market.

And so, Michael, Mary and little Seamus found themselves among the two hundred emigrants aboard a ship for Liverpool, where they were to re-embark onto a second ship sailing for New York.

Chapter 8

Norfolk, England

1849

It was May, and Dan and Frances strolled with their three children, through the fields on the edge of Renton. Jemima was now ten and in the intervening years, Frances had borne two more children, Edward now eight and John, six. Dan and Frances settled down in the soft grass while the children played their game of chase; their laughter ringing out across the fenland meadow.

Dan lay on his back looking skyward, pensively chewing on a grass stalk. Frances was the first to speak. 'I am worried about you going off tomorrow, Dan,' she said, her eyes focused on the children as she spoke. She wondered what might become of herself and the children should anything untoward happen to Dan. Tomorrow, he was leaving for Liverpool en route for America. Ever since Jemima's birth, she had dreaded the arrival of the day ahead. In her heart she had carried the hope that as the family increased and the children grew, Dan would have dropped the notion of making his fortune in America. She realised that being a husband and father had only strengthened his determination to make a fresh start. He had never kept his plan a secret and as a result Frances had never attempted to deter him. The plan he had held in his heart long before he had met, and married

Frances was at last about to materialise; albeit in a modified form and delayed by several years. In his childhood, he had thought of making the journey alone. The thought of taking a wife and family to America at that age never entered his head. In the early days of their marriage, their plans were to make the journey to the 'New World' as soon as they had saved enough money to finance their scheme, but as the children came along their plans had become more and more remote. Nature had not shared their plans, as every two years Frances had found she was pregnant. With Dan now almost thirty-two and Frances twenty-nine, Dan had come up with a compromise whereby he would make the journey alone. Once he was settled in and had raised enough money to buy land on which he could establish his own farm, he would send for Frances and the children to join him in their new home in America. Although Frances was not entirely happy with Dan's new arrangement, she knew he had nursed his plan for so long and there was no way of deterring him. 'You won't forget me and the little ones?' Frances asked nervously.

'You know I will never forget you, Frances, it's because of my love for you and the little ones that I must make this journey. I do not want to spend the rest of my days being a farm labourer and you skivvying for the farmer's missus. I want more than that for us all,' he said, 'and we'll achieve nothing else staying here,' he added indignantly.

Because Frances worked as a domestic servant up at the farmhouse, the Haywards had agreed to let her stay in the tied cottage until Dan returned for her and the children. This assurance gave him the courage to leave them behind and go ahead with his scheme; he doubted if he would have carried out his plan otherwise.

It was early evening, and the sun was still warm for May. High in the Norfolk sky, almost invisible to the human eye, a lark sang what Dan imagined was a celebratory hymn of thanks for the God-given gift of wings and the freedom they provided. Shading his eyes from the evening sun, now low in the sky, he looked towards the heavens to catch sight of this tuneful creature. Scanning the sky, his eyes eventually homed in on the lark hovering, as if stationary, high above them. 'Do you think I will hear a lark over New York, Frances?'

Dan's question fell on deaf ears as Frances unwittingly ignored the question. She had decided it was time to return home. Calling the children to her, they made their way back in the direction of the village.

'Have a good look around at what you are leaving behind, Dan; it may be some time before you see this beautiful landscape again,' she reminded him. An uneasy feeling came across her of cold water trickling down her back and she shivered. Was she trying to unsettle him in the hope he might change his mind? He could not leave her and the children without her approval. He needed that peace of mind to carry out his plan.

'Don't think it hasn't bothered me, Frances, this is not easy for me,' he reminded her. 'I have agonised repeatedly. In my bed at night while you slept, during my ploughing and whenever my mind was unoccupied, my thoughts would turn to whether I was doing the right thing, mainly by you and the children and least of all myself.'

'I understand fully what your mind must have wrestled with all these years. It is not in your nature to act selfishly Dan, and I am sure everything will work out for us. I am aware, what you are doing, you are doing for us all,' she said, not wanting him to reproach himself over his decision. He was pleased she had cleared the situation with him; knowing he had her support in what he was about to embark upon, was all-important to him.

That night in bed together, Dan was aware of the warmth of Frances's body next to him and wondered how long it would be before they next slept in each other's arms. He pulled her closer to him, nuzzled his nose into her hair and drank in the smell. He relished the smell of Frances. It was personal to her: but it was still *his* and he wanted to retain it in his memory for all the time they were to be apart. He kissed his wife on the nape of her neck, and she responded. She turned to face him, and her head became eclipsed between the moonlight streaming through bedroom window and the light from the single candle, creating a saintly aura; for in his eyes she *was* a saint. She was a caring and loving wife to him, and an excellent mother to their children. She searched for his lips in the meagre light of the candle. 'Oh, I love you so much,' she mumbled as their lips met almost by instinct and their bodies locked in a passionate embrace. Frances broke away and turned onto her back. She spread her legs in readiness for Dan's response, for she knew, she had to have him tonight more than any other night since their marriage. She wanted it to be the best lovemaking they had ever experienced. Dan responded to her urgency immediately and with his usual tenderness, he penetrated her proffered body…

*

Later, they lay side by side, their heads on the pillow, thinking of what had gone before, their heightened passion now sated and slowly abating. Frances was the first to speak. 'Please stay true to me, Dan, won't you? I cannot bear to think of anyone else sharing what we have experienced. Promise me, this is special to us and us alone.'

Dan searched for her hand and squeezed it gently. 'You know you are the only one for me and always will be, Frances, no one could ever take your place. You know ideally, you and the children would be leaving with me tomorrow if things had worked out as we planned. If only fate had not been so impatient and given us more time to save more money,' he said dolefully. She knew this to be the truth. Hadn't they talked of the move even before they married? Frances understood this was the last chance Dan had of ever realising his American dream. If he did not try this, the children would be getting older and the opportunity would be gone forever. He lay in his bed, his head heavy on his pillow until he dozed into a fitful sleep; but Frances never slept.

PART 2

THE PARTING

Chapter 9

Dan left first thing the next day on his journey to Liverpool, bound for New York. He was finally setting out on his voyage of a lifetime. This was not the way he had intended for it to happen and it worried him immensely that he was leaving behind his beloved Frances and their children. He fretted inwardly, not wanting to upset Frances and the children with his own misgivings. On his journey to Liverpool, he could not get the sight out of his mind, of Frances and their children seeing him off. He remembered Frances holding his outstretched hand until the horse-drawn cart quickened causing Frances to lose the hold she had on Dan and she stopped her pursuit and offered a forlorn wave of her arm. This too was short lived as the anguish within her heart overcame her. Cupping her hands to her face, she collected the stinging tears as they streamed from her eyes. Dan's last image of Frances was of her standing in the road with her apron up to her face, drying her eyes. He knew, to be strong enough for what lay ahead, he had to dispel this last vision and hang on to the one of his beloved Frances, waving him goodbye – but no tears.

The children also shouted their farewells, each in their own way. 'Bring us a present each from America when you come back for us, Da, won't y'?' Jemima had called as she ran alongside the cart.

'And you'll write to us telling us all about the mystical land of America,' Edward had shouted breathlessly. Little John, the youngest of the group had made no such special requests, doing well to keep pace with the other two. In his mind's eye, Dan remembered the three children continuing to run alongside the cart until, with fatigue overtaking them, one by one, they too gave up the pursuit. His lasting mental picture of his departure was the children waving with both hands like children do and loudly yelling their goodbyes until their voices trailed away and he was left with only the carter and the horse for company. Yet again, he wondered whether he was doing the right thing. He was convinced there was a better life out there for them all and this was his goal.

*

The journey while free of anything untoward was tedious, involving, cart, coach, and the final leg to Liverpool, by the relatively new railway system. This part Dan had found most interesting. As the railway coach swayed rhythmically, Dan thought of the time he had spent leading up to the day of his notice, teaching George Binney the skills of ploughing and harrowing exactly as old Ted had taught him. George Binney and Fred Gill had both matured into good reliable workers and Dan and James Hayward had discussed who would succeed Dan as ploughman. Physically, Fred Gill was of lighter build and for that reason alone they decided George Binney would be the new ploughman at Renton House.

*

On reaching the Liverpool dock area, Dan was amazed at the view before him. There were tall-masted ships and other smaller sailing vessels moored in the dock, and steam tugs towing ships out to the open water. Dan, being from the country, had never seen so many. The whole dock area was a hive of activity. People were to-ing and fro-ing. Ships from all over the world were being loaded or unloaded. The speed at which these human ants moved their loads amazed him. He could not believe the weight they could raise to their shoulders with consummate ease.

On the quayside, he met a group of people whom he learnt were lead miners from the Allendale area of Northumberland. A short, thickset man introduced himself as Edward Cranston. He appeared to be in his early forties and Dan could not help but notice how pale he looked. He had none of Dan's swarthiness brought about by years in the open air. 'How are ye lad?' he asked. 'Y'll be off to make your fortune no doubt.' Dan detected a slight sarcasm in the stranger's remark, which for the first time, caused him to doubt the validity of his venture and despite the hustle and bustle about him, he felt isolated there on the quayside.

Trying hard to regain his enthusiasm, he replied in a downcast manner, 'That's my hope for the future, if all goes well,' trying not to sound too forlorn as he revealed his plan to the lead miner. A troublesome feeling had come over him on meeting this stranger. He felt like a cork bobbing in a sea of strangers; out of his depth and ready to sink at any time. For the first time in his life he was far from home, albeit up to now, only as far as Liverpool. He was used to the closeness and the camaraderie of village life and was not used to unfamiliar faces all around him. These people too had been part of a close-knit community that they had to leave behind. The lead miners were travelling as families; Dan was travelling alone, his family left behind in Norfolk. He knew, for his venture to be successful he had to come to terms with these feelings, as the real journey was yet to begin. He drew upon Mrs Mullen's words all those years ago and he could hear her saying, *You can do anything you wish, Dan, if you only put your mind to it,* and it renewed his waning American dream.

'Where are y' from?' Edward Cranston asked, disturbing Dan's thoughts.

'Renton in Norfolk, I'm a ploughman but ideally I hope to have my own farm someday. My plan was for my wife and me to emigrate together as soon as we had raised enough to pay for the journey, but nature decreed we had a family first. Now, with three children, we have decided, I go ahead alone and return for the family once established in America,' he explained, hoping his plan sounded credible to the stranger.

'Why man, whether you are brave or a fool, only time will tell. At least you are doin' it of your own free will, which is more than can be said of the fifty-eight of us from Allendale. There's no alternative for us,' he continued in his Northumbrian accent.

'How do you mean?' Dan asked.

'It's a long story, bonny lad, but I'll try and keep it short. It all came about when the owners, W.B. Mines – W.B. bein' William Beaumont no less, Lord Allendale – tried introducin' new practices for producin' the lead ore. Better yields, they said. We all knew it would mean some of us were goin' to lose our jobs and our homes as well. So, we struck. We were out for five months before the owners brought in blackleg workers from Alston in Cumberland and they blacklisted us as well. We were all in tied houses, so we had nowhere to go. There were lots of ill feelin' in the community and some of us were gettin' death threats. Some of us already had relatives in Illinois and we decided to head out there and make a new start cos we would never get work in the Northeast anymore,' he said despondently.

'I wish you all well for the future and God go with you,' Dan said.

'Thanks, but you might need Him more than we do,' Edward replied rather irreverently and he began loading their belongings onto a large handcart.

'Oh, by the way bonny lad, y' travellin' alone, so watch out for the man-catchers and runners, they'll skin y' for y' hide n' fat if y'r not wise to them, so be warned,' Edward advised him grimly.

'Thanks, I will,' Dan replied, grateful for this crucial piece of advice.

'We're travellin' on the *Guy Mannerin* if you fancy a bit o' company.'

'Thanks, we may meet again,' Dan replied.

Left alone again, he had deep consternation as to what might lie ahead. The lead miner's conversation had sown seeds of doubt in his mind. Even amidst all the hustle and bustle around him, inwardly he realised how isolated he was and once more his thoughts went back to Frances and their three children at home in Norfolk. The thought of his family gave him the resolve to carry on and he mouthed quietly, '*I have to do it for them.*'

Dan managed to avoid the 'man-catchers', both male and female, who seemed to be everywhere. Watching the antics of these unscrupulous people who hunted in packs like wolves preying on the innocent traveller, Dan realised the value of Edward Cranston's timely advice. Notices of the daily sailings of the various packet ships to New York appeared on the walls of many buildings in the docks area and one notice caught his eye. It read: -

Loading Berth, South Side, Waterloo Dock.
THE ``BLACK STAR´´ LINE OF PACKETS.
LIVERPOOL TO NEW YORK.
'Packet of the 22nd May'.
The New York-built packet ship
``GUY MANNERING´´
William Edwards, Commander,
1418 tons register
Apply at our office for further details.

The illustration of the ship on the poster seemed to leap out at Dan. As he read, he realised it was the same ship that the lead miner Edward Cranston had mentioned earlier. Ignoring any would-be ticket sellers and after a few directional enquiries, he found the office of the ticket agents acting for the 'Black Star Line', situated around the corner from the waterfront. He entered the office and found it empty but for the passage broker who was balancing precariously on a stool to open the window. The elbows of his black frock coat were shiny through wear and the seat of his trousers had a greater shine, which almost dazzled. On hearing someone enter the office, he nervously extricated himself from his elevated position on the stool and eventually replaced both his feet back on *terra firma*. He was a tall, spindly, elderly man with a grey moustache occupying his entire upper lip. Dan deduced he was a snuff taker, for not only did the office smell of the stuff, but also, in the area below his nose, his moustache was stained brown by his use of powdered tobacco.

'How can I help you, young sir?' he asked, rubbing his hands together in anticipation of a ticket sale.

'I wish to purchase a passage on board the *Guy Mannering*, bound for New York,' Dan stated, in a voice even *he* did not recognise. *What have I said? Too late now*, he thought.

'Well you have certainly chosen the right vessel,' and to further encourage Dan to purchase passage to America on board the 'Black Star' ship, the passage broker continued to sing its virtues, repeating what Dan had already learnt from the poster. He provided extra information by revealing, 'She's a new vessel, built by William H. Webb in New York. She slid down the slipway only last March and she recently completed her maiden voyage to Liverpool. This will be her first East-to-West voyage,' he continued, with an air of pride, which Dan sensed was genuine.

'Guy Mannering was a character from a novel by Sir Walter Scott, don't you know. Two other ships of the Black Star Line namely, *Marmion* built 1846, and *Ivanhoe*, built in 1847, are plying their trade between Liverpool and New York. The owners have continued the trend in naming their newest vessel. Your passage will cost you £4 and 16 shillings, and in my humble opinion, still cheap at twice the price.' Dan admired the broker's determination as he worked hard to convince him that this was the ship for him.

'I'll take it,' Dan said and taking his pouch from inside his drover's coat, he placed five sovereigns on the counter. The ticket clerk took the cash and disappeared into an inner office. Straining his ears, Dan heard what he thought was a safe being opened slowly and more quickly he heard it close with a thump. *He is taking no chances in this neighbourhood,* Dan thought.

The clerk slid Dan's ticket across the counter along with four shillings change.

'You'll find your ship berthed in the Waterloo Dock; she sails in two days. If I were you, I would get on board today as you will be safer there than on the streets of Liverpool. There are some dangerous people in the dock area. Good day to you and have a safe journey and good luck to you in America,' the clerk said finally.

Dan made his way to the Waterloo Dock where he found the *Guy Mannering* floating proudly, her three main masts reaching to the sky. Her hull was painted black, with a broad band painted white from bow to stern. Along this white area was a series of hatches or vents, which at first glance were reminiscent of gun stations like those Dan had seen in pictures of Lord Nelson's flagship *Victory*, and he found this strange for a merchant ship. Maybe it was a deliberate ploy on the part of the designers to give the appearance from a distance, of an armed vessel. Flying atop her mainmast was the flag of the Black Star Line. The body of the flag was blue, with a white lozenge shape in the centre. In the centre of the lozenge was a five-pointed black star. Dan thought she looked magnificent. Her appearance and her newness gave him a good feeling about the whole venture. He boarded the *Guy Mannering* with his single chest of belongings and as he did so, he could not help but notice, he was travelling much lighter than many of the other passengers. The fact was, he could not afford any extra personal provisions to serve him during the forty-day or so voyage. It was less for him to protect from the *'runners'*, he thought. These people, like the man-catchers, also preyed on the waiting emigrants, offering to keep an eye on their meagre belongings and either running off with them or even having the audacity to demand payment for their return.

The ship was normally a two-decked vessel, but it had been fitted with an extra area referred to as *'atween decks'* and this was to be the quarters for all the steerage-class passengers. Once on board he made his way with the rest of the bemused souls, in the direction of the steerage deck, moving slowly with the crowd until he found one of the empty bunks, he could call his own. Rightly or wrongly, he chose one amidships and in the centre aisle away from either side of the hull, on the assumption, during rough weather, there might be less violent movement. These small bunks ran the full length of the ship on both sides and another double row ran down the centre, creating two aisles. The accommodation on board offered no privacy and Dan tried to contemplate what it would be like if the voyage was fraught with difficulties, like bad weather or worse still, disease.

As Dan was travelling without any extra personal provisions, the regulation issue by law would be his only sustenance during the voyage. According to the Passenger Act, no passenger-ship could put to sea until a medical practitioner appointed by the emigration office of the port of embarkation had inspected all the ship's passengers and the medicine chest, and certified the medicines etc. were enough, and the passengers were free from contagious disease. All this vetting for disease was carried out in a hasty fashion and almost everyone travelling to America were passed fit to travel. Once each emigrant had undergone this process, their passage tickets were stamped and they had nothing further to do before they went on board, but to make their own private arrangements and provide themselves with outfits of clothing to protect them from the Atlantic weather, or with such luxury foodstuffs and utensils on which to cook, which were over and above the ship's regulation allowance. As Dan had no further belongings, he hoped his drover's coat would provide him with adequate protection in any inclement weather in the coming weeks.

While Dan was arranging his things on his bunk, a couple and a young boy approached him. 'Would you be mindin' now, if we were to take up next to yez on the voyage?' the man asked. Dan recognised the man's accent was like the itinerant Irish workers who turned up at Renton House at certain times of the year. Having placed his belongings on the bunk, the man introduced himself. 'I'm Michael Crowley and this is me wife Mary. This young fella is me son Seamus, he's only four,' he announced proudly. 'We had a little girl, Breda was her name, but we lost her in April from the 'famine fever', God rest her soul. She would have been two later this year, had it pleased God,' he continued. 'So, with the crops failin', we had no choice but to take our chance with many other people from Kenmare who are making the journey to the 'New World'. Now we're setting up anew in the land across the sea, the name of which is on everyone's lips now. Everyone would have yez believe America is burstin' with all the world's riches,' the Irishman explained.

'Not at all, make yourselves comfortable,' Dan replied as he removed his few possessions from the adjacent bunk and stowed them underneath his own.

On realising Dan was English, the Irishman's mood changed. 'I don't know why I'm bein' so friendly with an Englishman. Is it not the truth now, they are to blame for all our troubles? Sure, they have never given a damn about us.' Although his wife said nothing at this point, Dan was sure she shared her husband's hostile feelings towards him. Little Seamus meanwhile hid behind his mother's well-worn skirt. Dan could not understand the Irishman's hatred of the English. How could he? He was not aware of the politics in Ireland and the absentee English landlords' attitudes towards their Irish tenants. In his naïvety Dan could only think, judging by the appearance of the Irish passengers, they had had a more harrowing journey to meet the ship than he had, and their wretched state was far worse than his. In his heart, he wanted to be friendly with these people. He could see quite plainly they had endured terrible hardship from one source or another and in their present state, the last thing he wanted was to make enemies of them. He was a deep-thinking

God-fearing man who considered all men equal. He always tried to follow his beliefs, and he hoped the anti-English feeling within the hearts of the Irish contingent on board ship would mellow as the journey progressed. He realised the cramped conditions between decks left no room for animosity, the weeks ahead could be a harrowing time for everyone on board ship, and it would be better for people to get on with each other than to make enemies on sight. Thinking discretion to be the better part of valour, he decided to defuse the situation by excusing himself and go back on deck. 'That's it now, off ye go! Truth's hard t' take is it now?' Michael Crowley yelled after him.

Dan had never personally experienced unprovoked anger like this from another man in his life before. He had had his differences with certain individuals in the past, but not often and not without reason. Having a confrontation because of his nationality was completely new to him. His sense of decency and fair play told him this man was nursing much pent-up bitterness and Dan did not want to judge him until he knew the full story of what was festering inside him causing all his anger.

No sooner had Dan arrived on deck, than the little form of Seamus Crowley came charging past him. He clambered up a pile of rope coiled on the deck against the gunwale of the ship. As he reached the top, his little foot caught in a loop and he pitched headfirst overboard into the murky waters of the dock below. His little body disappeared out of sight but soon he rose to the surface with his tiny arms flailing the water. Apart from the obvious danger of drowning, there was a greater threat from the hull of the adjacent ship. The two ships drifting together in the water could crush the boy as he struggled to stay afloat. Dan waited for the ships to drift apart and quickly grabbing a rope he lashed it around his waist. Without hesitation, he jumped over the side, landing in the water near to where Seamus was struggling to stay afloat. He grabbed the boy's body to him and holding him tightly, he signalled to a crewmember who had witnessed the whole incident to haul on the other end of the rope. By now, several other people had gathered and all hauling together, they raised Dan and the boy back onboard seconds before the two vessels came clashing together.

In the forefront of the excited crowd of people, gathered on the deck were Michael and Mary Crowley. Mary picked up her bedraggled offspring and cuddled him into her. 'We'll have to get y' out o' these wet rags,' she said through her tears of relief. A crewmember offered a piece of sailcloth and Mary gently set about rubbing down the naked young Seamus and at the same time remonstrating with him on the dangers of charging about on deck. Dan too took an offered panel of sailcloth and immediately began towelling himself down. Michael Crowley stepped forward and offered his outstretched hand to Dan who accepted it, shivering as he did so.

'Tis a brave man that y' are. I owe y' me thanks for what y've done. Forget what I said to y' earlier. I apologise to y'. I reckon not all Englishmen are bad,' Michael Crowley declared.

'I accept your apology, Michael. I did no more than any other man would have done under similar circumstances no matter what his nationality,' Dan replied, through chattering teeth. 'I hope we can get on together during the voyage on which we are about to embark.'

'I hope so too,' Michael Crowley replied and with that Dan went below to get a dry shirt from his belongings.

<h1 style="text-align:center">Chapter 10</h1>

Amid all the noise from the quayside, there was the noise of the crew going about their business of getting the ship ready for the open sea. During this time, the crewmembers carried out the search for stowaways. This exercise completed, the captain compiled his list of passengers by checking everyone's ticket. With over eight hundred passengers and crew aboard, the roll call was a lengthy exercise and took several hours to carry out. With the passenger list compiled, the anchor was hauled up by thirty crewmembers all working in unison to a tune sung by a single voice. *'Heave away, Boys,'* he sang, and the heavy anchor was slowly raised from the murky waters of the dock area.

The *Guy Mannering* left the Waterloo Dock, Liverpool, for New York on Tuesday 22nd May 1849. People were shouting a multitude of farewells and the waving of handkerchiefs and scarves signalled the ship's departure. Several ships were leaving simultaneously from different docks, multiplying the activity. Never had Dan heard such a noisy crowd of people nor had he seen anything like it in his life before and he marvelled at the spectacle. Even though it was a journey into the unknown, he found himself carried on the wave of euphoria. She passed a tower, which a crewmember explained, 'was the Observatory; built four years earlier to allow ships' masters to set their chronometers to Greenwich Time.' Clear of the docks and now in the middle of the River Mersey, the pilot ordered 'drop anchor'. The medical officer ran through the necessary legal requirements before the ship could put to sea. This necessity completed, the crew again weighed anchor and a steam tug began its task of towing the packet ship down the Mersey before casting her off into the open waters of the Irish Sea. Under the direction of the ship's mate, the crewmembers hoisted the sails for open water. In all this activity, the captain never shouted an order but instead he spoke quietly to his mate who called the captain's orders to the other crewmembers. With these final orders carried out, she was under way and as Dan looked up into the wind-filled sails, he realised his journey to America had begun in earnest and his thoughts once again returned to Frances and the children.

*

The ship, with a fresh wind in her sails, passed Fastnet Rock with the coast of Ireland in the background. The news soon spread through the Irish passengers and the deck quickly swarmed with a bedraggled crowd of Irish emigrants taking in what would be for most of them, a last look at their homeland. Dan too had left his homeland behind him and indeed his family too, but somehow his circumstances seemed to pale into insignificance set against these poor wretches milling around him and he found himself mouthing a prayer to God that all their futures irrespective of race or creed would bring them greater happiness than they had known so far.

As the Irish coast faded in the distance, only a small band of passengers remained, peering with difficulty, through strained eyes stung by tears to witness its passing and eventually they too returned to their bunks speculating amongst themselves as to what lay ahead.

Within hours of the *Guy Mannering* leaving the coast of Ireland behind, Dan became sick and he had to take to his bunk. This came without surprise. As a plough lad, he had never been onboard ship before, and his only sight of ships was on the rare occasions he had visited the port town of Lynn.

The passengers onboard ship especially in steerage class suffered from the cramped conditions and as with Dan, many more passengers were suffering the same effects of the ship's motion. The stench of vomit in these cramped conditions was overpowering. Dan felt he was spewing all the strength from his body with each new onslaught. Despite his weak state, he managed, with a great inner compulsion, to drag himself up on deck where he found a sheltered spot on the leeward side of the ship and there he stayed throughout the next two days. On the third day, he was much better, he had even made himself a small portion of porridge for breakfast, which he had managed to keep on his stomach and his strength slowly returned.

Once he had found his sea legs, he began to take in more of the voyage. He marvelled at the vastness of the open sea. Water as far as the eyes could see and yet seabirds foraged in the wake of the ship, so far from land. These birds were much smaller than the gulls that followed the plough back on the farm. One of the crewmembers informed him they were storm petrels commonly known by the sailors as Mother Carey's chickens, but the sailor could not say why they were so called. Seeing the gulls and hearing their screeching reminded him of his days behind the plough and his mind returned to Frances and the children and he quietly offered a prayer to God, not only for *their* safety in his absence, but for his own safety out on this vast ocean wilderness.

As Dan settled into the journey, he learnt more about his Irish neighbours, the Crowleys.

Michael Crowley related to Dan the tide of events that had brought them to a new beginning in America. He related in detail how the famine years beginning in 1845 had decimated the population. Michael had described how they had lost their youngest child Breda to the famine and how the workhouse had become an institution of death. He also told with bitterness in his voice, how the starving residents of Lord Lansdowne, had become an embarrassment and how his agent had come up with the idea of an assisted passage scheme to get them to America. Few tenants, if any, could afford to emigrate. 'Indeed, we no longer had the strength nor the means to work the land and so when the opportunity had come along, I decided t' grab it with both hands,' Michael explained.

Dan listened intently, hanging on Michael's every word as he described the circumstances that had brought them together. He understood Michael's bitterness. As he listened, he felt an affinity with this Irish family. Maybe it was the fact they had both worked the land for a living, meagre though it had been in the case of Michael Crowley and in the end, non-existent. Dan thought they might get on well together.

'What plans have yez about accommodation when we reach New York?' Michael asked him.

'I don't have any plans, I hope I can get fixed up with something on arrival,' Dan replied.

'Lansdowne's agent did say when he was explainin' all the details of this venture to us, that families with more than one wage earner in the household would qualify for better accommodation. So, I'm after thinkin', stick with us when we get to New York and it may work out better for all of us.'

'I will if you will have me,' Dan replied.

The idea Michael Crowley had come up with, removed some of the uncertainty Dan had about arriving in New York not knowing anyone and with nowhere to go. Now his plans were a little less haphazard and he felt a huge weight had lifted from his shoulders.

Chapter 11

One week into the journey across the North Atlantic, the weather up to now had been quite fair. There had been enough wind to fill the sails and apart from some squally showers, nothing to cause concern. A crewmember had spotted icebergs, huge mountains of ice, to the north, but the captain had ordered a change of course, taking them well clear of any danger.

Dan continued to spend all the time he could up on deck. With his drover's coat buttoned up to his chin, he would brave the squalls and he relished the sea spray lashing against his face. He was so used to the outdoor life and he hated the overcrowded conditions between decks. The noise and activity on deck; the songs of the crew and the order of things; the way the crew so skilfully went about their work, almost instinctively as though driven by some sixth sense; all these things fascinated him.

This person now enjoying his time at sea appeared far removed from the one who only one week ago was so ill with seasickness. The idea crossed Dan's mind had he not been a ploughman and with no ties, he might have considered going to sea for a living.

The time on deck Dan found most special was at night. With the moonlight lighting up the sea like a million shards of broken mirror glass, creating a myriad of constantly changing patterns of shimmering light. He also liked the sound the ship made, as it blindly cut its way through the black expanse, which in daylight seemed to stretch even to eternity.

Alone at night he wondered about God. From being a child, he had always believed God was everywhere. He thought about Frances and his children and he was confident that God was in Norfolk and would be protecting his wife and family. America was not Norfolk and until he arrived in New York, he had yet to learn whether he would find God here also. On deck, at night, he imagined the ship talked to him as it creaked and groaned its way onward towards its destination. The angry groaning of the timbers made him think, *was this the devil's voice, taunting him for leaving behind his wife and family?* His greed for wealth had been the driving force behind his yearning to emigrate to America and the devil was reminding him of his avarice. As quickly as the ship had chastised him, he was convinced the wind took on the voice of his beloved Frances as it soughed through the rigging telling him to take care in America and to return for them soon, safe and sound and this was the voice of God encouraging him that he was doing the right thing for his family. He gained solace from this windborne encouragement, his renewed thoughts of Frances made him realise how much he missed her, and he longed once more to take her in his arms.

It was during these quieter moments, out on this vast ocean, he felt closer to his God than he had ever been, and he prayed for a safe passage. When he eventually retired to his cramped quarters, he lay on his bunk thinking of Frances and the children and wondered how they were coping in his absence. Although he worried about them, he tried to fill his mind with all the happy times they had had together and the security they could afford in the future if this venture was a success. The offer of accommodation with the Crowleys also pleased him. This would help him raise the necessary funds to pay for his own land and home so Frances and the children could join him in America.

*

The next few days had seen the passengers in good spirits and the continued fair weather brought more of them up on deck. Much to

Dan's delight, there was impromptu entertainment from an Irish emigrant who had brought with him a fiddle, which he played with great passion and dexterity much to the delight of the Irish who urged him on. A fellow Irishman soon joined him, taking up the melody on the penny whistle. A third Irishman, skilfully beating out a rhythmic accompaniment on a shallow drum, completed the musical ensemble. Dan had not seen a drum like this before. The drummer beat the skin with both ends of a short drumstick with great dexterity.

Dan learned from one of the Irish passengers that the drum, a bodhrán, was common in Ireland. The Irish passengers who had decided to come up on deck soon joined in with the trio as they sang their Irish folk ballads. Although Dan did not understand the language, he was familiar with some of the melodies. The Irish travellers, who arrived on the farm at harvest time, sang them as they went about their work. It was probably good Dan was ignorant of the meaning of some of the Irish ballads, as some were anti-English; telling of the suffering of generations of Irish folk, exploited at the hands of English landed aristocracy.

The sound of the music brought others up on deck; more of the stronger passengers and soon others in the crowd took up the enlightened mood and spontaneously joined in and danced several jigs.

One of the Allendale lead miners also made his own contribution to the music on an instrument Dan learnt were the Northumbrian pipes. The lead miners also joined in the merriment and danced what some observers may have wrongfully thought was a parody of the Irish dancing, but Dan learnt later from Edward Cranston, it was clog dancing, popular in Northumberland. Clogs were the regular footwear of the lead miners. Dan was full of admiration for these people, both Irish and English who found themselves travelling together onboard a ship in mid-Atlantic, all having been driven from the lands of their birth, by the actions of uncaring members of the English aristocracy.

Next day the mood of all on board took on a serious tone when the news spread through the ship, of a twenty-year-old male passenger, Peter Muldoon, who had taken to his bunk with what appeared to be diarrhoea and dehydration. The captain summoned the ship's doctor and he immediately realised that the sick young man was seriously in need of rehydration.

The rationing of drinking water on board frustrated the ship's doctor in his treatment. He knew too well, without a plentiful supply of fresh drinking water, he would lose his patient.

Others gave whatever they could eke from their own rations but Peter's condition rapidly deteriorated. Sudden change in his features indicated to the doctor that his patient was suffering from cholera. News of the doctor's findings spread rapidly throughout the ship and soon, the cholera was spreading almost as quickly as the rumours. Four days later and despite the doctor's efforts, Peter Muldoon died on the 3rd of June, twelve days out of Liverpool.

Captain Edwards ordered the body to be committed to the deep with the utmost urgency in the hope it would prevent the spread of the disease. At first, it appeared this had indeed prevented further infection, but five days later the doctor diagnosed a second case when William Walsh aged 32 years, fell victim to the cholera and he died on the 11th June, eight days after Peter Muldoon. But the worrying thing for the doctor was, no less than eight other people had gone down within days of William Walsh contracting the disease including little Seamus Crowley who died on the 13th June. Mary Crowley was inconsolable and found it doubly difficult to come to terms with Seamus's death as she had now lost both her children.

The ship's doctor soon realised he had a serious outbreak on his hands and although he and the crew were working round the clock to make the victims as comfortable as possible, he knew there was little he could do. Fresh water and better sanitary conditions were required and neither of these conditions prevailed onboard ship. He knew, any poor soul contracting the disease under these conditions had little chance of survival.

It was Michael and Mary's turn to attend a burial at sea, that of their only son. Mary stood on deck, a pathetic sight with Michael's arm about her shoulders, trying in vain to suppress the trembling building up within her slight frame. The tiny, wrapped body lay on the narrow board: the same board used for all the previous sea burials now looked ridiculously oversized for Seamus's tiny corpse. Captain Edwards went through what was now becoming an overfamiliar service. Before he reached the committal, Dan moved alongside the little body now swathed in sailcloth.

Addressing Captain Edwards, he said, 'I would like to say a few words, if I may, sir.'

'Go ahead,' the captain replied. Dan remembered a poem from his own hand-written anthology. A poem by John Clare, the poet whose work his teacher, Mrs Mullen, had introduced him to, all those years ago. He quoted from the first verse:

> *'Infant grave mounds are steps of angels,*
> *Where Earth's brightest gems of innocence repose.*
> *God is their parent, so they need no tear;*
> *He takes them to his bosom from Earth's woes.'*

Although he realised there would be no grave mound covering little Seamus's body, Dan thought it added a little more dignity to the burial of a child at sea and he hoped Michael and Mary would find some solace in the words. He bowed politely to Captain Edwards and re-joined Mary and Michael. The captain once more spoke the words of the committal and nodded to the two crewmembers standing either side of the burial board. They slowly tilted the board until the little body was swiftly despatched to the deep.

As the body splashed into the sea without any great disturbance of the vast water, Dan remembered his rescue of little Seamus. The sea was now claiming the little body, which Dan had denied it so heroically only three weeks earlier. What others had seen as a brave deed then, now seemed so futile.

Captain Edwards joined the three mourners. He placed his hand on Mary's arm and offered his condolences. He took his leave of them and returned to his other duties leaving the little group to mourn alone on the windswept deck. The breeze carrying them to America, was rapidly putting distance between them and the spot where moments earlier the mighty ocean had swallowed up Seamus's tiny remains. Try as she might, Mary could no longer recognise the point where her child's body had entered the water. She once more broke into uncontrollable sobbing at the thought she would never be able to visit her child's grave and place flowers where his little body rested or mouth a silent prayer for his departed soul at the spot where his earthly remains lay. She tried to recall the words Dan had so recently recited, in the hope they may bring her solace; she could not recall them. Those well-chosen words, which at the time of utterance had comforted her, had evaporated on the wind.

The following day, the 14th June, Margaret Walsh, William's wife, died aged forty years. She had survived her husband by only three days. Within a week of William Walsh's death, eight more deaths had occurred.

At this point, Captain Edwards had to take whatever measures were available to him. He ordered everyone from the steerage class to muster on deck. This gave the crew and a few able-bodied passengers the opportunity to place barrels of tar the full length of the area *a'tween decks*. Into these barrels, they plunged red-hot iron rods that gave off acrid clouds of carbolic-laden fumes in the hope it would fumigate the steerage area and halt the spread of infection. These measures were less drastic than those suggested by a wealthy farmer from Scotland who was travelling to America to set up anew with his wife and family. His suggestion was, anyone who became ill with the disease, be despatched to the deep forthwith to improve the chances of the healthy to reach their destination. The captain immediately dispelled this murderous notion, knowing it would create a great outcry from the Irish passengers who were the main victims of the scourge. The crew had a job on their hands to safeguard the irrational Scottish farmer and his family.

The captain's ploy of burning tar, appeared to have brought about the right result, and eight days passed before the next outbreak. These latest victims were Thomas Stanton aged 37 years and Steven Cullen aged 27 years.

Ironically, two days later, the *Guy Mannering* stood off, outside New York harbour.

Fate had dealt the Irish passengers who had perished on the journey, a double blow. Having survived the famine, albeit in a malnourished state, they had not realised their dream of a better life across the Atlantic and Dan wondered what his own fate might be.

PART 3

LIFE IN AMERICA

Chapter 12

Thursday 28th June 1849 and the steam tug *Swallow* drew alongside, and the river pilot boarded the *Guy Mannering* into whose hands Captain Edwards temporarily passed control of his ship. The journey through the lower bay to the berths at Manhattan on the East River waterfront took them past Norton Point on the southern tip of Brooklyn, to the right, past Fort Hamilton, through the narrows, past Governor's Island and into the East River. As the ship slowly manoeuvred into berth 29, the bowsprit almost touched the building on the quayside. As the gangplank lowered, an air of excitement swiftly passed through the passengers thronging the deck. It was a similar scene to the one Dan had witnessed in Liverpool. The same hubbub and frenzied noise greeted the arriving passengers. He also recognised similar undesirable types here in New York to those Edward Cranston had warned him about in Liverpool. As soon as the gangplank touched the quayside, a crowd of these undesirables rushed aboard offering accommodation and all manner of services to the passengers about to disembark.

'Dan, you mind now, stay with us an' let me do the talkin', as far as Lansdowne's man is concerned y'r me brother Seamus,' Michael Crowley reminded.

'I'll remember,' Dan assured him, 'and I'm grateful to you,' he added.

'Lansdowne estate workers over here and form an orderly queue,' yelled a man in a stovepipe hat. Both the hat and the man had seen better days. Soon a long queue of desolate Irish immigrants had formed. He steered them in the direction of a man seated at a trestle table. After shuffling slowly along, Mary, Michael and Dan found themselves facing a weasel-faced man seated at the table. On the front edge of the table was a roughly fashioned nameplate bearing the name Richard Snell. In front of him were two thick piles of papers through which he was constantly shuffling and reshuffling. One contained the names of the Lansdowne tenants from Kenmare and the other contained the available accommodation addresses.

'Name!' the weasel demanded.

'Tis Michael and Mary Crowley and me brother Seamus, sir,' he declared, trying to be as convincing as possible.

'Does your wife intend to work too, Crowley?' he asked brusquely.

'To be sure, she will indeed, sir, we'll all be seekin' work – there's no mistake about that now,' Michael replied emphatically.

'Right,' said the agent, and once more resumed his frantic shuffling of the papers. After some deliberation, he looked up; first at Michael and he cast a suspicious glance in the direction of Dan. Dan held his breath, hoping Richard Snell asked no questions of him.

'You will be living at 38, Orange Street, apartment 5B, in the district known locally as the 'Five Points', in the city's Sixth Ward. I can exchange any remnants of money you may have, into American currency as it will not be of use to you now and I will give you a better rate of exchange than the money changers will on the streets.'

Although it did not amount to much between them, Richard Snell assured them; if they were prudent, they had enough to furnish their new home modestly.

Modestly. How modestly? Dan wondered. The exchange done, they had American money in their hands for the first time.

'Thank ye kindly, sir,' said Michael, almost grabbing the keys and his money out of the agent's hand before he had a chance to change his mind. Dan remained silent while Richard Snell exchanged his money.

'Over here, boy,' the agent demanded of a young black male, who Dan assumed to be about fifteen or sixteen years old, who was waiting with his primitive handcart.

'Show these people to their quarters in Apartment 5B, at 38 Orange Street, you know where it is, I hope?'

'I sure do; left off Anthony, sir, at the 'Five Points',' he confirmed confidently.

'Well let's be off now, we're in your hands, young fella,' Michael said quickly before Dan could speak and so reveal his English accent.

Thomas loaded their few belongings onto the handcart and off he led the three expatriates through the unfamiliar streets of New York City. Leaving the waterfront behind them, they progressed towards the 'Five Points' district in which Thomas had said Orange Street was.

Once they were out of earshot of Richard Snell, Dan realised Michael's ruse had worked.

Turning to their guide he asked him his name, realising it was the first time he had seen a black person in his life other than blackamoors he had seen portrayed in book illustrations.

'Thomas Mays,' the youth replied, grinning from ear to ear causing his black face to beam like a beacon.

'And how old are you Thomas?' Dan continued with his questioning.

'I ain't rightly sure but my mama, she says she thinks I's fourteen,' he replied and once more a broad smile lit up his round black face. If he was fourteen, to Dan, he did not look it. His frame suggested his mother's estimation was out by two or three years or indeed he was mature for his years.

'And where in these parts do you live, Thomas?' Dan queried of him.

'Well I reckon you wouldn't know if I told y', seen as y'all only just got here,' Thomas replied, being more honest than insolent. 'But I'll tell yer anyways,' he continued. 'I lives in what's called The Old Brewery, on Cross Street, along sides hundreds of other people mainly Irish and Negras,' Thomas concluded.

'Hundreds?' Dan questioned incredulously. 'Do you really mean hundreds, Thomas?'

'Sure do, ain't much furniture in the place, we all squats on the floor in the spaces we've claimed for ourselves.'

'Without any privacy?' Dan asked.

'Privacy, what's privacy?' Thomas asked in bewilderment. Dan realised he had asked a futile question and ended the inquisition. During this exchange, Michael and Mary had remained silent.

The journey from the waterfront to the apartment took, at Thomas's pace, about fifteen minutes. Dan could not help but notice how the conditions hereabouts had worsened the further they had travelled into the city. The conditions underfoot and the smell were almost unbearable; but to Dan's surprise, his three companions raised no objection. Dan found this strange and realised he was the only one affected by the conditions hereabouts. At this stage, he thought it might be prudent, for the time being, to keep his thoughts to himself. After all, the Crowleys had been kind enough to offer him accommodation with them, even though somewhat contrived, which could have easily been detrimental to themselves.

The drab building marked 38 Orange Street was in keeping with the rest of the properties in the area. The frontage was of clapboard design some of which was coming away from the rest of the building. If these buildings had ever known days of grandeur, the previous wealthy occupants had left for finer neighbourhoods a long time ago.

'This is it, folks,' Thomas announced, 'your new home in America, not much to look at but better than my place any day,' he added in his American drawl, which Dan found fascinating. *Where on Earth must Thomas live for it to be worse than this?* Dan asked himself.

'You folks require any more of me?' he asked, wanting to be back to the waterfront and another pick-up. 'That'll be a penny straight,' Thomas stated, trying to sound rather business-like. Dan took a few of the coins the agent had exchanged for them from his pocket and looked at them rather nonplussed. 'Which one of these is a penny? None of them looks like the pennies we have back in England,' he said naïvely.

'Don't you know that much?' young Thomas said rather rudely. 'Let me show you guys, it's easy, Liberty on one side and it tells you on the other side, One Cent,' he said emphatically.

Taking the coin from Dan's palm, he turned it over under Dan's nose, illustrating his point. *At least he is honest,* Dan thought. Pocketing the chosen coin, he said, 'Been nice doin' business with y'all, now be sure to look for 5B which you'll find on the first floor,' he added. 'If you need furniture, go to Black's second-hand store, first around the corner in Cross Street where you can get whatever you need at a reasonable price,' Thomas informed them. 'But don't settle for the first price; try to knock him down as he always tries to get the most he can out of his customers,' the black youth added.

With that final piece of advice, he turned his cart quickly and off he headed back in the direction from which he had brought them. With one backward glance, he called out, 'Y'all stay safe now, there are dangerous people about these parts,' and he tore off faster than he arrived: his handcart, now empty, almost overtaking him.

The trio of immigrants entered the main building and made their way up the stairs leading to the first floor. The stairs smelled of dampness and the whole place lacked ventilation.

To the left of the landing at the top of the stairs, was a small window. To the right a corridor ran the full length of the building. The window while inadequate for lighting the full length of the corridor was in keeping with the general ambiance of the establishment. All the rooms on this floor led off this corridor. As they passed along the corridor, the new arrivals were greeted by all kinds of human noise emanating from each occupied apartment. Passing the open door of apartment 1B, children screamed, and a demented woman's voice yelled obscene warnings at them to be quiet. In doing so, she only added to the cacophony. Further, down the corridor at 3B, sounds of a fierce domestic argument filled their ears. They eventually discovered apartment 5B at the darker end of the corridor. Dan deduced from this, there were probably five apartments on each level making fifteen apartments in the building in total.

Michael placed the key in the lock and opened the door leading off the dimly lit corridor.

The Crowleys were quite pleased with the accommodation and entered the place rather excitedly. Dan was less impressed and on seeing, what was to be his '*home*', his only thought was of his home back in Renton and of Frances and the children.

What have I let myself in for? he asked himself, not wanting to appear ungrateful to Michael for the kindness he had shown in offering him accommodation.

Inside the apartment and immediately opposite the main entrance, was a large grimy window, which had it been clean, would have allowed light to flood into the room. That could easily be remedied, he thought, trying hard to see a way of improving the conditions before him. In addition, the curtains hanging at the window were little more than rags and did nothing to improve the scene. He followed the Crowleys into the room. In the centre of the room were two rickety chairs and a rough table left behind by the previous occupants. A stove stood against the wall to the left. This would provide heating and a means of cooking food, he thought. Dirt and grease encrusted the floorboards around the stove. The walls behind the stove were also filthy and Dan knew, the caked-on filth would need scraping off and the wall and floor cleaned to make the place fit for habitation. To the right, two more doors led in turn to two bedrooms.

The bedroom to the left was the larger of the two. A window in the wall to the left offered little light and the buildings opposite restricted the amount of light entering the room.

In the smaller of the two bedrooms, they found a urine-saturated palliasse made of rough hessian. Wet straw was spewing out where the hessian had rotted. In this state it was not even fit for burning.

Dan offered to take this room; after all, he *was* the Crowleys' lodger and as such, he recognised he was last in the pecking order. His priority was to get rid of the stinking palliasse; but how?

The Crowleys continued their high appreciation of the place much to Dan's surprise as he saw it as a much-neglected hovel and could not help but wonder what type of people had previously existed here. The few pieces of abandoned furniture did not look out of place with their filthy surroundings.

After the initial investigation of the place, the three decided to make their way to Silas Black's second-hand furniture store and following Thomas's directions they found it first time. Passing through the streets of the 'Five Points', Dan again wondered what he was doing in this godforsaken place. What he saw here did not match the image he had built in his mind of the America Mrs Mullen had described to him all those years ago. As he looked about him, a sense of guilt crept over him for abandoning Frances and the children to come to this. *Is this what you have left your wife and family for? Have you come thousands of miles across a vast ocean chasing a schoolboy's dream, only to find this?* he chided himself. At this moment he vowed his family would benefit financially from his journey to America and he promised himself he would get a letter off to Frances and the children the next day. He also decided he would not reveal to them the full truth of what he had found on his arrival in America. Being a religious man, he knew this would weigh heavily on his conscience for he had kept nothing from Frances in the past.

By contrast, in all the time from leaving the ship, the Crowleys carried on with an air of elation. To Mary and Michael, the situation in which they now found themselves, was a reincarnation, a rebirth. This accommodation even in its present state was much superior to the conditions they had suffered in the last few years of trying to eke out survival in Ireland.

Mary knew she could make a home of this place. Dan did not share her enthusiasm: to him, all he felt as he looked about was disappointment.

Chapter 13

Silas Black was a thickset man, with muscular arms suggesting he might have been a prize fighter in his younger days.

'You've come for a few bits and pieces for your new place, have y'?' he asked. 'Well, have a good ferret round, I'm sure there'll be something to fit the bill, there usually is, never failed yet to meet my customers' needs,' he claimed confidently. 'Tell me, who put y' on to me?' he queried. 'I like to know who is spreading the word,' he continued.

'A young black lad called Thomas Mays who we met on the waterfront on arrival,' Dan informed him.

'That boy sure is something else, I tell y',' Old Black said.

After 'ferreting around', they found a double bed and a single bed with flock-filled ticking mattresses and a dresser, which Mary called a 'press', a small chest of drawers and an oak cabin trunk, which Dan said, would do for his few things.

They also managed to find a chair to match the other two left behind in the apartment. Their money also ran to some moth-eaten bedding, which even in this state would have to do as they could ill afford anything better. Some odd pieces of crockery and cutlery, a couple of slop pails and a wooden bucket for fetching clean water completed the deal.

'We can add things as we get settled in and have some money comin' in,' Mary stated, enthusiastically. Thomas had been right about haggling for they had indeed been able to knock Old Black down on his original prices. Old Black was a businessman, and he got a kick out of letting the customers think they had put one over on him. He deliberately marked up his original price knowing full well the true value of the goods. This worked every time and the news spread that you could get a *'deal'* out of Old Black.

Later that day, Old Black turned up at their address with his horse and cart to deliver the essential furniture and effects to their address. He showed an air of annoyance, saying his carter had left him in the lurch for more money down on the Bowery digging out a new culvert. Dan not slow to spot the opportunity immediately offered himself as the replacement for the carter's job. He explained to Old Black, he had worked with horses all his working life and would be able to start whenever he was required.

'How about tomorrow?' Old Black suggested and his mood improved at the thought of an instant replacement for the defector.

'It suits me,' Dan said excitedly, hardly being able to believe his luck.

'Report tomorrow at nine o'clock sharp and we will discuss pay,' Old Black stated. 'If I were you, I'd catch the black kid who brought you here; he'll act as your guide until you get your bearings. He may be a kid, but he has a shrewd head on his young shoulders. I bet he told you to knock me down on your purchases,' he said, knowingly and turning to Michael, 'You, young man should get yourself down to one of the many building works taking place all over the city and see if you can get signed up.'

'I will be doin' that for sure now, sir, and I thank ye for the advice; that's right kind of yez,' Michael replied.

'There are many people with lots of money in New York and they keep having grand houses built in better areas. I can remember when I first moved here, the 'Five Points' was *the* place to live. The money people have been long gone from here. Moved to the north side, every one of them. That's why you find it the way it is now.'

Silas Black continued to tell the newcomers about the area in which they now found themselves. 'The 'Five Points',' he continued, 'as you may have noticed, gets its name from the intersection of Orange Street and Cross Street and where Anthony Street running in from the west of the city ends. The area extends to the Bowery to the east, Canal to the north and Elm to the west. During the last century, there was a lake here called the Collect Pond. In those days, the pond was a beauty spot where the people would picnic in the summer and skate in the winter. Industries sprang up on the shores such as tanneries, rope works, and slaughterhouses and of course the brewery. This led to severe pollution and they filled it in with earth taken from a nearby hill, levelling it in the process. They didn't do too good a job, as the Tomb's Prison, built eleven years ago on Centre Street, between Franklin and Leonard is subsiding already. This, despite building it on a huge platform of hemlock logs,' Old Blake concluded. His comments on the 'Five Points' area once more pricked Dan's conscience, filling him yet again with misgiving about his venture to America.

Turning to Mary, Old Black asked, 'You my dear, have you any children?'

'No,' Mary replied nervously, not knowing what was coming next. 'We had two children, but we lost our first child to the famine and our second died at sea on the journey over from Ireland,' she revealed.

'Well, I'm sorry to hear that. I am indeed,' he said sympathetically but without real conviction. 'You should get off down to Tatum's wash house on Canal Street; I don't know what they put in the water down there, but the women are always leavin' to have babies, so there are always vacancies.'

'Young Thomas told me he lives in The Old Brewery,' Dan stated.

'Well it don't surprise me one bit, seen as how it's full of Negras,' Old Black said, adding, 'At least he's occupyin' himself and not runnin' with any of the gangs of juvenile felons who operate out of that den of iniquity. The building at one time was Coulter's brewery.

In its heyday, Coulter's beer was famous all down the eastern seaboard. The building was painted a bright yellow colour at one time but now the paint is nearly all peeled off and the clapboards with it. After the brewery fell into decline, it became dilapidated and no longer fit for its original purpose. About twelve years ago, it became a dwellin' place housin' them Negras, lots of them havin' white wives,' Old Black concluded with contempt.

'Come on Beauty, let's get back to the old place, this is costing me business, talking,' and with some difficulty he attempted to turn his horse in the street. 'Here let me do that for you, Mr Black,' Dan said, as he jumped up alongside Silas Black, keen to show off his expertise with the horse. He turned the horse and cart at the first attempt. 'There you go, Mr Black,' he said, and he handed the reins back to his future boss.

'Nicely done, son. You'll do for me,' and he set off back to his store, with a parting shot of, 'Don't forget nine o'clock on the dot tomorrow,' for the benefit of Dan.

'Oh, before you go Mr Black,' he shouted, 'we found a stinking palliasse in one of the bedrooms, how do we get rid of it?'

'Well if I were you, I'd do the same as everyone else around these parts. Drape it over the railings around Paradise Square and I can guarantee it will not be there for long before someone will take a fancy to it. It works every time.'

His suggestion of how to deal with the rotten palliasse left Dan perplexed as to who on earth would find any use for such a dilapidated and filthy article. He thought the name Beauty, was somewhat wasted on the rather scrawny animal. Its conformation was slight for a working horse. While not malnourished, she lacked the condition of the horses back in Norfolk, a sure sign her diet contained too much hay and too little oats. The smell of the horse filled Dan's nostrils and the thought of Norfolk once more sent his mind back to his days on the farm. In his mind's eye, he could see himself back there ploughing on a cold autumn day, with the steam wafting from the horses' hot backs, drifting up his nostrils as he got the land ready for the winter wheat. *At least she smells like a horse*, Dan mused as he drew in the ever-familiar smell and it pleased him to think he would be working with a horse once again, even if it was this run-down mare.

With Old Black gone, the next job for Dan and the pair was getting their purchases off the street and up to apartment 5B. They decided the two men would carry out this task while Mary kept an eye on the stuff left on the street. From the little time they had been here, they realised it would have been naïve to leave anything unattended. With everything carried inside, they set about tidying up the place as best they could. Before Dan did anything else, he gingerly dragged the stinking palliasse out into the street and up to Paradise Square, which was the area at the top of Orange Street and doing as Old Black had suggested, he draped it over the railings and made a rapid retreat hoping nobody had seen him. No way did he want anyone to think *he* might have been the owner of such a filthy article. At various places around the fence, there were articles of clothing and bedding hanging out to dry. On his return, he cleaned his room and set up his bed for the night while Mary worked in the other bedroom.

They removed the dilapidated curtains from the windows and used them for cleaning rags. 'I'll be off t'get some coal for the stove. On the way up here, I spotted a grocery store with bags of coal stacked outside,' Michael shouted through to them.

'That'll be new t' y' Michael, seein' how we've always burnt peat in the past,' Mary reminded him.

'Remember to get some kindling,' Dan added.

'And see if you can get some food, we must all be starvin', I know I am,' Mary added.

'I will now. It wouldn't do at all, to come all this way to starve when we were doin' that anyway back home, Mary,' Michael reminded her.

Michael retraced his steps, until he found the grocery store they had passed on the way to the apartment. On reaching the store, he found crates of fruit and vegetables stacked outside, some of which were bordering on rotten. A short, round woman, with eyes set close together, which gave her the appearance of having a permanent scowl, met him.

'I don't think we've met,' she claimed.

'Well that would be the truth now,' Michael said.

'Your accent tells me y' probably a Kerry man,' she speculated.

'A Kerry man I am, and proud of it, Michael Crowley is the name, pleased to meet y' now,' Michael replied.

'I'm Bernadette Finnegan, the owner of this place, what can I get for y'?'

'A bag o' coal and a few things to throw in the pot, to make a bit of a meal,' Michael said.

'I'll fix you up with a few things to tide you over 'til you find your feet; us Irish have to stick together.'

'That's right kind o' y', Mrs Finnegan,' Michael said, trying to show his gratitude.

'Oh, call me Bernie, none of that 'Mrs' nonsense now and I'm sure you'll be needin' a drop o' the hard stuff,' she added. 'Hoist a bag o' coals onto y' shoulder while I get you the rest of the stuff.'

She threw a selection of sad-looking vegetables and a bottle of cheap whisky into a big paper bag and offered it to Michael.

'I'll be payin' y' as soon as I get fixed with some work and that's me word,' Michael promised, as he took the bag in his free hand.

'That's no problem, pop in anytime; all y' Kerry men come in here and I always keep a drop of the hard stuff thru' the back,' Bernie Finnegan informed him, gesturing with her head in the direction of the inner room.

'I'll be biddin' y' good day now and I'll see y' again, Bernie; been nice meetin' with y'.'

And with that, Michael was about to leave the store, when Bernie shouted after him, 'Oh by the way, I've thrown a pig's trotter in t' add a bit of flavour to the stew, free of charge, Michael.'

Back at the apartment, Dan attempted to clean his room. He realised it would be a hopeless task. Although humble, Frances kept their cottage neat and tidy and it was a palace compared to this place.

*

Michael duly returned and dropped the bag of coal by the stove, causing a cloud of dust to spread across the room, undoing any good Mary's efforts had achieved so far. He dropped the bag of vegetables clumsily on the table, spilling the contents. Mary saw the bottle of whisky roll along the table top.

'Can we afford that now, Michael?' Mary asked, as Michael frantically grabbed at the bottle as it rolled toward the edge of the table.

'Oh, don't y' be given' out to me now, woman, sure they are almost given the stuff away,' Michael replied, not realising how truthful he was being. After a long swig from the whisky bottle, Michael set about getting the fire going in the stove. Using strips of rags from the old curtains, and the kindling, he soon had it back to life. Water was carried from a communal tap situated on the landing and once the stove was up to temperature, Mary cooked a simple vegetable broth flavoured by the pig's trotter. It was not a feast by any stretch of the imagination but as they had not eaten since they left the ship, they ate it ravenously.

That night Dan wrote to Frances and the children telling them he had safely made the journey across the Atlantic Ocean. It had been a hectic day for the three of them, settling into what would be their new home and he soon passed into a deep sleep.

Chapter 14

The following morning Dan was back on the waterfront early, to seek out Thomas Mays to offer him the opportunity to work together fetching and carrying for Old Black. As expected, he found him trying to negotiate a deal with a family of immigrants newly arrived off one of the many ships noisily disgorging her passengers onto the quayside. Luck would have it, from Dan's point of view, his little hand cart was too small for the job in hand, but Thomas being Thomas he was suggesting doing three journeys. At this suggestion, the head of the family with whom Thomas had been trying hard to strike a bargain, turned his back on him, indicating no deal.

'The very lad I want to see,' Dan said, taking Thomas by surprise.

'Lad?' Thomas retorted. 'That's a new one on me; most people calls me '*boy*', 'specially the white folks, they even calls the negra' men 'boy', tha's the way tis, tha's the way t'will always be, 'spose,' he concluded.

'Well that may be, Thomas, but to me you will always be lad or Thomas,' Dan declared, immediately realising the contempt in which the white people must hold the black members of the community. What struck Dan more was the way Thomas took this for granted. This attitude, Dan found hard to come to terms with, for his religious teaching made it difficult for him to comprehend the inhumanity of one race of people toward another.

'How would you like to come and work with me?' Dan suggested.

'Doin' what?' Thomas asked, curtly.

'Helping me with Old Black's carting,' Dan replied. 'Collecting from the sellers and delivering to the buyers,' Dan explained. 'You will be my guide and you can mind Beauty while I am inside with the customers. How's that sound to you, Thomas?'

'What's in it for me?' he asked, guardedly.

'Well, regular income,' Dan offered.

'What d'ye calls income?' Thomas asked.

'How does three cents a day sound?' Dan replied.

'Sounds to me I'm short-changing m'self, I make six already on a good day with my handcart,' Thomas countered, prepared for an argument.

'Four cents guaranteed. Final offer, Thomas,' Dan said emphatically.

Thomas cautiously considered the offer trying not to let any facial expressions betray his thoughts. After a moment of further consideration, Thomas spat on the palm of his right hand and offered it to Dan like an older man would have done when clinching a deal.

'Done,' he said, giving Thomas a dubious look when he saw the spittle-besmirched palm. Seeing that broad smile spread across Thomas's face, he took his outstretched hand and shook it firmly.

'You will not regret your decision, Thomas, lad,' Dan said sincerely.

With the deal done, Dan suggested, 'How about starting right away? Old Black wants us there for nine o'clock sharp. Let's not be late on our first day,' Dan warned.

*

Postman Martin Woods was in good spirits that September morning as he made his way to the cottage annexed to Renton House Farm, for in his bag he had a well-travelled letter, bearing an American stamp in the right-hand corner and addressed to Mrs Frances Swain.

Not often you get one of these to deliver, he thought to himself, which caused his chest to puff out so much it threatened to burst open the top buttons on his waistcoat. As he approached the cottage door, young Jemima greeted him.

'Hello Mr Woods, have you got anything for us today?' she asked hopefully.

'This must be what you've all been waitin' for these past few months,' he called, as he teasingly held the letter high above Jemima's head.

After several failed attempts at gaining possession of the long-awaited letter, Jemima gave up and tried pleading instead, at which the postman relented and lowered his up-stretched arm to the point where Jemima was able to grab it from his hand.

'Thanks Mr Woods,' she called behind her as she dashed inside the cottage.

Postman Woods continued his rounds. *I hope it is all good news; I hope I am not the harbinger of bad tidings. It never crossed my mind, that didn't,* he reminded himself, and in doing so, his chest deflated as he quickly put some distance between him and the cottage.

'It's here, Ma,' Jemima shouted as she brandished the letter in front of her mother. 'American stamps an' all,' she added. Frances took the letter from Jemima; the two boys abandoned their game of five stones and came scurrying from the corner of the room to join her and Jemima. With the children gathered about her, she carefully opened the envelope and withdrew the letter.

'Hurry Ma, tell us what Da has to say,' Jemima shouted impatiently.

'Are we all going to America now?' John asked, hopefully. Edward remained silent, not wanting to delay further his mother's reading of the letter. Frances began reading aloud.

Apt 5B
Orange Street
New York City
U.S.A.
30th June 1849

My Darling Frances and children,

I hope this letter finds you all well, if indeed, it finds you at all, since this is the first time I have availed myself of the American postal service.

The sea crossing, while extremely interesting and a wonderful adventure, was fraught with illness and many of my fellow passengers succumbed to an outbreak of cholera onboard ship. Despite the sterling efforts of the ship's captain, his doctor, and his crew, in all, more than thirty souls perished, and their remains were despatched to the deep. Thanks be to God I have survived to write this letter.

I have made friends with a young couple from South West Ireland from whom I am renting a room within their apartment. Unfortunately, their young son was one of the victims of the cholera outbreak. He was only four years of age. This was the second tragedy they have suffered, as they lost their other child last year, to famine fever (a form of typhus brought on by the potato blight), aged but one year and named Breda.

They are members of a large group of Irish emigrants who have fled the scourge of the great potato famine. Consequently, these Irish people were the most vulnerable onboard ship but despite all this they have shown great resolve and the majority, by the Grace of God, have survived. My friends are Michael and Mary Crowley from Kenmare in County Kerry. Tell the children I have seen some remarkable sights on my journey, such as flying fish. Fish that leap from the water and fly for several yards, out of the water. While out of the water, they flap their fins as though they were wings, giving them the appearance of birds. This way they kept pace with the ship for some time.

I also saw small gulls far out to sea which, a crewmember informed me were storm petrels but the sailors called them 'Mother Carey's chickens', but when I asked him for an explanation as to why they were so called, he was unable to do so. The sight of these small birds made me wonder how they survived so far out in this watery wilderness, so far from land. I also saw an iceberg to the north of the route we were following. A huge mountain of ice floating in the sea. Thankfully, this was during hours of daylight and as a precaution our captain set a more southerly course and so it remained far enough away from us, to be of no threat and eventually it passed without hindrance.

In all, the journey across the Atlantic had taken thirty-seven days and the lives of thirty-four unfortunate passengers, God rest their souls.

As I said earlier, I now find myself living in New York City with the Crowleys and I have secured a job with a Mr Silas Black who runs a second-hand furniture business. I am to be his carter, so I am lucky enough to be still working with one horse at least. I see the opportunity of making sufficient money here to give us a good start in America and I have a great idea which I plan to put to Mr. Black, at the first convenient opportunity which, if he agrees, will allow me to make more money still, but I will tell you more about that as it develops.

I have also met a young black youth with skin as black as coal. A more pleasant soul you never did see. He carried our belongings on his handcart and guided us to our new place of abode. His name is Thomas Mays. He would have me believe he is fourteen years of age according to his mother, but he says he is not sure; but I think he looks older.

That is all the news for now, but I will write again soon. In the meantime, I remain your loving husband and father...
Daniel

On completing the reading, Frances placed the still-opened letter against her lips and kissed Dan's signature. Taking the letter from her lips, she ran her finger slowly over his signature, tracing every single letter that formed his name. As she did so, she pictured him in her mind's eye, to close the miles between them.

She calculated the letter had taken almost ten weeks to reach her. As she folded and replaced the letter in the envelope, the back of her hand brushed against the swelling now developing once more in her stomach. She was four months pregnant with their fourth child, following their last night of passion before Dan had left for America.

Dan had deliberately omitted from the letter, any account of the squalor he had witnessed in the short time he had been in New York City, especially in the 'Five Points' district.

99

Chapter 15

'Y're prompt, that's a good start, I like that, and I see you've got the boy with y',' Silas Black stated. 'I've three drops for you; local, so you should soon have them finished but after that, we will have to see.'

'I've got an idea, Mr Black,' Dan said, rather tentatively.

'Whoa there! I am always cautious when people put ideas my way.'

'But I think this will benefit both of us,' Dan said, not too convincingly.

'OK, I'll hear you out, but it's got to be good, and I mean good from my point of view,' Old Black retorted.

'Well, what I have in mind is this. When work is slack, I suggest young Thomas and I can operate down on the waterfront using Beauty and the cart to shift cargo from the warehouses to the ships, and from the ships to the warehouses. I will pay you a percentage of all the trade I drum up, say ten per cent.'

'That's not a good idea from where I see it. I see it more as twenty,' Old Black replied.

'Well how about ten, as I suggest, and I will take on Beauty's feed?' Dan replied, knowing Beauty would require a change of diet including a daily measure of oats to boost the energy required to withstand the rigours of work down at the docks.

'You're on,' Old Black said, emphatically, realising the work would be ongoing even when his second-hand furniture business was quiet and now Dan was taking over Beauty's diet, he knew he was onto a good business proposition.

They shook hands and Old Black turned to Thomas. 'You boy, heed this man, he will teach you a thing or two, mark my words. Not that he can teach you anything new about the ways of these parts; you're already well versed on that score. Let's say you're good for each other,' and once more the now familiar smile spread across Thomas's face.

*

Dan had grasped the opportunity, in creating for himself the business of working for Old Black when needed and working down on the waterfront for himself. As each week passed, Dan was building up his business. The system was proving most profitable. So much so, he had opened an account at the newly established Emigrants' Savings Bank in Chamber's Street and each Saturday morning, Dan stopped off at the bank where he would deposit his surplus cash. Moving the cargoes down on the waterfront was a lucrative business and he soon found himself in a position to make Old Black an offer of buying Beauty, but he now realised he would need a bigger cart for the waterfront operation. He also realised, the business relationship between them was disrupting his earning potential and he now needed to be his own man, concentrating his efforts on his new enterprise.

He reported to Old Black's place the next day and put his latest idea to him. Wary of how Old Black might react, he tried to broach the subject as diplomatically as possible.

'Good morning Mr Black, I've been thinking…'

'Hold it right there, young fella,' Silas Black said, stopping Dan mid-sentence. 'Whenever I hear you start talkin' that way, it puts me on my guard. You are provin' to have a shrewd business head on y' and I'm tryin' to keep abreast of y' here,' he concluded.

'Well I know you have been good to me by giving me the opportunity to make a start for myself. I need to spend more time down on the waterfront, which is where the money is good and it's regular business. I know you need to transport your wares to and from your customers' dwellings and for that you need your horse and cart. I have got used to Beauty and since I have been feeding her myself, she has put on condition and she is now well suited to the work she does shifting the cargoes. I do need a bigger cart, so I am proposing to buy her from you at a good price. You can buy another horse suitable for your needs and pocket a profit from the deal,' Dan suggested rather tentatively. He already knew Beauty was up to the rigours of work on the waterfront and he preferred to continue working with her than taking a chance with an untried and untested new horse of his own. After what seemed to Dan to be an eternity, Old Black finally responded to his proposition.

'Well now, first thing that comes to my mind is, if I say yes to this, you've got yourself a horse and no cart and I've got a cart and no horse. That ways we're both out of business,' Silas Black replied with a wry smile on his face.

'I've considered that,' Dan responded, 'and what if I suggest we go together to the dealers and you get yourself a horse and I get myself a cart, as yours is proving too small for my needs these days.'

'You still ain't mentioned money,' Old Black reminded Dan.

'No, I was coming to that, how does $30 sound?'

'Don't sound like music to my ears, $50 would be more in tune, I'm thinkin',' Old Black replied.

'$40 and we're both in harmony,' Dan retorted, taking up Old Black's musical connotation.

'Done!' said Old Black and they shook hands on the deal.

'Now it's me doin the thinkin', like where do you intend keepin' Beauty?'

'Well I was hoping I could keep her here as usual as there is an extra stall and room for the extra cart and I could pay you livery,' Dan suggested.

'Sounds fine by me,' Silas Black agreed.

*

Within the week they were on their way to the Hoers' Brothers, Otto, and Jorgen, of German extraction, who dealt in livestock, *'and all things horsey,'* as Old Black had put it.

During the journey to the horse dealers, Dan had enquired if Silas was a religious man.

'You could say I was, a long time ago when I was a boy,' Silas admitted. 'But, when I was thirteen and before my Bar Mitzvah which, had I gone through with it, would have *obligated me to God,* I ran away from home and ended up here in New York,' he revealed.

Dan remained silent in the hope Silas would continue and his ploy proved successful.

'My original family name was Schwartzman. Imagine, Blackman in English; with all the Negras about, I had to change it once I arrived in New York,' he said with a laugh. Dan failed to see the joke.

'My parents left Germany in 1795 and they settled in Philadelphia. They were Jews and they thought they could follow their religion in America, free of persecution. Therefore, in answer to your question, Dan, I suppose, as a lapsed Jew, I am now an atheist, as I do not believe in gods, of any form. I have not been near a synagogue to this day. What about you, Dan, you strike me as a religious man, are you a churchgoer?'

'I was a regular churchgoer back in England, but I am afraid to say, I have neglected my churchgoing since arriving in New York. It is something I mean to attend to soon,' Dan replied.

'I take it you are a follower of Christ,' Old Black suggested, and Dan detected an air of sarcasm in Silas Black's remark.

'I am indeed a Christian, Silas, excuse me, may I call you Silas?

'Course ye can, seein' as how well I've taken to you, Dan,' Old Black replied.

'I must admit, after witnessing the deaths from the cholera on the journey out here and the suffering of the Irish who were fleeing the potato famine, and to top all, the squalor and ungodly things I have seen since arriving here, it has seriously put my faith to the test. The thought has passed my mind of late, where was God when the Irish Catholics needed Him? Why is He not doing something to help the wretches living in the 'Five Points' and the Old Brewery in particular?' Dan queried.

'Well Dan, you seem to have to do some wrestling with your faith too. You appear to be at the same impasse as I was all those years ago. My religion taught me to believe the same god as you until I decided I did not want to commit myself to any god. The difference in the religion to which I was born and your own, is your religion accepted Jesus Christ as the Messiah; my religion ceased at your 'gospels'. Those Jews, who were unconvinced, by this upstart, chose not to accept his claims and they are still waiting for the 'real' Messiah's arrival. These same Jews had your Messiah killed off as an imposter. I will give you this, Dan; I do believe your Jesus of Nazareth did exist and he was probably the best politician to walk on this earth. Tell me one politician down at Tammany Hall today, being remembered almost two thousand years on. Believe me, not one of them will have a new faith established in his name, despite the physical force they employ to get across their views. Your Jesus as I see it had to be a good politician. He had much to deal with; the hierarchy of his church was corrupt and in the pay of the Romans who were occupying the country of his birth. They allowed the moneylenders to do business within the temple and at the same time, he was preaching passive resistance, or as he allegedly put it, *'to turn the other cheek'*. Now that could prove a fool thing to do, especially if the other person packs a mighty punch. Having said all that, I do not go for the miracle working. Walking on water can be a mighty dangerous game to play,' Old Black remarked cynically.

The word blasphemy was on Dan's lips, but he said nothing. He wanted to offer some argument in support of what he believed but he could not do so. As he pondered Silas's words, he realised no one had put their views of Jesus Christ across to him so forthrightly before. The more he thought about it the more he was convinced he had left his God back in Norfolk, where he had known the love of Frances and the children and the peace and quiet of the fens and the comfort of a good home. His faith had gone unchallenged until now. After a brief silence, Dan was the first to speak.

'I know you no longer believe, Silas, but if you can cast your mind back to when you were small, did you believe God could see all our actions and hear all our utterances? Because I think, He has His eyes tightly closed to what is happening in the 'Five Points' area. Before I arrived here, I believed in the all-seeing eyes of God. I am now having doubts,' Dan confessed.

'Well, I understand what you're saying, young man, and I do not intend to try to influence you in any way. The way I see things regarding your god in his heaven up there is this; he's a long way from the truth, and from that distance, maybe he don't see things as they are down here. If he *is* watching us, to him, viewing from way up in his heaven, things may appear all hunky-dory down here,' Old Black said.

Dan was uneasy listening to Silas Black's deliberations; they had left him with much to ponder over. They both remained silent for the rest of the journey, but Dan was turning Silas Black's comments over repeatedly in his mind.

Silas Black reined Beauty into the Hoerst Brothers' yard and called her to a halt.

After viewing what was available within their price range, they were able to buy Old Black his new horse, a dappled grey gelding of fifteen hands and of good conformation. Going by the name of Major, Silas's new acquisition was a bit ribby, Dan thought, but nothing diet correction could not put right. Jorgen Hoerst, the younger of the two brothers, claimed the gelding was half Morgan, half Percheron cross.

'It will be the Morgans that will open up the West,' Jorgen Hoerst predicted.

'A nice horse you got yourself there, Silas, and at $35, including tack; a real bargain,' Dan enthused. 'All in all, a nice profit too,' he added, alluding to the money he had paid Old Black for the purchase of Beauty.

Dan also got the cart he was looking for. A bigger vehicle, with detachable side rails which could accommodate wider loads. They yoked the new horse into the shafts of the new cart and with Dan taking charge of the new horse and cart they headed back to Silas Black's premises; the same premises that in years gone by, had been a furniture emporium selling quality items in a quality district. The size of the business at the time, meant the emporium had been built with its own stables and years later Silas Black had acquired the premises for a knock-down price. Therefore, there was ample accommodation for both horses and carts.

Once they were back, they saw to the horses' needs.

'Don't forget, Silas, a good measure of oats besides his hay ration on the days he's been worked hard, will help his condition,' Dan suggested.

'May I remind you oats ain't cheap Dan,' Old Black replied.

'Please yourself, but a working horse needs oats in its diet and if you deny it that, it's a false economy.'

'Well how's about you letting Major have a few of Beauty's oats?' Old Black suggested, adding, 'You wouldn't deny Major the odd scoop now and again, seeing how they're goin' to get on fine together. Pity he's a gelding, we might have set ourselves up as horse breeders,' he finally added, laughing at the idea.

'Don't give me any more ideas,' Dan replied.

'Not a bad day's work, young Dan,' Silas Black said with a hint of satisfaction in his voice.

Dan didn't reply, not wanting to reveal what he was thinking; he was more than satisfied in his mind he had got the better of Old Black on the deal.

'Until you get yourself a new man, Silas, I will be prepared to help you out whenever I can. I wouldn't want to leave you in the lurch after all the help you have given me,' Dan said with conviction.

'That's real considerate of you, Dan; I might take you up on that, young man.'

Chapter 16

Dan was quickly building up his business working on the waterfront. Through hard work, his reputation for reliability was growing and so too was his bank balance. He had helped Old Black with his deliveries until he had found himself another deliveryman, leaving Dan to devote all his time and energy to his own business. He was happy down on the waterfront, but he detested living in the 'Five Points'.

Mary Crowley was working hard to make a home of the apartment. She had not acted on Silas Black's suggestion of seeking work at Tatum's washhouse, not her own decision but Michael's. He had decided, rather dictatorially, her place was in the home and they would have enough money to see them through, from his earnings as a labourer and Dan's rent. Michael had taken Old Black's advice and had found work digging out footings on a building site in the Bowery district for which he was earning eighty-seven cents a day, $5.22 cents per week. Most men working on the contract were also Irish immigrants.

The Crowleys were paying rent of $5 per month for the apartment, to which Dan contributed a dollar a week for his room and meals and a further five cents a week for Mary doing his laundry. With this amount of income each week, they had been able to make further visits to Old Black's to add more furnishings to the original purchases they had made back in June. Now in mid-October, Mary was well pleased with the home she was making for the three of them. She had hung curtains at all the windows. When drawn closed, the curtains in the bedrooms provided privacy when needed. Although still simple, the new curtains were *'grand'*, as Mary had described them, compared to those they had found on first arriving at the apartment. To Mary, the place was her palace.

Once in conversation, Dan had asked Mary about the home, which they had left behind in Ireland. 'Well, it was nothin' like this, for sure.' She continued to describe it as having only one room with a dirt floor and a hole in the centre of the roof through which the smoke from the peat fire was supposed to vent. On days when the wind was blowing strong off the Atlantic, which was quite often, the smoke filled the room making it necessary to keep the rickety door ajar to improve the atmosphere within. In turn, this let in the bitterly cold Atlantic winds especially in the winter months. As Mary surveyed her new home, she felt a sense of contentment. At last they had food in their stomachs, enough money to live on without the morbid dread of famine hanging over them and free of the threat of the workhouse. To Mary and Michael, already the move to America had transformed their lives. Dan on the other hand, knew he could not share their enthusiasm until he was out of the 'Five Points' and into his own place with his wife and family.

The next day he was in conversation with one of the warehouse captains.

'What we're y' engaged in back in England; surely not this work?'

'Well I did work with horses. I was a ploughman and one day I hope to own my own farm,' Dan revealed.

'A ploughman? Well, they say, arable land like what you have set your sights on, young man, is available to the north of the county,' he advised.

'Any idea how much good farming land like you describe costs?'

'I ain't rightly sure, but I have heard it said it can go for as little as $6 an acre. Some say you can get a huge tract of land for next to nothin' these days as they encourage people with the right experience, to open up the country; it would be a much better prospect than bringin' yer wife and kids to the 'Five Points'.'

With the conversation over, Dan went back about his work, but the warehouse captain had given him something to think about and he soon decided this would be his aim for the future.

While Dan appreciated the improvements Mary had made to the apartment, his opinion of New York City's Sixth Ward in general and the 'Five Points' district in particular, had not changed from the day he arrived at Orange Street. This only steeled his determination to earn as much money as he could, as quickly as possible and seek out the farming land to the north of the county, mentioned to him by the warehouse captain.

A strong anti-English feeling existed among the Kerry men. Indeed, one of the gangs operating in the 'Five Points', the 'Kerryonians', did little else but pick fights with the English immigrants. Luckily, for Dan, Michael had made it known to all the Irishmen his reason for having an Englishman as a *friend* and how Dan had risked his own life in saving Seamus from the murky waters of the Liverpool docks. This earned Dan a fragile immunity within the Irish fraternity. He knew if he fell out with Michael he would be in real danger. He realised his situation was worsening as regards lodging with the Crowleys. Michael's attitude to working on the building project down on the Bowery was rapidly changing. He was spending less time in his labouring job and more time hanging out with the 'Dead Rabbits' gang, one of many gangs operating throughout New York City. These gangs were both territorial and sectarian. Michael was excited about his acceptance as a gang member and he enthusiastically explained to Dan how these gangs had originated out of the need for self-preservation and operated all over New York City.

'We've got to protect ourselves against the 'Native Americans'. If we do not, they'll do for us,' he had argued. The 'Native Americans' were formed, as the name suggested, from the original white Protestants residing in New York before the burgeoning influx of immigrants from Europe. Dan viewed all the gangs as organised criminals and for his own safety, he kept this opinion to himself.

Michael revealed to Dan that the 'Dead Rabbits' were a breakaway faction of a bigger gang named the 'Roach Guard'. 'Sure, we're all Irishmen and proud of it. Some time ago, there was a bust-up in the 'Roach' and several members broke away and formed the 'Dead Rabbits'. Now there is bad blood between the two gangs. Since the breakaway, we fight each other constantly. If other gangs, especially the 'Native Americans' or the 'Bowery Boys' were to confront either the 'Dead Rabbits' or the 'Roach Guard', we would unite in a common cause. The 'Native Americans', sometimes referred to by the rival gangs as the 'Know Nothings', look upon all immigrants, regardless of their origin, as nothing more than interlopers and as such should be kept in their place,' Michael explained.

Michael had Mary sew a red stripe down the side of his trousers, another emblem of the gang. Dan was not impressed with this request and he found it rather childish. Indeed, with the task completed, and Michael regaled in his emblazoned trousers, Dan thought they looked rather bizarre on a so-called Irish hard man and he was not impressed; he had never lent himself to things military and he found pseudo-military ridiculous.

The leaders down at Tammany Hall, the headquarters of the Democrat politicians in New York City, used the 'Dead Rabbits' to threaten the electorate to vote in their favour and to break up their opponents' meetings. In general, they were involved in mugging, pickpocketing and robbery, and indeed sometimes murder. Michael's involvement in these activities brought in more money than he made working as a labourer. Apart from the money, he enjoyed the rough and tumble of the gang's activities.

The gang would meet up in the back of Bernie Finnegan's place. There they would plan their next operation or review the previous night's activities and to share out any ill-gotten gains while partaking of Bernie's rotgut whisky. Michael was no longer the quiet, caring man who had arrived from Ireland. He was drinking more and more; his whole personality was changing rapidly.

With time, Dan had become more familiar with the geography of the district in which he was now living and as such, he had learnt more about the gangs operating in the various districts.

The 'Bowery Boys' as the name suggested operated out of the Bowery district. These gangs also operated voluntary fire services, but the overzealous rivalry between them was quite often detrimental to the service they were supposed to be providing.

PART 4

EVENTS BACK HOME

Chapter 17

Norfolk, England

November 1849

Frances was busy preparing breakfast for her and the children before she took up her duties at the farmhouse. A hard frost had settled on the fens overnight, freezing any surfaces exposed to the bitterly cold wind blowing off the North Sea. A loud commotion emanating from the farmyard broke the calmness of the November morning. People were yelling frantic instructions and garbled advice. Above all this commotion, Frances could hear Mrs Hayward's erstwhile calm voice, wailing as though in distress.

Leaving Jemima in charge of the younger children, Frances rushed round from the cottage to the farmhouse to see what was happening. The scene on turning into the yard was one of chaos. 'What has happened?' Frances asked, addressing no one in particular.

'The master's slipped on the icy steps leading from the hayloft and

I fear he has broken his leg,' Mrs Hayward explained, dejectedly. 'Oh, my poor James, what on earth have you done?' she cried, wringing her hands in anguish.

Taking a knife from his pocket, George Binney slit the right leg of his master's trousers up to the knee, exposing the damaged leg. 'Get him up off the ground, steadily. His leg is badly broken,' he said, confirming Mrs Hayward's worst fears.

'He'll need the bone setter,' someone else declared.

'I'll get Dan Cutler,' Fred Gill volunteered, with urgency in his voice.

Despite the commotion, they managed to get James Hayward indoors and made him as comfortable as possible on a settee situated below the window.

After a few minutes, which seemed like hours to Frances, Dan Cutler arrived. He took one look at James Hayward's damaged leg and shook his head. 'It's well beyond me to attempt anything with this break, it is a compound fracture and far too complicated for my capabilities. I'm afraid we need to get him to Durnham hospital with great haste or the blood won't be gettin' to his foot. Get the brake round here,' he said with urgency.

George Binney soon had Dolly yoked into the limbers and brought the brake round to the side door of the farm. They loaded their injured master onto the brake and made him as comfortable as possible for the ten-mile journey to Durnham.

During all this preparation, James Hayward was in great agony and he kept drifting in and out of consciousness. 'Keep him awake!' shouted Mrs Hayward. 'Do not let him go to sleep, talk to him throughout the journey!'

With George Binney at the reins and Fred Gill tending to his master, they set off for Durnham with as much haste as was practically possible considering Mr Hayward's dilemma. Frances spent the morning trying to console Mrs Hayward, without any real success.

As the days following James Hayward's accident passed, the news from the hospital got worse. Mrs Hayward, on her return from her most recent visit, had reported that despite all the efforts of those concerned at the hospital, the break was so severe they had no alternative but to amputate the leg below the knee. The time lapse in getting James to the hospital had caused the leg to become gangrenous and this was now the bigger threat to his life.

Within four days of the original partial amputation, the gangrene was moving so rapidly the surgeons expediated a full amputation of the leg. Notwithstanding this, Mrs Hayward received the sad news from the hospital that her husband's condition had deteriorated rapidly and he died in his sleep the following night.

*

Two weeks from the time of his accident, they laid James Hayward to rest, in the churchyard of All Saints, Renton, in the vault that now contained the remains of three generations of Haywards. Their son Richard and daughter Arabelle together with their respective spouses had made the long journey from London. The funeral had been a grand affair and the whole village turned out as was the usual thing on these occasions. People from all over the county joined the family mourners, to pay their respects to James Hayward; such was his popularity within the local community and beyond.

Frances found Richard and his wife Diana pompous and standoffish, while she found Arabelle and her husband most amiable. It came, as no surprise to Frances when they announced to their mother, they were returning to London the day after the funeral, which in Frances's opinion, showed no respect for their widowed mother.

*

The appointment of James Hayward's successor brought serious problems for Frances and her children. Following the death of her husband, Mrs Hayward had received notice to vacate the farmhouse in readiness for the arrival of the new bailiff Robert Hart and his wife Rachel.

In turn, it was necessary for Frances and the children to vacate Renton House Cottage so Mrs Hayward could move in.

Her next conversation with Mrs Hayward confirmed her worst fears; she only had two weeks in which to find alternative accommodation. 'Robert Hart will be taking up his new position on 1st January,' Mrs Hayward informed her. 'If it was up to me, my dear, you know I would take you in until Dan's return, but my tenancy is only a courtesy arrangement on the part of the estate managers and as such I am not allowed to take in boarders. In fact, if any members of the present staff were to marry, they would qualify as tenants and would claim precedence over anyone else. As you know very well George Binney and Sally Groves, have been engaged for over a year now, should they decide to name the day, my own tenure of Renton House Cottage would be in jeopardy. I am so sorry it has come to this, Frances, and so close to the Christmas festival. I've come to love you like my own daughter,' she added sadly.

The irony in all this was Robert Hart was the boy Frances had gone to school with and whom she had admired for his academic ability. The same boy, who had gone on to study modern agriculture on leaving the village school, was now being instrumental in displacing Frances and her children.

*

Try as she might, over the next two weeks, Frances was unable to find any alternative accommodation. Filled with anxiety, she hardly slept. In her desperation, she had gone to her parents' home at Ditchington, a six-mile journey to the east of Renton to see if they could help, taking Jemima with her and leaving the boys with Mrs Hayward. The reception she received on her arrival was welcoming at first. Her mother's mood soon changed when Frances revealed the predicament in which she and the children now found themselves. Her father knowing his wife well, sensed her mood change and took himself off to the 'Green Man' before her mother launched herself into one of her vitriolic tirades.

'I don't know how you expect us to take you in, there's hardly room for us all here as it is, without you and *your* three and another on the way. Your daydreamin' husband should be here for y', y' bein' in your condition. Y' always had ideas above your station, our Frances, ever since y' went to live with our Polly, her filling y' head with fancy readin' as she did. When you did start work, you couldn't settle for workin' as the dairymaid or scullery maid; no, not you, it had to be the mistress's maid.'

'I knew what to expect when I came here. You don't understand, what Dan is doing in America is to make enough money to give us a fresh start in life; and that is what he *will* do. I have already penned a letter to him telling him of our plight and I have every faith in him returning as swiftly as possible once he learns of our predicament. By the time he receives the letter, books his passage, and makes the voyage home, it will be at least three months hence. It is only during this period, I would seek your help, to tide us over until Dan's return. Surely, you could find it in your heart to offer us a roof over our heads during the crisis now facing us. After all we are your own flesh and blood,' Frances pleaded.

'Y' know what I said when y' told me you were planning to marry that poetry-readin' man of yours. "Once y' marry, y'll make y' bed and lie on it,"' her mother reminded her unsympathetically.

'It's not his fault recent events, that are not of his own making I might add, have overtaken us and I think it is unfair of you, Ma, to condemn him this way; especially in his absence,' Frances shouted back angrily in defence of her husband.

The argument with her mother and the long walk from Renton had left Frances drained of strength. Realising her mother had made up her mind on the matter, she decided further argument would be futile and she still had to make the return journey. Gathering Jemima to her, she turned and headed for the door, knowing she would probably never see her mother again and she left with a deeper fear of what was to become of them.

'What are we to do, Ma?' Jemima asked, sensing even at her young age, the seriousness of the situation.

'The truth is, Jemima, I don't know; for the life of me, I don't know,' Frances replied with tears trickling down her cheeks.

During the long and arduous journey back to Renton, Frances reflected on her mother's attitude towards her. Frances could not believe her mother could dispel her so readily. Even at Aunt Polly's funeral, her mother must have held Dan in such low esteem without revealing her true feelings towards her son-in-law. She had thought she knew her mother well, but today her mother had proved that was not the case. Frances had not realised in the time she had been away from home, she had lost something that she had thought would endure the test of time – her mother's love; it grieved her immensely to learn otherwise.

Chapter 18

Four days before the day of her eviction from Renton House Cottage, Frances had faced the ten men who formed the Board of Guardians of the Durnham Union Workhouse at their weekly meeting; an occasion she would rather forget. The inquisition was both harrowing and embarrassing. On hearing her account of her recent misfortune, like her mother, they too thought Dan's idea of seeking their fortune in America, speculative and thus, foolhardy. The most hurtful thing in their interrogation was when one of the Guardians inferred that Dan had been neglectful of his wife and family.

'I regard your husband's actions as a complete and utter dereliction of his duty towards you and your children,' said a rather pompous member of the board.

An overweight member, who until now had slouched in his chair, saying nothing, shuffled sideways, and pulling himself upright with some effort, pointed his silver topped cane directly at Frances's distended midriff and snarled, 'Did he know of your condition before he embarked on his ill-conceived plan?'

'No, he did not, sir,' Frances replied almost in a whisper, for her ordeal had dried her throat.

'Speak up, we shan't hurt you, my dear, can I offer you some water?' asked another member of the panel whom Frances thought showed the only friendly face. He poured a glass of water and offered it to Frances, which she accepted and took a couple of quick sips. Not wanting to slow down the procedure too long, she took two more quick sips and handed back the glass.

'No, he did not, sir,' she replied for the second time.

'Let us regard that as the one thing in his favour so far,' said the pompous member.

'As you are aware, the widow of your previous employer has been in touch with us and she has explained the circumstances which have led to your present dilemma. We will now retire to deliberate your request,' said the chairman. 'If you would wait outside, we will call you back once we have made our decision,' he concluded.

Frances thanked the Board politely and left the room.

She was ushered to a bench seat to the left of the door, where she awaited the board's decision. Under their present circumstances, admission to the workhouse, while daunting, was the best outcome for which she could hope. She had no idea what lay ahead of them and it was this fear of the unknown that daunted her. After what seemed an age, the door opened, and Frances entered the chamber for the second time. She took up a position again in front of the ten men and the bearded member addressed her.

'We have reached our decision and the outcome is this. We are prepared to offer you and your children accommodation within the institution. I take it you can read and write?'

'Yes, I can, sir,' Frances replied, meekly.

'Then fill in this form for you and your children and following your eviction, you will return here and present the said form to the Relieving Officer. In your condition, it will be necessary for you to see the Medical Officer also. You will probably be confined within the hospital wing until your child is born. I must also inform you, we operate a segregation policy for all inmates of the institution. This means, no male or female co-habitation, not even within families. I understand you have two boys and one girl; the boys will be together, but your daughter will be within the girls' quarters. Your baby will remain with you until the time he or she be weaned from your breast. There will be no family meetings.'

'But the oldest is only ten and the youngest but only six years, surely I will worry myself sick about them and in my condition,' she implored.

'I am afraid we need to have rules to maintain the smooth running of this establishment,' said the friendly face.

'Is there anything else?' the chairman asked, curtly.

'No,' said Frances, knowing full well, she wished to ask many more questions. She wanted to run from the place. The board's announcement of the splitting up of her family had knocked the life out of her.

'If that is the case, your business with us is concluded and you may leave,' the chairman said finally.

'Thank you all for your charity, I and my children are most grateful,' Frances said politely and she left the room.

*

It was the day of their eviction from Renton House Cottage. Frances was saying goodbye to Mrs Hayward. 'I am so sorry it has come to this, Frances,' Hannah Hayward said apologetically.

'None of this is your fault, Hannah. You have had your own share of misfortune. I am fortunate in as much as my husband is still alive even though he may be the other side of the ocean. Can I ask you to take care of the few belongings I treasure; the two china cups and saucers that meant so much to Aunt Polly?'

'Of course, my dear,' said Mrs Hayward, 'and anything else you may cherish,' she added as an afterthought. With a final hug of Frances and the children, she bid them all goodbye. Neither of them were able to hold back their tears.

*

Frances had passed the arched entrance to Durnham Union Workhouse on numerous occasions when visiting Durnham market with Aunt Polly. In those happy, carefree days, she remembered reading the name fashioned in wrought iron, which spanned the entrance gates. Instinctively, their pace had always quickened as they passed this austere building and was not relaxed until they had cleared the place. No respectable member of the public ever wanted to be associated with the 'Workhouse'. Any such association, was regarded as a slur on one's character and 'The Workhouse', instilled fear into the community. Designed to repulse rather than attract, it gave the impression that it was a place one should strive to avoid. As such, the word 'workhouse' filled every man, woman, and child with trepidation. Now, Frances found herself and her three children, and heavily pregnant with her fourth child, about to make the ignominious entrance through the same menacing arch. This time, no quickening of pace would take them safely past the entrance of this fearful place; today they would be entering under the dreaded arch of despair.

Through the arch and across the yard was the main building. Built of stone, there was an air of foreboding about the place. They nervously passed through the arch, not knowing what was in store for them and Frances found the building very intimidating. She had a quick glance behind her to see if anyone from the outside world had seen her make her entrance. The sad little group walked with heads bowed in shame, across the yard and into the main entrance to the building. To the right was a large desk on which a sign stated, 'RELIEVING OFFICER'. Two women dressed in workhouse uniforms stood to the left of the desk.

'Your name?' asked the man behind the desk rather abruptly. His whole persona was that of an undertaker, which did not help Frances's present state of mind.

'Frances Swain,' Frances said meekly, and once more, as in the interview with the Board of Guardians, her throat had dried up. This time there was no kind offer of water, after all this was an employee of the Board of Governors and he had a job to do.

'Are these all your children?' he asked, continuing in his now familiar abrupt manner. 'No father I see,' he continued. 'Has he abandoned you?'

'No, he is working in America,' she replied, trying hard to make her version of the truth sound convincing.

'Well that's what it states in my book,' the officer replied, sarcastically. 'Have you completed the forms, which the chairman of the Board of Guardians gave you on your interview? Your man can't be sending you any money, or you wouldn't be standing here in front of me now, looking all forlorn and your little'uns hangin' on to your skirts. Make the most of what little time you've got with them before you all go your separate ways, once I've got my paperwork together,' he said coldly. Frances sensed an air of pleasure in his final remark, which filled her with despondency. She wondered how many poor souls in the past, had stood at this man's mercy, subjected to his veiled concern. *What sort of person could do such a job as his?* she asked herself.

'You filled the forms in yourself and without any help?'

'Yes sir, I did,' Frances replied.

'You have a good hand, I'll give you that and it might stand you in good stead when it comes to finding you work,' he said, raising a grain of hope as to what lay ahead.

'Your two boys will be taken to the boys' probationary ward and your daughter, to the girls' ward. You, because of your condition, will go to the hospital ward for assessment. If deemed fit to work, a job will be found for you. With your standard of education, a light job within administration is possible. When the birth is imminent, you will be transferred to the hospital wing. After the birth of your child, your confinement in the hospital wing will last for ten days. At the end of this period, you will return to the women's quarters along with your baby. The baby will stay with you until such times as it is weaned off your breast, then it too will be taken to the children's ward,' he declared, reiterating almost verbatim what the Board of Governors had told Frances.

Hearing this for the second time made it no easier for Frances to accept and she silently prayed to God for Dan's safe return home as soon as possible. She was sure Dan would sort everything out; if he were only here. He would find somewhere for them even if it meant moving to another area and ending this terrible ordeal, she told herself.

With little respect, he asked her abruptly, 'How far on are you?'

'I think I have another four weeks to my baby's birth; possibly early next month,' Frances replied nervously. She had the date of her baby's conception indelibly etched in her mind. Dan had set forth for America on the 19th May, last, and she had calculated she was thirty-two weeks into her pregnancy. She knew she had conceived on the night before Dan had set off for New York.

'In that case, if you are found to be of sound health following your medical assessment, you will be found work for the next four weeks or so.'

There was a long silent pause… Frances thought the officer was allowing her time to mull over the situation in which she and her children now found themselves.

The silence was broken by an abrupt, 'Take them away!' causing Frances's stomach to pitch. The two women who had stood in silence up until now stepped forward and ushered them into an adjoining room. The room was large and had cupboards from floor to ceiling running along one wall. A pile of rectangular wicker baskets was stacked in one corner.

Five cubicles stretched along the wall at right angles to the cupboards. There was only one chair in the room, placed in the centre. The taller of the two women took Jemima first and sat her on the chair. Without any announcement, she produced a pair of scissors from the large pocket of her apron and commenced cropping Jemima's hair.

'Oh! No!' Frances shouted, at the same time as her daughter broke into fearful crying. Frances watched on helplessly as more and more of her daughter's hair littered the floor in a semicircle around the back legs of the chair.

Each in turn, the children had their heads cropped mercilessly by the tall woman, while Frances had to stand and watch. Finally, it was Frances's turn to have her raven black hair cropped in this barbaric initiation to workhouse life. The same black curls Dan always found so attractive fell to the floor in huge clumps. This woman's would-be act of barbering was completely void of any skill. In fact, the more she cut the clumsier she became. She must have performed this task a countless number of times on other poor souls in the past, but it appeared that no improvement in her skills had been achieved.

While her colleague was busy with the hair cropping, the smaller woman rummaged in the large cupboards as she assembled the regulation uniforms they would wear during their stay in the workhouse. Having finished the hair cropping, the taller woman was the first to speak.

'All this is necessary; you will have to have a bath. We will confiscate and sterilise your clothes along with your other belongings and they will be stored until the time you leave the workhouse. The uniforms always remain the property of the workhouse. If you leave the premises dressed in your uniform, you will be arrested and charged with the theft of workhouse property, unless you are a member of an outside working party. On the other hand, if you give three hours' notice, you are free to leave at any time and your own clothes and belongings will be returned to you,' the small woman explained.

Their haircuts completed, they had to bathe, and dress in their uniforms. Frances and Jemima's uniforms were ill fitting and consisted of course, calico shift, woollen petticoats, day caps, worsted stockings, and canvas slippers. The three boys' uniforms consisted of a strong cloth jacket and breeches, striped cotton shirt, cloth cap and boots. Although all the clothing was clean, none of it was new.

With the grooming, the ablutions and the fitting-out process completed, the tall woman turned to Frances. 'It's time to say your goodbyes; you all have to go your separate ways. I'll give you five minutes and it will be time,' she said without any emotion.

The group of four huddled in a tight circle hugging and crying.

'You must be brave, my darlings; you, my little men will have to be brave indeed, and Jemima, believe me your Da will get us all out of here as soon as he gets back from America, believe me,' said Frances hopefully.

The two boys, despite Frances's request for bravery, were too young for such valour and being afraid of the unknown, were now crying uncontrollably.

Jemima, ever mindful of her mother's condition said, 'Will you be all right, Ma? Will they look after you?

'I'm sure they will, after all, this isn't a prison,' Frances said. Jemima was not convinced and seeing her mother with her beautiful hair ruined, made her doubt whether there was any difference between the two institutions.

'Time's up,' said the tall woman and she took Frances by the elbow and led her from the room.

On reaching the door, Frances turned and said, 'Remember I have written to your Da and he will return.' With this parting comment, the orderly led Frances into the inner part of the institution. Immediately after, the other woman led the children to *their* quarters.

PART 5

END OF A DREAM

Chapter 19

New York, January 1850

Down on the waterfront, Beauty munched hay from a nosebag and Dan and Thomas were having a bite to eat during a quieter period. Dan preferred to take a break around midday to get some proper food into Thomas on a regular basis as he was never sure of Thomas getting anything to eat at all when he returned to the Old Brewery.

It was the first week in 1850, it was Dan's first experience of a New York winter, and it was a particularly cold one. The cold spell had begun at the turn of the year and it showed no sign of relenting. Indeed, he had found it necessary to fit rubber cleats to Beauty's hooves to get a purchase on the frozen cobbles of the quaysides. Luckily, the snow had stayed away and although there was much ice underfoot, Dan was able to carry on with his business uninterrupted. Seated on a bale of cotton, sheltered from the wind, Dan had drawn Beauty in towards them and they could feel the heat from her steaming body.

'Tell me a bit more about yourself and your family, Thomas,' Dan asked.

'Ain't much to tell about family I guess – only me and my ma.'

'What about your dad, Thomas. Isn't he around anymore?'

'From what I know, my ma and pa had been slaves to a rich family in Boston and came to New York when they were freed. I don't know exactly when. During the time when I's still a baby, my pa, who was workin' on the railroad, gets himself killed in a blastin' accident.'

'I'm sorry to hear that, Thomas, how awful for you.'

'Don't bother me none, never knowed him any roads,' Thomas said, philosophically.

'What my ma did tell me is he was a hardworkin' man and he died tryin' to give me a good start in life and that's why I's a good worker too and not runnin' with those gang-kids in the Old Brewery. In those days, my ma tells me, we had our own place.' Thomas's reasoning had an air of pride about it, which impressed Dan.

'That is honourable of you, Thomas.'

'What's hon-err-bull, Mr Dan?' Thomas asked.

Since Dan had taken him on as his helper, and of his own choosing, he now addressed Dan as Mr Dan, saying he preferred it that way.

'Honourable, Thomas, means something or someone is worthy of praise, good, upright,' Dan explained, and once more Thomas's face beamed with his huge smile Dan found so infectious.

'I reckon that's a good enough word to remember, Mr Dan, and to try to live up to,' he added.

'What about your ma?' Dan queried further, for he was curious to learn more about Thomas's circumstances.

'She don't do much, but I know she goes with the white fellas at times; word is they pay more money than the black guys do. I gets worried for her. Some of those guys, they treats her rough and she lies cryin' herself to sleep of nights, helped by the gin from the stone bottle she keeps under her pillow,' Thomas disclosed.

'Is this going on under everyone's nose?' Dan queried incredulously.

'All the time, even with the kids.'

'Let's get this right, Thomas, are you saying grown men are doing to young girls what they do to your ma?'

'Sure do, as long as they pays them, that is. The ma's gets their gin, and the kids gets their candy.'

This latest disclosure shocked Dan more than he had ever been shocked in his life. It was beyond his comprehension to imagine mothers prostituting their children to feed their alcohol dependency.

Furthermore, the matter-of-fact way Thomas related these happenings shocked him. 'Does no one try to prevent it from happening? Has no one done anything about it in the past?' Dan asked with anger in his voice, which frightened Thomas and made him think Dan was angry with him for what he had told him.

'I hope you ain't angry with me, Mr Dan, I'm only tellin' yer as it is in there,' he continued.

'What else goes off in there, Thomas?' Dan asked, wanting to learn as much as he could while Thomas was prepared to talk.

'Well, a little girl died a few weeks back and her body lay in the corner for three days before they dug into the wall and buried her in the hole.'

'Is this common practice, Thomas?' Dan asked.

'Let's say there's hundreds buried in there that I knows of; there ain't nobody in there can afford fancy funerals and black horses with black plumes in their manes.'

Dan remained silent for a while as he tried to take in what Thomas had told him about life in the Old Brewery. Thomas waited for Dan to speak but the silence continued. Eventually, Thomas, trying to pre-empt Dan's thoughts, said, 'Don't get any ideas of goin' in there tryin' to change things, will you now? Because if you did, they'd skin you alive and I mean that, Mr Dan. Even the police don't go in there unless there's a gang of them and that ain't too often. An alley runs down the outside wall of the Old Brewery and at the end is a large room, called the 'Den of Thieves'. In there about seventy people are livin', both blacks and whites together. Runnin' along another wall is Murderer's Ally. They say there must be a thousand people in the whole of the place. Sure, ain't no place for good people like you, Mr Dan. Come to think of it though, there's a couple that's been goin' in there lately and gettin' away with it,' Thomas recalled.

'Who are they, Thomas?' Dan asked eagerly.

'The Reverend Pease and his wife who have been handin' out religious pamphlets and talkin' to some of the women saying they are goin' to try to get them some work doin' sewin' and stuff. Don't know what good the pamphlets will do, as most folks can't read,' he concluded.

'Can you read and write, Thomas?'

'Never been to school in all ma born days, but I know ma numbers, Old Ma' Baker showed me usin' stones and scratchin' in the dirt with her walkin' stick.'

'Who is Old Ma Baker?'

'She was a friend of my ma who kept an eye on her until she upped and died about two years this fall. Ma ain't never been the same since. I sure miss Old Ma' Baker. She was kind to me like you is, Mr Dan,' Thomas concluded.

'Time we were getting back to work, Thomas,' Dan said, still reeling from Thomas's incredible revelations, but thinking he would like to meet the Reverend Pease and his wife. For the rest of the day, Dan's thoughts kept switching back to what Thomas had described earlier and he realised how corrupting this place could be. He recalled what Thomas told him of the work Rev. Pease was trying to do in the Old Brewery. *Maybe if I could immerse myself in some of the Rev. Pease's work, in alleviating the plight of these women and children, it might help toward salving my tormented conscience,* he mused. From first arriving in the 'Five Points' district, he had begun to doubt whether his God was a loving god. *Is there some divine retribution being imposed on these people for their transgressions?* he wondered, and he felt his faith being pulled this way and that.

As he lay in his bed, he mulled over what Thomas had revealed to him concerning life in the Old Brewery. While in this inquisitive mood, his thoughts went back to his old teacher and her indoctrination of the young minds within her care, on life in America. Convinced as she was, on how good life could be across the Atlantic, why had she fled to England with her footman-lover and not America? How naïve he had been, to swallow completely, what this fugitive from a titled life of full and plenty had told him all those years ago. It must have been an intense love she and her footman shared to compel her to take the route she had done, leaving such a comfortable life behind her. It now made no sense to him to leave his wife and family back in England and come to this godforsaken place. Each day he spent in this place, his faith weakened more and more. The more he pondered over the predicament in which he now found himself, he knew he had to push these negative thoughts to the back of his mind and make the most of this opportunity to earn money quickly. At least that side of Mrs Mullen's teaching, was correct. His present situation and the jeopardy in which it placed his faith, left him asking himself, *Will it all be worth it?* He knew more than ever he had to make this work to achieve his goal and successfully return to England for his family.

*

The following week, by some strange quirk of fate, the Rev. Pease found Dan rather than Dan finding him. He was making his way back to stable Beauty, when a 'man of the cloth' stopped him. 'Excuse me, sir, may I trouble you for a moment? Let me introduce myself. My name is Lewis Morris Pease, and I am a minister in the Methodist Episcopal Church.' The man wearing the 'dog collar' looked younger than Dan.

'I'm pleased to make your acquaintance; the name is Dan Swain and I live close-by in Orange Street,' Dan replied as he reached down to shake the stranger's up-stretched hand.

'I would like to ask a favour of you if I may,' the Reverend continued.

'I'll certainly try to help you, Reverend, if I possibly can,' Dan replied, seeing the possibility of a restoration of his faith by association with this churchman.

'Well what I would ask of you is this. I have had the offer of off-cut cloth remnants from the many Jewish tailoring establishments in the Broadway area, which I would need collecting and delivering to the Old Brewery. There, I hope to get some of the women who are capable, to use the cloth to sew shirts etcetera, thereby giving them the opportunity to earn money with which to keep themselves and their children. You know what the Lord said about idle hands doing the devil's work.'

'It is a strange coincidence but although we have never met, I already know of you. God indeed *works in mysterious ways,*' Dan said to the somewhat surprised Rev. Pease.

'What do you mean?' the Minister asked with surprise.

'Well, Thomas Mays, my young assistant, lives in the Old Brewery with his widowed mother. Last week, he told me of the work you and your wife were doing to provide work for the women living there. He also told me about the female inhabitants of the Old Brewery, who at present are prostituting themselves and their daughters to raise money for gin. I must say, his revelations appal me, and I am pleased someone is trying to do something to improve the situation and I would be pleased to help you in any way I can,' offered Dan.

'It grieves me to say, what your young assistant has related, is indeed correct. I am afraid it is only one aspect of this quagmire of humanity, which I wish to address here in the 'Five Points'. Your offer is more than generous; I will draw up a list of the premises taking part in my scheme and a letter of introduction to the tailors involved. Where can I contact you?' the Reverend asked.

'I stable my horse at Silas Black's second-hand furniture place in Cross Street. Tomorrow is Saturday and I usually go to the

Emigrant's Bank in Chamber's Street in the morning. So, you will catch me about ten thirty at Silas's stables and we will take it from there. I must point out to you at this stage, I will only be able to give you an hour of my time each Saturday morning as I need to get down to the waterfront where I do most of my business moving the cargoes to and from the ships at the wharfs,' Dan explained.

'Excellent, since taking up my post, my wife and I have set up home in Cross Street, so I know exactly where Mr Black has his business premises.'

'As we are heading in the same direction, we can carry on our conversation as we go. Jump aboard and save your legs,' Dan suggested. The two men chatted as Beauty trundled her way through the streets that formed part of the 'Five Points'.

'I am much obliged to you. It is so kind of you to offer your services. The Ladies' Home Missionary Society has commissioned me to set up a mission in the 'Five Points' in an attempt to *reform the area and save the souls of the inhabitants*', the Ladies' words, not mine. I am afraid, in their eyes I would appear to have got off to a bad start in my commission.'

'In what way? Surely your plans are most commendable.'

'Well, they would rather I was saving souls and converting all the Catholics living in the 'Five Points', to Methodism, and I must admit I am not preaching many sermons of late. Sermons though, do not put food in mouths and warm clothes on backs during this severe New York winter.' The Reverend Pease continued the conversation. 'My wife Ann and I are determined to get our work scheme established in the Old Brewery and, if successful, move the work to better, more purposeful premises once we have it running smoothly. Ideally, with all my dreams fulfilled and all these languorous souls gainfully employed, by the grace of God, we could set about removing them to better living accommodation.'

'I think your plans are most admirable and I will help in whatever way I can,' Dan promised.

Soon they were outside Silas Black's place. 'Here we are,' Dan said as he drew back on the reins and called Beauty to a halt, knowing without the restraint, the old mare would have headed straight into Old Black's stables and her evening feed.

The Rev. Pease jumped down from his incongruous mode of transport for a man of his calling. 'Until tomorrow,' he said as he shook Dan's hand for the second time and bade him goodbye.

'One more thing before you go, Reverend, there will be no charge for my services,' said Dan.

'That is most Christian of you, Dan,' the Reverend said. 'Goodbye once more; it has been my pleasure meeting you. See you Saturday at ten thirty,' he added.

With that, they parted, and Dan reined Beauty into the stable yard. As Dan unhitched Beauty from the cart, he reflected on his fortuitous meeting with the Rev. Pease and he felt better for it. He thought being with him would help him re-establish his faith, which had suffered since leaving England. Subjected, as he had been, to so many irreligious happenings of late, he had questioned his faith more and more, particularly after his conversation on religion with Silas Black and the revelations of his young assistant. He hoped he could look to the Reverend Pease for the sound counselling with which to regenerate his flagging faith. The work in which he was about to get involved excited him. At least he could now make some small contribution towards alleviating the plight of the poor and destitute people living in the 'Five Points' area in general and the Old Brewery in particular. He believed the Rev. Pease's scheme, once established, would give the women of the Old Brewery something which would gainfully occupy their time, instead of having to resort to prostitution to survive. He realised by throwing himself into the Rev. Pease's scheme too whole-heartedly, might prove costly. He had set up his business down on the waterfront, for the sole purpose of making money quickly. His primary objective was still to get his own place for Frances and their children, and he realised he must remain focused on the real reason for being here in New York City.

*

The recent Warehousing Act of 1849 meant the hauliers like Dan, engaged in moving the commodities between ships and warehouses had to be reliable and totally dependable. They had to be able to move as and when required. The Act allowed the merchants to store their commodities and to release them from the warehouses at the precise time when the markets decreed it advantageous to the merchants to do so. This was a lucrative business both to the merchants and the people like Dan engaged in the transference of the commodities and through his hard work and business acumen, in less than eight months from arriving in New York, he had amassed more than $300 in his bank account. His sobriety and his frugal life style had made this possible. Yet again, his conscience troubled him. Was he now making money his god? What more could he find with which to chastise himself?

Chapter 20

Mary Crowley never knew from one day to the next where Michael might be. He would return at any time of the night or day, bearing wounds from his gang fights. After being missing for three days, he arrived back from his latest sojourn, tanked up with Bernie Finnegan's cheap liquor and began verbally abusing Mary.

He barged into the room. 'Would y' be after havin' me dinner ready?' he bellowed at Mary. She knew at once that he had been with his cronies, the 'Dead Rabbits'. She hated him when he was in this mood. Up until now, he had not been violent towards her, but she thought it was only a matter of time before the gang violence would manifest itself in their home life and she was becoming more and more afraid of him.

'I haven't got anything ready for you, Michael, as I never know where you are or when you'll be back half the time, but I can soon be gettin' something ready for you, to be sure,' she reasoned timidly.

'Don't start givin' out to me about what time I get home now will y',' he yelled at her.

'Y' know I would never give out to y', Michael,' she replied, hoping in his drunken stupor he would believe her. Dan listened from the other room knowing if he made an appearance while Michael was in this mood, it might be enough to provoke him to violence. Although it seemed cowardly, he decided to keep his own counsel, for Mary's sake as well as his own. Sometime soon, he might have to step in to protect her. This environment had changed

Michael, and Dan tried hard to imagine the man he had met on the boat on the journey over from Liverpool; the man who had been so caring towards Mary and young Seamus. He thought the death of both of Michael's children had had a bad effect on him and this was probably responsible for his present behaviour.

Mary quickly prepared some food for her husband. She carved several thick chunks of soda bread and three thick slices of cold ham from a boiled shank. She sliced some hard cheese and placed the food on a tin plate, which she placed nervously on the table, in front of him.

'Now would y' be gettin' me some beer to wash it down,' he demanded.

'Don't y' think water would be better?' Mary suggested, cautiously.

'Y' said y' wouldn't be givin' out to me,' he bellowed, banging his fist down so hard on the table the plate bounced into the air, spilling all its contents onto the table except for one slice of ham, which landed on the floor at his feet. He looked down, fixed a drunken stare on the slice of meat, and for some reason an inane grin creased his face. The hint of irrational humour disappeared as quickly as it had appeared, and his foul mood returned as he reached down and attempted to retrieve the meat. The chair creaked and groaned under his considerable weight and after teetering on one leg, it appeared to defy gravity as it miraculously settled once again on four legs. After wiping off some offending grime on his filthy shirtfront, he stuffed the errant piece of ham into his mouth and after a minimal number of munches he ravenously swallowed it down. Picking up another slice of ham, he tore off a large mouthful with his teeth without chewing on it; he stuffed the remainder of the ham into his mouth and despite his filthy hands he munched on his food.

The brief humour the scene evoked quickly dissipated as Mary ran in fear to get a tankard of the beer from the press. She returned to find Michael gormandising the rest of the food from where it had landed on the table. She placed the tankard of beer on the table in front of her husband and put the plate upright again, but she did not attempt to replace the remainder of the food, knowing to do so would probably provoke further commotion. Michael stuffed more food into his mouth as though he had not eaten for days. He grabbed the tankard and gulped most of the contents down his throat. He finished most of the food and the last of the beer and lolled back on his chair. Mary knew her husband would soon stumble his way to the bedroom and crash out on the bed. She had seen it many times since he had taken up with the 'Dead Rabbits' gang. Sure enough, her prediction turned to reality. She heard her husband collapse heavily onto the bed and soon his loud snoring emanated from the open bedroom door. With her drunken husband ensconced in their bed, she began to cry, in a mix of relief and desperation.

Dan, on hearing Mary sobbing, came out of his bedroom to join her. He placed his arm around her shoulders. 'Come on now, Mary, keep your spirit up or you will be destined to this existence for the rest of your days if you let yourself go,' he reminded her.

'I don't know if I can stand any more of this, Dan,' she sobbed. 'I am about at my wits' end. He is a completely different man from the one I married.' Mary was conscious of Dan's arm around her shoulder. It gave her a warm comfort to feel the attention he was showing her. She turned to face Dan and let her head, rest on his shoulder. As she did so, her lips lightly brushed his neck. It was some time since Michael had shown her the same consideration and she drank in the warmth and comfort for as long as it would last. Her breasts swelled within her bodice at the closeness of Dan and the need for love coursed through her veins. The close contact of Mary made Dan realise how long it was since he had last taken Frances in his arms and his thoughts winged back to the night before he had left for Liverpool. Mary neither smelt like Frances, nor was she as beautiful. Despite this, he was becoming aroused by her close presence and he found himself battling with his conscience. Despite loving Frances, he knew he had to have Mary. His animal instincts were taking over his mind. Mary raised her head slowly from his shoulder and looked up into his eyes. Her red hair tumbled about her face emphasising the paleness of her skin. Dan was seeing Mary as he had never seen her before. Her face had taken on a new sultry appearance, creating in her, an attractiveness which, until now, he had not noticed. Placing her hand on the back of Dan's neck, Mary pulled his head down to her parted lips and kissed him almost violently, full on the mouth. From the look in Mary's eyes, he knew where the situation was leading. By now his sense of reason had diminished to such a level that try as he might, he knew the outcome was inevitable. The raw animal instincts surged through his body.

'Take me, Dan, take me now, I need y',' she whispered pleadingly. They both needed each other but for different reasons. She hungered for the love and affection, which she was no longer receiving from Michael, and Dan, despite his religious beliefs, needed sexual satisfaction.

Mary took him by the hand and led him into his bedroom. He could almost hear his heart pounding in his chest, but he did nothing to prevent what was happening. A voice in his head was yelling at him to be strong for Frances's sake, but his conscience was losing the battle as he succumbed to the flesh. Things were happening quickly now. Mary knew her husband lay in the other bedroom and at any minute, he could awaken from his drunken sleep. If he did, Dan knew all hell would break loose. For some strange reason, this seemed to add to the excitement of the situation.

They entered the bedroom and Dan quickly drew the curtains closed in what was a strange act of modesty. On reaching the bed, Mary quickly removed her undergarments but nothing else and hitching her clothes around her waist, she lay on the bed with her knees bent and her legs splayed in readiness. Dan joined her on the bed and undoing the fly buttons on his trousers and not waiting to remove any clothing, he straddled her. Both now acting hastily, he entered her... It was all over quickly. Dan got up immediately and quickly rearranged his clothing. He sat silently on the edge of the bed with his back to Mary who was still lying on her back, the bed untidy from their illicit actions. Full of remorse and consumed with guilt he was unable to face Mary who unsatisfied, turned onto her side and stroked Dan's back in the hope she might re-kindle the fire within him, but she soon realised the fire had already burnt out.

Dan rose from the bed quickly and moved to the window. The room seemed full of an almost audible, guilt-laden silence. He knew he should be saying something apologetic to Mary, but words escaped him. She sensed a cowardly reaction on his part and without saying a word, he was blaming her for what had taken place. He parted the curtains with one hand and without attempting to draw them open, he stared out. He could have been looking out into deep space, for his eyes focused on emptiness as though he was trying to distance himself from Mary. His mind was not concentrating on anything other than what had taken place between them and he was filled with deep remorse. What he had done with Mary, was no different from what might have happened had he taken one of the many prostitutes who frequented the 'Five Points' area. To take advantage of Mary of all people, he thought was despicable.

Mary left him staring out of the window and passed through into the living room, not knowing what was going through his mind. Dan did not join her. Too embarrassed to face her, his thoughts returned to Frances and the children and his sense of guilt deepened, gnawing at his very being. All he had held so dearly, now destroyed in one moment of madness. He had violated the sanctity of two marriages. *How could things ever be the same?* he agonised. His precious love for Frances, now sullied as though he had taken a delicate flower and ground it between his dirty palms. He had let them down and he had used Mary when she was most vulnerable. These were not the actions of a good, God-fearing man, and he hated himself for what he had done. Taking to his bed, he laid on his back, his mind in turmoil. The sexual act in which he had indulged himself had been bereft of any love. It was nothing more than lust for the flesh and it kept flashing through his mind, torturing his very soul. He wished he could turn back the time and wipe this sordid incident completely from his memory. Maybe in the morning he would awake to find it had all been a horrible dream. He knew the sickening truth; it *had* taken place. With all these things running through his mind, he eventually fell into a fitful sleep.

*

Mary woke the next morning, stiff and aching, having spent the night curled up in the corner near the stove rather than risk disturbing her drunken husband, asleep in their bed. She was becoming more and more afraid of him and there were times, especially now with both her children dead and indeed her marriage heading the same way, she found herself wishing she had died in Kenmare. What had taken place the previous night had not had the effect she had hoped it would. She wanted some small moment of distraction from what her life with Michael had become and she ached for love and tenderness. How she had hoped she could get this from Dan, but she now realised, while Dan's body had been weak, his conscience was too strong to forget Frances completely and so, the full sex act enjoyed between two loving people had been nothing more than a dangerous dalliance. The love and tenderness, which she and Michael had once enjoyed and which she hoped to find in Dan had not materialised. She realised, the kind of love, which she craved from Dan, was for one person only and *she* was back in England.

Dan lay awake on his bed where the previous night he had had the brief sexual liaison with Mary. Now filled with unbearable remorse, his mind was in painful torment. He tried in vain to rid his mind of what had happened. He was in great mental agony; it was as though some demon had taken a sharp-nibbed pen and indelibly written the details of his actions painfully on his brain and he could do nothing to shift it. He knew it would remain there forever like some punitive tattoo.

Dan shuffled around his room causing Mary to sense his guilt by his reluctance to emerge from the scene of their indiscretion. He carried out his ablutions paying attention to his groin area and scrotum and, trying hard to cleanse himself of what had taken place. As he vigorously dried himself, Mary appeared in the doorway. 'Don't y' worry, Dan, you'll catch nothing from me, I've not even been with that drunken husband of mine for months. Trying to cleanse your conscience, now that will take more than soap and water,' and she returned to the kitchen. Eventually steeling himself to face Mary, he left his bedroom and passed through to the other room, where he found her rekindling the stove in readiness for breakfast. 'Would you be wantin' some rashers and eggs now, Dan?' she asked him as though nothing had happened between them. He still found it difficult to look at Mary, let alone speak to her. He ran a few opening phrases through his mind before he eventually broke the silence.

'I am so sorry Mary, what I did last night was unforgivable,' he said sheepishly.

'Oh, think nothin' of it, sure I did not,' she said, somewhat sarcastically. The innuendo was lost on Dan who continued to apologise, he was not ready yet for Mary's humour.

'I don't know what came over me—' But Mary interrupted him.

'Stop right there, will y' now, Dan? Y' wouldn't be about to moralise with me now, would y'? We both knew what we wanted and what we were doin', we are not children and we both needed that. I admit we were in a bit of a rush now, but it was good while it lasted, I think it could have been much better if we had taken our time. Maybe next time we might not be in such a rush.'

'There can't be a next time, Mary. I must get out of the 'Five Points'; I think this place will eventually destroy all of us. As soon as I have raised enough money, I will return to England and buy my own plot of land there, with my family and my God around me once more. I have seen enough of America to last me the rest of my days.

Are you sure you'll be all right, Mary?' Dan asked.

'Sure, I'll be fine. I've been through much and taken all life has thrown at me up to now. I'll get by. As you say, I'll have to,' she replied, adding, 'About last night, Dan, I got a bit carried away with your kindness. I *am* sorry; it was not my intention to put y' in danger. I hope you can find it in y' to forgive me.'

'Think nothing more about it; it was not your fault, I have nothing to forgive you for. It should be me asking for *your* forgiveness. I took advantage of you when you needed my support.'

'Thanks for takin' it that way. What d' y' say we forget about it now?' Mary suggested, adding, 'But if ever y' change y' mind now…' and she tilted her head quizzically and smiled.

'I don't want breakfast this morning, Mary. Thanks all the same. Somehow I have lost my appetite.'

'Don't go losin' yer strength now will yer? Yer never know when y' might need it now,' Mary said, with continued innuendo, as she nervously tried to make a joke of what had happened. She wasted her time on Dan as he was too guilt-ridden to see the funny side to her remarks. His overwhelming guilt would not allow him to find her conversation amusing. He had been weak, and he knew it; nothing could reconcile him.

Although they had talked quietly, Michael had woken from his sleep earlier than Mary had expected and was listening to their conversation through the half-open bedroom door. He was aware Mary had not slept in her bed all night and immediately jumped to the conclusion she had spent all night with Dan Swain.

'Yer a filthy English bastard, to be sure, I'll do for y', but not yet. I'll bide me time. Y'll pay dearly for this,' he mouthed in a barely audible whisper.

Chapter 21

Exactly one week after his transgression with Mary, Dan picked Thomas up as usual and on his way to the waterfront, he stopped off once more at the post office to see if a first letter had arrived from Frances. This time he was successful. The clerk behind the counter handed him a letter sheet bearing a British stamp and addressed in Frances's familiar hand. He was overjoyed at the thought of receiving news from Frances and the children. Dan eagerly opened the letter, but the joy soon changed to gloom as he read the contents.

Renton House Cottage,
Renton,
Durnham,
Norfolk.
15th November 1849

My dear husband,

Thank you for your letter from America in which you described your journey and your good progress so far. But, with great sadness I must report on the sudden death of Mr Hayward following a fall on the frozen cobblestones in the farmyard. This sad event happened in the first week of November. I have also to report you are to be a father again. I must have conceived after our last night together before you left for America and the baby is due in early February. Indeed, I may even have given birth by the time you receive this letter. I have been keeping all this from you Dan in the hope something would work out, but the death of Mr

Hayward has had a devastating effect on our standing here at Renton House Cottage.

Mrs Hayward is under instruction by His Lordship's agent, to vacate Renton House Farm to make way for the incoming bailiff, Robert Hart, and his wife Rachel. Therefore, she is to occupy our present home in the cottage on our departure, someday early in January, after which time, we shall be homeless with Durnham Union Workhouse as our only prospect.

With these new circumstances, the children and I now find ourselves in crisis. I realise how much your plans lie in America, but in my present condition, I beseech you to return home to us with great speed. My dearest Dan, I am at my wits end with worry for the future, of myself and our children.

Your ever-loving wife,

Frances.

Dan stared at the letter sheet without saying a word. The contents had completely stunned him. In his mind's eye, he saw all his great plans collapsing about him like a tall tower built from playing cards and he knew his American dream was over. The thought of his darling Frances and his beloved children incarcerated within the walls of Durnham Workhouse left him wanting to jump on the first ship leaving for England.

His mind once again returned to his adulterous act with Mary and he thought the Devil's own courier had delivered the letter from England.

It is time to pay penance for all my wrong thoughts and deeds. I have neglected my churchgoing. I have questioned my faith and I have acquired a growing love for money, by working on the Sabbath and my adultery with Mary Crowley. All these things have come about in the short time since I set foot in America, he thought as he remonstrated with himself.

'What's up, Mr Dan; is it bad news? You sure do look shocked,' Thomas interjected as Dan still stared at the letter.

'It is grave news indeed, Thomas, so much so it is imperative I must return to England immediately, but before I do so, I am handing the business over to you.'

His mind was racing; he knew he had to act quickly. His getting back to his family was of the utmost importance. He had important things to do in what little time he had available otherwise his journey to America had all been in vain. In his mind, he was already prioritising the things he had to do before he departed for England.

I will hand over my business to Thomas Mays, he thought. He was young but Dan had great faith in Thomas's ability, and he was not afraid of hard work. It would give Thomas a great start in life.

'Are you sure, Mr Dan? I knows nothin' about readin' and writin'.'

'But you know your figures and you know how to add up, so no one can short change you and that's the main thing in business. I am sure, sometime soon you will be able to read and write. Before I go, I will ask Mrs Pease if she can find time to teach you. I have great faith in your ability, Thomas. Grab this opportunity with both hands. It is the best chance you will get in your lifetime,' Dan said with great conviction. 'Our next port of call is the Emigrants' Savings Bank to make an appointment for us to see Mr Chapman, the manager. I will need to sponsor you in opening an account in your name. Each week place all the money you can into your account. Take from your earnings only that amount which is required for you and your mother's daily needs, and I do not mean your mother's gin; the rest you save. You will receive a passbook. Always keep this safe and do not let anyone else in the Old Brewery be aware of your affairs, not even your mother. At the earliest opportunity, find better accommodation for you and your mother away from that den of iniquity, and clear of the 'Five Points'. Soon you will be able to afford it. This is your first move on the road to a better life, Thomas. Tomorrow will be our last day working on the waterfront, together. Today I will explain to the warehouse captains and the stevedores who all know you, that you will be running the business from now on. I will explain to them that I have lodged a *Letter of Intent* with Mr Chapman, the manager of the Emigrants' Savings Bank, stating that you will now oversee the business. One final thing, Thomas, keep away from alcoholic drink in any form. It is the Devil's drink. We must move quickly as we have much to do today,' Dan stated.

During Thursday, notwithstanding his worries, Dan managed to make all the arrangements prior to leaving for England. This included a passage booked on the packet *Patrick Henry*, sailing on Saturday evening bound for London.

While Thomas was having his break, Dan had gone to the bank where he explained to the young clerk his need to return quickly to England and he would be closing his account. He also requested an appointment with Mr Chapman, the manager, as soon as possible with a view to sponsoring Thomas Mays in opening an account with the bank.

On seeing Dan in his working clothes, the clerk took on an air of superiority.

'Wait a moment while I have a word with the manager,' he said curtly and turned and knocked, politely on the door behind him where a skilled sign-writer had fashioned in gold leaf, the words Donald Chapman, Manager.

'Come,' a voice from within beckoned and the clerk passed into the inner office and closed the door behind him.

After a few minutes, the clerk returned to his post and addressed Dan again.

'I have spoken with the manager and he sees no problem with your request to close your account and the accumulated funds from your account will be ready for you to collect on Saturday morning. Concerning your other request, Mr Chapman would like to discuss it further when you collect your funds. Your appointment is for Saturday – ten o'clock. The manager asked me to point out to you, Mr Swain, that the establishing of this bank was mainly for Irish Catholics, and people outside that faith would require special sponsorship, as indeed, was the case with your good self. He also asked me to say, were it not for the fact that you are a good and respected customer of ours, and the circumstances, which have necessitated the closing of your account, the sponsorship of Mr Mays, would be out of the question. We will see you on Saturday morning, Mr Swain,' the clerk concluded with an air of triumph.

'Thanks, you will indeed. Those arrangements suit me perfectly as it gives me a whole working day to hand over my business to my partner,' Dan explained, and he left quickly to re-join Thomas down on the waterfront.

*

'How has it gone while I have been away, Thomas?'

'Sure seemed strange, you not been around an' all that, Mr Dan, and I took a bit o' raggin' off the men. But I know's they're only joshin' me, and I'll get used to them and with a bit of luck, they'll get used to me,' he said hopefully.

'Tomorrow, Thomas, I want you to tack up Beauty yourself. You have seen me do it many times in the past and I am sure you will find it quite easy. I want you to meet me down on the waterfront instead of at Silas Black's place. I want you to do things without me whenever possible tomorrow in readiness for the handover. I will be there to lend a hand, but in the main, it will be you doing all the planning of the work. You will have to get used to doing all this in the future,' Dan reminded him.

On returning to Silas Black's yard at the end of work, Thomas set about removing the tack from Beauty, hosing her, and bedding her down for the night, which he did competently. In the meantime, Dan relayed his enforced new plans to Old Black, and he disclosed the contents of the letter from England and what effect this had on his future in America.

'I have decided to hand over the reins to young Thomas here, he's coming up sixteen and he knows the job inside out. What is more, everyone down on the waterfront knows him and can depend on him being there as and when required. As you said to me when you suggested I took him on, he is a shrewd fellow. Can I depend on you,

Silas, to keep a watchful eye on his well-being, as I have become fond of him and I would like him to make something of himself?' Dan asked.

'I'll do what I can, but I can't promise him my total attention, I have my own business to run but I'll do what I can Dan for your sake.'

What bothered Dan was Silas's attitude towards the black community and this worried him.

That is why he wanted Silas to be a counter signatory to his *Letter of Intent* thereby binding him to the arrangement over the stabling at Silas Black's place.

'I have drawn up this *Letter of Intent* outlining my handing over of my business to Thomas Mays. As I have no time to do it legally, I would like you and the Rev. Pease to countersign it allowing him to continue with the business I have established down on the waterfront. I would like to think Thomas will be able to continue with the same arrangements you and I have about the stabling of Beauty.'

'Of that you have my assurance,' Silas Black replied.

'Thank you, Silas, now I must go to see the Rev. Pease and arrange things with him. I have an appointment with Mr Chapman at the bank on Saturday morning where I will ask him to sign it and I will lodge it with him for safekeeping. I may be too busy tomorrow and Saturday to see you before I leave for England so before I do, I must thank you for everything you have done for me, Silas. You have given me a great opportunity to set up my business and that is why I want to hand it over to young Thomas. He should do well out of it. In the meantime I must now go to see the Rev. Pease,' Dan concluded.

Having said their goodbyes, the two men shook hands. As Dan was about to leave, Silas Black said, 'And don't you be forgettin' that scoop of them there oats for Major, I want things to carry on as normal with that arrangement,' he added. Silas watched as Dan disappeared around the corner of Cross Street and he wondered if Dan was doing the right thing leaving his business to Thomas Mays. He hoped Thomas Mays would not let Dan Swain down, knowing how much faith he had placed in the project. *Only time will tell*, Silas Black thought.

As he had done with Silas Black, Dan explained to the Rev. Pease the reason for his immediate return to England and that Thomas would be taking over the business. 'Nothing will change with the collection and delivery of the off-cuts of material each Saturday. Thomas will now provide that service and I have passed on to him the list of participating tailors.'

Dan showed the Rev. Pease the *Letter of Intent* and explained its significance concerning safeguarding Thomas's future as the new owner of Dan's burgeoning haulage business. The Reverend read the letter, which was signed *Dan Swain,* and he countersigned it *Rev. Lewis Morris Pease* alongside that of *Silas Black* and waiting briefly for the ink to dry, he handed the letter back to Dan.

'On Saturday morning, Thomas and I have an appointment to see the bank manager, Mr Chapman, at the Emigrants' Bank, where I will ask him also to add his signature, whereupon I will lodge it with him for safekeeping,' Dan explained.

'Rest assured, Dan, I shall give it my full support should the need arise. You have my promise.'

'Do you think you could keep an eye on Thomas, Reverend, until he gets established? You never know, he could be your first convert. One final thing I wish to ask of you, Reverend.'

'What is it? I will help in any way I can. I seem to remember I owe you a favour, Dan.'

'Well Thomas is quite clever with figures, but he can't read or write. Do you think your dear wife could find the time to give Thomas lessons in reading and writing?'

'You know we are both busy with our work at the Old Brewery. Between us I think we can manage at least one lesson or so a week.'

'Excellent, I think that finalises my arrangements with your good self and Silas Black. I have secured a passage onboard the packet the *Patrick Henry* bound for London, sailing Saturday evening. Therefore,

I will take my leave of you, Reverend. Pray me and my family good luck in undoing the misfortune that has befallen us of late. Pass on my goodbyes to Mrs Pease.'

'I most certainly will, Dan; you will always be in our thoughts and prayers. God speed your journey to England and your troubled family.'

The two men shook hands and Dan turned and headed back to the apartment. There, Dan found Mary and Michael sat at the table. For the first time in a long while Michael was sober although still his usual sullen self which had been his countenance for some time now.

'There is tea in the pot if y' would be fancyin' a cup now Dan,' Mary said kindly.

'That would be nice,' Dan replied as he took off the drover's coat, which had been his salvation during the cold wet New York winter.

Michael said nothing as he sat looking into the bottom of his cup. For no apparent reason he flung the dregs contemptuously from the cup across the floor of the living room in the direction of Mary and Dan. His silence did not surprise Dan, as there had been little exchange between the two men since the business with Mary. This made Dan wonder, *Does Michael suspect something?*

Over the cup of tea, Dan told them of his letter from England and once more went over his urgent plans for the next couple of days.

'I will be busy on Saturday; first I will close my account at the Emigrants' Bank on Saturday morning. I have booked a passage on the *Patrick Henry* bound for London,' he revealed to them.

Still without saying a word, Michael Crowley gave Dan a long hard stare. *Now I have y'; come Saturday I'll be after havin' me day with y'. You'll never see that family of yez again,* he thought as he ran through his own plans for Dan.

'Will y' be returnin' with y' family when y'll be after gettin' all yer troubles sorted out?' Mary asked.

'No, Mary, I will not bring them here. The money I have saved will be enough for me to make a fresh start back in England free of the tied system,' he explained.

'I will miss yer,' Mary admitted.

I'm sure y' will, Mary, Michael Crowley thought. *I'll have both you and y' money, English maan; I said I would have me day with yer and that day is Saturday,* Michael thought, as he ran his heinous plan over in his mind.

On the Friday morning, Dan met Thomas down on the waterfront where he found him already into his work. Thomas had tacked-up Beauty himself for the first time and proceeded to the waterfront where he had to withstand more banter from some of the men. Most of the exchanges were friendly except for the comments from one burly labourer who Thomas recognised as having lived a short time in the Old Brewery. He sidled up to Thomas and leaning in towards him said, 'You lucky little black bastard; is the Englishman havin' it away with y' ma?'

This hurt Thomas, especially the lewd reference to his mother and remembering what Dan had said, about getting out of the Old Brewery, he resolved there and then he would make this opportunity work.

Other than the one incident, most of the warehouse captains and stevedores accepted the planned transfer and Dan was quite happy the way his last day was going.

On their return home, they stopped off at a second-hand clothes shop where Dan had Thomas fitted out with a pair of breeches, a waistcoat, a shirt, and a flat tweed cap. A pair of decent boots completed the ensemble in readiness for his appointment with the bank manager.

'You have to look your best now you are the young businessman meeting his bank manager for the first time,' Dan reminded him.

With this task completed, they headed back home. When they reached 38 Orange Street, Dan turned to Thomas and said, 'Bed her down for the night, Thomas, and don't forget the scoop of oats for her. Remember also, part of the deal with Silas is, Major gets a scoop too if he has been worked today. Let's not get off to a bad start under new management.'

He jumped down from the shafts and walked round to front Beauty and taking her head in his arms he nuzzled up to the side of her head.

'Goodbye, old girl, Thomas will be looking after you now,' and the old mare took a friendly nip on the collar of his coat. Dan was sad he would not be working with Beauty again.

Saddened as he was, he knew she would be safe with Thomas and more importantly, he had to get back to England.

'Take good care of her, Thomas, and don't forget I will meet you tomorrow for our visit to the bank. You may keep in mind, once you get enough money saved, about getting a second horse and cart and consider employing someone to work it for you. That is what I had in mind if I had not to return to England, there's certainly enough work to warrant it,' Dan suggested.

*

On the Saturday morning, as planned he met Thomas for their bank appointment. On their arrival, the clerk recognised Dan. 'Good day Mr Swain, I will finish Mr Finley's business and I'll be right with you,' he said. The said Mr Finley left, and Dan moved up to the counter.

'I'm sure you remember our conversation on Thursday when I requested closing my account and my request to sponsor my friend and business partner in opening an account in his name?'

'I do indeed, Mr Swain,' said the astonished clerk as he eyed young Thomas up and down. 'I had no idea he was a young… err… negro; you never said.'

'You never asked,' Dan retorted, adding, 'is there a problem with that?'

'Well that is for Mr Chapman to decide; I will see if he can receive you now,' he said, aloofly, 'but first let me get the application forms in place.'

The clerk gave Thomas a rather dismissive glance and proceeded to search the drawer for the required forms. Having found what he was looking for, he placed the forms on the counter and proceeded to see if his manager was ready to receive Dan.

The clerk returned. 'Mr Chapman will see you now, Mr Swain. Maybe your friend and business partner could stay with me and complete the forms while you have your appointment with Mr Chapman,' the clerk said in a rather sarcastic manner, looking down his nose at Thomas as he did so.

'Oh no that would not do at all, seeing that the appointment is for both of us. If you would bring the forms we will fill them out, in Mr Chapman's office.'

'As you wish,' the clerk said reluctantly and proceeded to usher Dan and his young successor to the manager's office.

'Mr Swain and err… Mr Mays,' the clerk announced, still unable to do so without the same air of superiority, which he had shown when first setting eyes on Thomas.

'Good morning, Mr Swain, I am sorry to hear of your domestic problems back in England,' the manager said, almost ignoring Thomas altogether apart from a cursory glance in his direction. He was a middle-aged man with a moustache, which was bushy under his nose and curled in wisps at the ends which Dan thought gave him the appearance of a circus ringmaster rather than a bank manager.

'I understand time is of the essence regarding your return to your wife and family. Therefore, I have everything ready for you. I have had your account with us closed and all that remains is for you to sign to say you are in full receipt of all your funds, which amounts to $339 and 25 cents. May I have your passbook to stamp it 'closed' please?' he continued.

The money was stacked tidily in front of Mr Chapman who slid it across his highly polished desk towards Dan together with a form for him to sign acknowledging he had received the amount of money stated. Dan signed the form and handed it back together with his passbook.

'I am sure you will find the amount correct,' Mr Chapman stated as he stamped the word 'CLOSED' with a heavy hand diagonally across the open passbook and taking a pair of heavy scissors he continued to clip a corner from the outer cover; an outward sign that the account was 'dead'.

'It is a pity we have lost your business, Mr Swain, when you were doing so well. In the short time you have had the account open you have amassed a tidy sum of money. Make good use of it back in England. Are you sure, you want to take it in cash? It would be prudent of you to take a banker's draft. There is still time for me to make one out if you so wish. Your bank back in England would honour it and you would receive a better rate of exchange,' Mr Chapman suggested.

'No, that won't be necessary, Mr Chapman. I appreciate your concern and your advice is sound indeed but as you rightly said earlier, time is of the essence and I shall need cash immediately I step off the boat back in England. I will not have time to open a bank account over there to transact your draft. Thank you for your concern but I will always have to be extra vigilant during my travels. You have not lost the business altogether; this is where this young man comes in. Let me introduce him to you, Mr Chapman. This is my successor, Thomas Mays; Thomas… Mr Chapman.' Thomas rose to his feet and reached across the desk, extending his arm to its limit to offer the bank manager his hand. Chapman remained seated, not making the gesture any easier for Thomas. He took Thomas's right hand with great reluctance and only by the fingertips. Dan, noticing Chapman's reaction to Thomas, immediately spoke up.

'This young man is taking over all of my business down on the waterfront. He may appear young, but he is a hard worker, and he has worked alongside me throughout my business venture. There is nobody more suited to take over from me. As such, I would like to open an account in his name thereby continuing your link with Thomas's business matters in the future. He knows all our contacts down at the wharfs and they know him. Therefore, you see Mr Chapman, your business with us is not lost. Indeed, with good luck on Thomas's side and with the help of people like your good self, the business should grow faster in the future than it has hereto.'

Chapman wriggled in his seat; the conversation was making him uncomfortable. His business head could see the sense in continuing to handle the young executive's affairs, but his prejudices precluded this.

'I must say, Mr Swain, notwithstanding the boy's age there is a somewhat more delicate issue here. I am sure you are aware that I, as a good person of this city, must always act responsibly and what you ask of me is rather sensitive to say the least. After all, I have my other customers to consider.'

'Surely, Mr Chapman, what I am asking of you should not, as *a good person of this city*, as you put it, compromise you in any way. Thomas himself is *a good person of this city,* is he not? He has never fallen foul of the law. He is free of any convictions and hard working. He had the misfortune to lose the guidance of his father who died developing the railroad that is opening up this country and has brought vast wealth to the area on which your bank was established. On the death of his father, what did he do? Run with the young gangs of New York that are everywhere throughout this city? No, he enterprisingly built himself a crude handcart and worked for his living. Your bank is young, Mr Chapman, and so is Thomas and so is his business. Allow for all three of you to grow together, that way you have it in your power to nurture his desire to succeed. Many years ago, when I was a child at school, my teacher told me about America. She had spoken of how it was the country of opportunity where, through hard work and endeavour, a man could make something of himself, irrespective of his status. I carried that dream into manhood, and it is that, which brought me here to America. I was chasing the dream. All I ask of you is not to let the narrow-mindedness of some of the so-called *'good people of this city'*, cloud your views. I would like to think I could depend on you to rise above any prejudices and act in the best interest of everyman who comes to you with a will to work hard and to prosper through that desire. Was it not the principles of the founding fathers of this great nation that made the USA the land of opportunity… for everyman? If not, I have been naïve in believing blindly what my teacher told me all those years ago. Please do not shatter that dream. Circumstance has robbed me of my opportunity to prosper here in your country, please do not let me return to England with a feeling that all was lost. If you can find it within yourself to give this young man the start in life he deserves, I will have achieved something from my short stay here, thus restoring my faith in the dream I have carried since my childhood and my faith in this great country of yours. I am sorry; I cannot control myself once I start on a subject about which I am passionate. I beg your forgiveness; maybe I was too outspoken,' Dan Swain concluded.

The bank manager sat forming a triangle with his fingers and thumbs and resting his index fingers against his upper lip as he pondered Dan's oratory. After a moment, he spoke. 'Not at all, Mr Swain, I thought you put your opinions across both eloquently and forthrightly. I think that teacher of yours, sowed the seeds within you of a budding lawyer or politician or maybe both. If I grant young Mr Thomas Mays the right to open an account with us, you realise I would need further sponsorship from another eminent member of the public, some professional man for instance,' Chapman explained.

'I come prepared,' and he immediately took from his pocket the copy of his *Letter of Intent* indicating the handing over of his business to Thomas Mays and which bore Dan's own signature and countersigned by the Reverend Lewis Morris Pease and Mr Silas Black.

'I would have had this done legally if time had allowed but you know how long these things can take and time is of the essence in this matter. So, this is the best I can do under the circumstances,' Dan explained as he passed the letter over to Donald Chapman, 'and I would like you to sign it and I wish to lodge it with you for safekeeping.'

As Chapman perused the letter, he said, 'Although I am aware of the Reverend Pease and the noble work, he and his good wife are attempting within the sixth ward of the city, I have not had the pleasure of meeting them. I cannot say I know of Mr Black,' and he continued to read. Without waiting for him to finish, Dan explained Silas Black was a businessman dealing in second-hand furniture with his premises in the sixth ward. He had deliberately avoided being specific with his geography and had not referred to the 'Five Points'.

Looking up, Chapman said, 'I see no reason why this would not carry sufficient credence in a court of law, should there be any controversy arising from your intention of transferring your business over to young Thomas here. I can tell you now, an account *can* be opened in his name,' he said as he also added his signature to the other three.

'At this moment Thomas is learning to read and write, so he will make his mark in the appropriate areas on the application documents and I will countersign on his behalf,' Dan said.

'That will not be a problem as many of the immigrants who, sponsored by others, are in the same position as your young friend,' Chapman assured them.

'May I add,' Dan said, 'he is numerate, and it will only be a short while before he is literate.'

Right on cue, a knock came on the door.

'Come!' shouted Chapman and in walked the clerk with the account documents, which he placed, in front of the manager.

'There are one or two outstanding details like Mr May's full name and date of birth,' the clerk said, and Dan detected a hope in the clerk's voice this would cause problems with Thomas's application.

Thinking quickly and before Thomas could speak, Dan said, 'Thomas Mays is his full name, and today is his sixteenth birthday which means he was born on the 23rd February 1834.'

Resting on the manager's desk, the clerk filled in the missing details, placed the application forms in front of Thomas and left the room. Chapman dipped a pen into the silver ink well and shaking the surplus ink from the nib, he offered it to Dan who in turn handed it to Thomas.

'Now Thomas, I want you to make a cross like this,' and he crossed the index fingers of each hand, 'right here on the paper where I have my finger tip,' he concluded. Thomas slowly and purposefully made a cross as Dan had shown him, and alongside, Dan wrote, *this is the mark of Thomas Mays,* and having signed the addendum, he passed the forms to Chapman who added his signature before rocking the ink blotter back and forth across the wet ink.

'That's it, all done,' said Chapman as he passed a pristine passbook over to Thomas, who on opening it, recognised the figure 1 and 0 alongside each other with a $ sign in front indicating an entry of $10 which Mr Dan had deposited in his name.

'Thank you, Mr Dan, I never did have so much money in my life before,' he said gratefully and placing the passbook in front of him, he removed his cap from his inside pocket in readiness for the cold walk home.

'Make the most of this opportunity, young man, for you are fortunate indeed to have such a benefactor as Mr Swain here,' said Mr Chapman.

'I sure am,' replied Thomas and that famous beam creased his shiny black face once again.

'I am most grateful to you, Mr Chapman. I can leave for England this evening in the knowledge that Thomas is in a sound position and I can concentrate my mind on what needs doing on behalf of my wife and family.'

Chapman shook hands with Dan and this time he shook Thomas's hand with a little more enthusiasm than he had previously. He bid Dan, *'Bon voyage,'* and turning to Thomas, he said, 'And as for you, young man, I hope to see your newly acquired business flourish and as a result I may see more of you in the future. Good luck to you both.'

Chapter 22

As Dan and Thomas walked from the bank, the journey took them along Cross Street. As they reached the junction of Cross Street and Centre Street, Thomas realised he had not picked up his passbook.

'That's a good start, Thomas, I thought I said keep it safe. Get back quickly and retrieve it, you can catch me up,' Dan scolded.

Thomas turned and ran back to the bank. Dan continued his way knowing Thomas would quickly catch him up. Walking on, Dan reached the junction of Cross Street and Little Water Street. He had travelled this route regularly without any need to be over cautious.

From the shadows to his left, a figure lunged at Dan dragging him backwards into the darkened ally. As he fell backwards, he caught a glimpse of steel as it flashed across his left arm and the cold blade of a knife entered his chest above his ribcage. He slumped to the ground, his lifeblood oozing from the wound to his chest. He was still conscious as his assailant rummaged through Dan's pockets and removed the leather pouch containing Dan's lifesavings before running off down Cross Street in the direction of Orange Street, leaving Dan dying in an ever-expanding pool of blood.

Meanwhile, having retrieved his passbook, Thomas quickly retraced his steps along Cross Street. He was almost at the junction with Little Water Street when he saw Michael Crowley tearing out of the ally to his left and fleeing down Cross Street ahead of him.

In the entrance to Little Water Street, Thomas found Dan dying in a large pool of blood.

'Murder, murder!' he yelled at the top of his voice. People quickly came flocking from the nearby grubby tenements.

'There goes another one,' someone remarked unconcernedly.

Another member of the crowd squatted down by Dan's body. Placing two fingers on his throat he declared, 'Not quite, but he's goin' fast,' and rose to his feet.

Another took up the vacated position and quickly proceeded to rifle through Dan's pockets with expertise that suggested he was used to robbing the dead. He commented in a disappointed way, 'Whoever did this left nothing of any value,' as he clumsily stuffed Frances's letter and his now superfluous boat ticket and bank passbook, back into the inside pocket of Dan's coat.

'He'll be off to the morgue soon,' someone suggested rather hastily.

'Not before we inform the law officers,' someone else interjected.

'I think that's where the black kid's headin',' said the robber of the dead.

'For what good they will be to this poor soul,' a cynic remarked.

The crowd that had gathered, more out of morbid curiosity than a sense of compassion, were slowly dwindling away, back to their dreary hovels. After all, death on the streets was commonplace to the people of the 'Five Points'.

Thomas, while wanting to stay with Dan, knew he had to get to the police as quickly as possible before Michael Crowley made a run for freedom and dashed off toward the sixth ward police department.

A large dark stain had rapidly formed on Dan's chest as the crimson liquid merged with the green fabric of his coat. On the ground, the crimson patch was creeping wider and wider as the life ebbed from his aching body. With great difficulty, he propped himself up on one arm, his free hand clutching his injured chest. All manner of thoughts rushed through his shocked mind. In the shadows of the alley, he thought he saw Frances and the children standing weeping, in the dwindling crowd still standing over him. With his free hand dripping with his blood, he tried to reach out to them, but they seemed to evaporate away before his weakening eyes. With what little breath he had left, he painfully and stutteringly began quoting from the Ten Commandments. '*…for I am a jealous God… visiting the iniquity… of the father upon the children… unto the third and fourth generation… of them that hate me*'.

In his last moments of consciousness, he blamed himself for the predicament in which Frances and the children would now find themselves.

'He's spoutin' religion but it sure is a bit late for that. Hang on; I reckon he's the haulier that carts the rags for the bible thumper that's tryin' to spread the gospel round here, and the black kid's his helper. How do we know it ain't the kid who done it? Maybe we should 'ave nailed him before he ran off,' said one of the now thinning crowd.

'They'll be carting *him* off soon,' said the last to leave.

Dan, now alone and abandoned by the dispassionate crowd, as indeed Jesus Christ had been that day at Calvary, gathered up what little strength was left within him and uttered his last words as he lay dying in that gloomy New York street. 'God, I have sinned against you and this is my day of divine retribution.'

There was no one to hear his confession as his last breath passed from his lungs. The arm that was propping up his body collapsed under him sending his body face down into the dirt of Little Water Street. God in his Heaven seemed too far distant from the 'Five Points' to hear the weak last words spoken by a poor mortal as he lay dying on a dirty street in New York City. The city, in which Dan as a boy had placed so much hope, was now the scene of his cruel demise.

Thomas ran all the way to the station house of the sixth ward Municipal Police Force, in nearby Mulberry Street and rushed up to the desk. 'Quick, Quick! There's been a murder. He's been an' done for Mr Dan, and I knows who done it. I sure as heck knows who done it,' he shouted.

'Whoa, slow down, boy,' the desk officer said as though there was all the time in the world, which only added to Thomas's frustration.

'We ain't got no time; he'll get clean away. I know where he lives, and I can take you there right now. Come on, please believe me. He lives in Apartment 5B, 38, Orange Street,' and Thomas headed for the door.

'Hang on, boy; you don't think I'm goin' runnin' round the 'Five Points' with some young negra kid lookin' for a murderer. How am I to know I ain't bin' set up and run straight into a gang of police-bashin' thugs. I'm too smart to fall for that one.'

The attitude of the desk officer was now annoying Thomas who knew Michael was a member of the 'Dead Rabbits' who could easily conceal Michael among their ranks, long enough for him to make his escape later, after the trail had gone cold. 'Please believe me, I ain't out to get yer, I want you to catch Michael Crowley the Irishman who runs with the 'Dead Rabbits'; I'm tellin' yer he's stabbed Dan Swain, my boss whose dead body is lyin' in a pool of blood in the entrance to Little Water Street.'

'Say, ain't you the kid who works for the English guy down on the waterfront doin' the haulin'?'

'I sure is,' Thomas said proudly but not in any mood to wait for any accolades.

'I recognise you now you had me goin' for a moment. You ain't no gang kid. I'll summon the troop.' The desk officer hurried through to the back room and quickly returned with six officers with truncheons drawn.

'He says the body is lyin' at the junction of Cross, and Little Water. Two of you check the body, the other three come with me, said the senior officer. 'Where did you say he is holed up, kid?'

'I'll show yer,' Thomas said enthusiastically. He ran off with Mr Dan's leather pouch containin' $339. All his money he drew from the bank in Chambers Street,' he concluded.

'Oh no you don't, boy. You stay right here and tell the desk officer the full story exactly as it happened; now that address again.'

Thomas related the address of the fugitive once more and the troop rushed from the station. Two officers found the body of Dan Swain exactly as Thomas had reported.

Meanwhile the four other officers arrived at the entrance to 38 Orange Street and cautiously climbed the single flight of stairs leading to the first floor. Turning right on the landing they quietly made their way along the corridor until they reached number 5B at the far end. They stood for a few moments listening at the door. The voices of a man and a woman talking in Irish came from within. The officer in charge of the operation nodded to the one nearest the door who carefully turned the handle slowly and quietly. Finding it unlocked he threw the door back wide and the four officers burst into the room catching the two occupants completely by surprise.

Two of the officers grabbed Michael Crowley one at each arm while one grabbed him by the waist, lifting him off the ground. He kicked and snarled like a mad dog for several minutes before the officer who had him by the waist finally managed to wrestle him to the floor where the two either side pinned him to the floor with their knees on his arms. With great difficulty, they turned him onto his stomach and eventually managed to force his arms behind him and manacle his wrists.

During all the commotion, the senior officer had restrained Mary.

'Let her go,' shouted Michael. 'She had nothin' to do with this. Let go of her.'

Realising how calm Mary had remained throughout the raid, the senior officer decided she was not a threat and released her. She sat on a chair at the table, with her head on her chest, saying nothing. The leather pouch belonging to Dan was under the table by her feet, empty. Strewn in front of her were the dollar bills which less than an hour ago Dan had collected from the bank. To the right side of the table was a pile of dollar bills stacked tidily, which suggested Michael Crowley had made a start at counting the money.

The senior officer made the formal arrest of Michael Crowley while one of the other officers retrieved the pouch from under the table and collecting the money up, tidily replaced it into the pouch.

The two other officers took the shackled Michael and frog marched him from the room and down the corridor. Several of the occupants of the adjoining apartments poked their heads out of their doors to see who was causing all the commotion.

'Y' put up a grand fight, Michael, by the looks o' things. It took four of 'em to nail y' I see,' said an Irish neighbour.

'That's enough of that now or you'll be keepin' him company in the cell as well,' warned the officer nearest to the doors. 'I'm afraid you will have to come along as well for now, Mrs Crowley; it is Mrs Crowley, I take it? You never know round here,' he added sarcastically, and the final two officers left apartment 5B and headed back to the station with Mary between them.

Following his arrest, Michael Crowley was taken to 'The Tombs' or to give the building its formal title, New York Halls of Justice and House of Detention. It got its nickname because of its design, which resembled an Egyptian mausoleum. Situated in Lower Manhattan, it occupied the whole area bordered on four sides by Centre Street, Franklin Street, Elm Street and Leonard Street, with its façade in Centre Street. Although designed to be impressive at street level, the whole building, as young as it was, was already sinking into the landfill that once was the Collect Pond. The wall and floors were cracking and water seeped up through the cracks in the floor making it a miserable place to be, both for prisoners and those employed there.

Chapter 23

The trial of Michael Crowley began on Monday March 18th, 1850, in the Egyptian Hall of the New York Halls of Justice, presided over by Judge Melville Stansfield, a judge with a reputation for not suffering fools gladly, including counsel and he was renowned for keeping proceedings moving along at a fast pace. Not trusting lawyers and not in the position of paying the high fees they demanded, Michael Crowley decided to defend himself. The prosecuting counsel was Morton Anderson.

Michael Crowley stood in the front of the court, flanked by two police officers with everyone else seated, waiting for the arrival of the judge who stood in the doorway to the left of the dais.

The Bailiff announced, 'All rise.' There was a noisy shuffling of chairs and feet as everyone rose. The Bailiff continued, 'The Supreme Court of the City of New York is now in session. The honourable Judge Melville Stansfield is presiding.'

The Judge entered and took his seat. 'You may be seated,' he declared, and everyone noisily followed his lead.

Judge Stansfield said, 'The Clerk will call the first case.'

The Clerk announced, 'The State versus Michael Joseph Crowley.'

Judge Stansfield spoke. 'Michael Joseph Crowley, you stand before this court accused of the murder in the first degree of one Daniel Swain. Are the lawyers in this case ready?'

Only one lawyer took to his feet, the prosecuting lawyer. 'Morton Anderson, Your Honour. I shall be representing the State in this case.

I understand the defendant chooses to represent himself,' he said.

'You realise, you can be defended by counsel if the state thinks you qualify,' the judge reminded Crowley.

'I do indeed, Your Honour, to be sure,' Crowley replied.

'And you still choose not to be represented?'

'That would be correct now,' Crowley said.

'Well, let us begin,' said the Judge impatiently and feeling relieved he had been spared any delay caused if the defendant had changed his mind.

In his own defence, Michael Crowley took the stand and related to the court the events on his return home on the night of Thursday 14th February and the conversation he was privy to the following morning, between his wife and Daniel Swain.

'Sure, the pair of 'em drove me to it. That English maan – I'll call 'im that for I cannot bring meself t' mention his name – had taken me wife while I lay sleepin' in the other bedroom. I'd arrived home with a fair load o' whisky inside o' me; maybe more than was good for me ye might say, and after a bite t' eat, I was after taken to me bed to sleep it off. I slept like a baby all through the night but like a baby I woke, earlier than they hoped, that is when they were discussin' what had gone off between them. They were talkin' about what they had done together, through the night. It was easy for a blind man t' see he had taken me wife under me own roof. I was beside meself with anger,' Crowley explained.

There was a long pause… Everyone in the court waited for him to continue. Judge Stansfield looked over at the defendant in amazement and said, 'Is that it? Do you have nothing more to say for yourself? You do realise, do you not, the seriousness of the charge ranged against you and if the members of the jury find you guilty of murder in the first degree, I have no alternative but to sentence you to death?'

'No, Your 'onour, I've nothin' more to say for the moment other than to say he 'ad it comin' and I can't deny that. I place myself at the mercy of this court,' was all Michael Crowley offered in reply to the Judge's reminder.

'Well Mr Anderson, I think the defendant has made it easy for us. He has given us the motive for the murder and stopping short of an open confession, he has admitted in his opinion, and I use his own words, 'he had it coming', meaning, I take it, the deceased. What remains for you to do is to prove to the jury that it was murder in the first degree. I think this is going to be one of the quickest murder trials I have had to preside over. It seems Mr Crowley here is out to enhance my reputation for expediency,' Judge Stansfield said, rather facetiously, considering the gravity of the occasion.

Morton Anderson began his cross-examination of the defendant. 'You have told this court, on hearing your wife and the deceased discussing what amounted to an adulterous act on their part, and I quote, *you were beside yourself with anger*', may I remind you, these are your words not mine, Mr Crowley. Is this so?'

'It's the truth now; y' have it spot on there, so y' have.'

'Yet you chose to do nothing about it at all?'

'Y' have it right again, sir.'

'It comes as a great surprise to me and I think more importantly, to the members of the jury, to hear you say that. You, a member of the notorious 'Dead Rabbits' gang, standing up and saying, on learning your wife has had sexual intercourse with another man, right under your own roof and with you in the next room, you were beside yourself with anger, yet you did nothing at all. Come now, Mr Crowley, I think the jury will find that difficult to believe.'

At this point, the Judge interjected. 'Mr Anderson, where is the proof the defendant is a member of the so-called 'Dead Rabbits' gang leading us, if indeed he was a member of this gang at all? May I remind you, the defendant is on trial for the murder of Daniel Swain and not for being a gang member, no matter how nefarious the gang may be? Without this proof, this is nothing more than conjecture on your part and as such, cannot remain on record.'

'Thank you, Your Honour, for the reminder. I will reveal, later in the case for the prosecution, that Michael Crowley was without doubt a member of the aforementioned gang and I have two witnesses who will testify to that effect.'

'Are these witnesses in court now?' Judge Stansfield asked.

'They are indeed, Your Honour and I shall be calling on them both to give evidence later.'

'I will allow as fact, the defendant was a member of this gang to remain on record. Carry on.'

'Thank you, Your Honour. I will also reveal his passive acceptance of his wife's adultery with Daniel Swain, on hearing their conversation on the morning of Friday the 15th February, was because he had other premeditated plans for Daniel Swain, with much more serious consequences. He sat alone in the other room, doing nothing, because he was also putting into place plans for a more devastating revenge than a good hiding.'

Morton Anderson continued with his cross-examination of Michael Crowley. 'Let me explain to you, Mr Crowley, why you stand before this court today facing a charge of murder in the first degree and not a lesser charge of grievous bodily harm. You stand here accused of murder in the first degree because you planned the murder of Daniel Swain from the moment you became aware of the conversation between your wife and your lodger when they discussed their indiscretion the night of the 14th February last. The instinct of a hardened member of a notorious gang on learning first hand of your wife's adultery under your own roof would be to give the transgressor a good hiding for their actions. I am not condoning this action, you understand…'

At this point, Judge Stansfield interrupted Morton Anderson's cross-examination.

'Please, Mr Anderson, try not to make too much out of my laxity over the issue of the accused's gang membership. As you told us earlier, this is to be established and I look forward to your revelations at some later point in this trial.'

'Thank you, Your Honour, for your direction, which I will indeed heed.' Turning to the accused, he continued his cross-examination.

'The point I make is this: you realised you could make capital out of this whenever it was to your best advantage. You did indeed, have other plans for Dan Swain. Your callous and calculating mind was planning a more exacting punishment, as and when the time was right. I suggest to you, Mr Crowley, you decided the time was right for revenge when you learned Dan Swain was returning to England.'

'It wasn't like that at all; I did nothin' at the time because I was carryin' a hangover from Bernie Finnegan's rotgut whiskey of the night before. Sure, it's brutal stuff. I hadn't the strength to raise me head from me pillow let alone box anyone and that's the truth now, I lay listenin' to the two of them discussin' their actions. If I'd been fitter that mornin', I would have boxed the two of them and that's for sure now. They can thank the whiskey for getting away with what they did,' Crowley concluded.

'Can they indeed, Mr Crowley? I'm sure the members of the jury will bear that in mind when they come to make their decision later.' Addressing the jury directly Morton Anderson said, 'What I would like you to concentrate on, is the time when the defendant first became aware that Daniel Swain had received a letter from his wife in England telling him of a serious domestic crisis. A crisis, which needed his immediate attention, and he had to return to England as soon as possible.' Shifting his attention back to the accused, he said, 'Mr Crowley, allow me to elaborate to you and the jury. On Thursday 21st February, Daniel Swain returned to your apartment 5B, 38 Orange Street, where he lodged with you and he told you and your wife of the letter he had received from his wife in England begging him to return. Serious developments back home affecting her and the children, necessitated his immediate return. Is that the case?'

'That is true,' Crowley replied.

'Moreover, he told you he had secured a passage on the packet

Patrick Henry, sailing on the Saturday evening for London, England. Would you agree?'

'I would indeed, sir.'

'Good. What I think the jury will find particularly interesting is the fact that Daniel Swain, when asked by your wife if he would return to America with his wife and family, as was his original plan, once the crisis was resolved, he had replied emphatically, he would not. Furthermore, he disclosed to you and your wife, rather naively I might say with hindsight, he was withdrawing all his money and closing the account which he held at the Emigrants' Savings Bank, on the following Saturday morning. A substantial sum of money totalling $339, the same amount of money, which the arresting officers found on the table in your apartment less than an hour after Daniel Swain left the bank on the morning of his murder.

'Mr Crowley, may I remind you, your wife is in the court building as I speak, and I will be calling her to give evidence against you later. She will confirm what I have described as a true account of the conversation between Daniel Swain, your wife and yourself when he returned to your apartment on the evening of Thursday 21st February.'

'I never said a word to the man followin' the business with me wife. So, I wasn't included in any conversation between the two o' them,' Crowley said and for once, he was telling the truth.

'Maybe so, Mr Crowley. You heard all of Daniel Swain's plans. While your tongue was disengaged at the time, your ears most certainly were not. I suggest to you and the members of the jury, that this vital piece of information was the catalyst that sealed Daniel Swain's fate. On hearing of his plans, your own plans were set in motion. The moment for which you had patiently waited since your wife's transgression with the deceased, had now arrived. This knowledge clearly illustrates your actions on the morning of Saturday 23rd February were those of premeditated murder in the first degree. You knew your victim's route from the bank in Chambers Street to 38 Orange Street would take him along Cross Street, so you secreted yourself in the shadows at the junction of Cross and Little Water Streets. There you lay in wait for your victim to pass. As he did so, you pounced upon him and cold bloodedly murdered him by a stab wound to the heart. Moreover, while your victim lay on the ground, his lifeblood draining from him, you removed from his now defenceless body, the large sum of money, which you knew he would be carrying. Gentlemen of the jury, I put it to you, this final act of theft from the murdered man, makes the defendant, who you remember, has not denied he was involved in the death of Daniel Swain, indeed he said, and I quote, 'he had it coming,' guilty of murder. Moreover, guilty of murder in the first degree. I am finished with this witness, Your Honour.'

'Have you anything to add in your defence, Mr Crowley?' the Judge asked.

'No, Your Honour,' Crowley said weakly.

'You may stand down,' the Judge said curtly.

Morton Anderson continued. 'I now call upon Mary Crowley,' he announced.

Mary Crowley took to the stand and took the oath.

'Would you please tell the court your name and your place of abode?'

'My name is Mary Elizabeth Crowley of Apartment 5B, 38 Orange Street, New York City.'

'And you are indeed the wife of the accused, Michael Joseph Crowley?'

'That would be the truth now, sir,' Mary replied.

'May I say at this point, Mrs Crowley, I think, what you are doing in giving evidence against your husband, who stands accused of murder, is both unusual and brave and I am most grateful to you.' He continued, 'I would like you to tell the court, in your own words, what life was like, living with your husband.'

'Well now, we were married in 1840 and at first we were happy. Before all the troubles came with the famine years. Our first baby,

Seamus, arrived in 1845, and he was the apple of Michael's eye. We lost him on the journey over here, fallin' victim to the outbreak of cholera onboard ship. Our second child, Breda, was born in 1847. Michael doted on her, but God took her from us, when the crops failed in 1848, God rest her little soul. Sure, 'twas not only us. Nearly everyone lost somebody durin' those hard times back in Kenmare.'

Morton Anderson interjected there. 'Am I right in saying, Mrs Crowley, the man who your husband stands accused of murdering, indeed bravely risked his own life to save the life of your small son?'

'That is the truth,' Mary replied.

'Would you care to explain to the court how this act of bravery came about?'

'Seamus fell overboard while the ship was still tied up alongside the dock in Liverpool and Dan Swain dived into the dock and saved his life, so he did.'

'I find it quite remarkable that someone who saved your son's life would later be murdered at the hands of your husband.'

At this point Judge Stansfield interjected. 'May I point out to you, Mr Anderson, that fact has yet to be established by this court,' he reminded the prosecuting counsel.

'Thank you for pointing that out, Your Honour, I stand corrected,' Morton Anderson replied.

'Please carry on, Mrs Crowley,' the Judge said.

'Michael continued to be the lovin' husband who had seen me through all those bad times. Things changed when he joined the 'Dead Rabbits'. At first, he said he joined to safeguard the jobs and to look after the interests of the Irish people who had left their homeland to settle on foreign shores, as he put it. At first, I believed him, and I think Dan did as well, but he was spending more time with the gang and less time with his job and that's when he changed quickly. I think that was when Dan once said to me, the gangs were a form of organised crime, as he had put it. At the time, Michael thought God had done him a bad deal in takin' the children from us.

He had little time for the church and less time still for the priests. He would go missin' for days on end. It got to the stage where I never knew when he would be comin' home and I so much wanted him to be as he was, lovin', kind, and carin' for me. I cannot remember the last time he attended mass or indeed when he last took confession. He was growin' away from me and this was down to his involvement with the 'Dead Rabbits'. I knew I was losin' him forever. The night Dan and I succumbed to the flesh, it was entirely my fault. I was the temptress. Dan was fightin' with his conscience, but he was too weak in the end. I take all the blame for what happened that night. I was upset when I saw the state Michael was in again, havin' been away for three days. More and more, I was gettin' afraid of him and his anger. I wanted comfortin' and lovin' and I turned to Dan for somethin' I had missed for a long time. I saw in Dan, what I had seen in Michael all those years ago. Truth is I think I was fallin' in love with Dan. I needed someone to love me, and Dan was there. Though he was married, I still made a play for him. I know now it was wrong to do so, but I couldn't help myself that night. Bein' starved of love for so long, I was desperate for comfort. Sure, Michael and I occasionally had sex, but since his running with the 'Dead Rabbits' gang, all the love in our marriage had long gone and the sex act had become nothing short of rape. Even that was well over six months ago. Despite what Michael may think, sex with Dan only happened the once. It was over quickly, and I never spent the night with Dan. In fact, the truth is, we quickly had sex and I spent the rest of the night curled up on the floor next to the stove. The last thing I wanted was to wake my drunken husband. It was my actions that led to Dan's death and that will stay with me forever.'

Mary concluded her evidence with tears trickling down her cheeks.

'Are you alright, Mrs Crowley? Let me say to the court I admire your frankness and honesty in relating what happened between you and Daniel Swain and I would remind you, it is not you on trial here for murder, but your husband. Thank you, I shall not be asking you any more questions,' and turning to the Judge he said, 'I am finished with this witness, Your Honour.'

'Thank you, Mrs Crowley,' Judge Stansfield said and addressing Michael Crowley he added, 'Do you wish to question this witness on anything in your defence?'

'No, Your Honour, I have nothin' to ask this witness, but I would like her to know, I still love her and I'm sorry I've brought this upon her, to be sure.'

A ripple of half-stifled laughter spread through the courtroom, which Judge Stansfield quickly suppressed.

'May I remind the court of the gravity of this case.' And addressing Michael Crowley, he said, 'Be that as it may, I think your renewed feelings for your wife have come too late to help you now.' And turning to Mary Crowley, he said, 'You may stand down now, Mrs Crowley.'

Morton Anderson called Thomas Mays to the stand.

'Would you please tell the court your name and where you live?'

'Yes sir, my name is Thomas Mays, and I lives in the Old Brewery,' he replied.

'Now Thomas the evidence you are about to give is vital to this case, so I want you to think carefully and tell the court exactly what happened on the morning of Saturday 23rd February of this year... Take your time, I want you to be accurate about what happened that morning. Remember this is a court of law and you are under oath to tell the truth,' Morton Anderson reminded him.

Thomas went over his account of what happened that fateful morning. How he and Dan Swain had gone together to the Emigrants' Savings Bank and on the way back, he had to return to the bank for his passbook, which he had left behind. He described to the court how on his return, as he approached the junction of Cross Street and Little Water Street, he saw someone dash from the entrance to Little Water Street, turn left and flee along Cross Street at speed, in the direction of Paradise Square. Thomas went on to tell how he had found Dan Swain lying in a pool of blood in the entrance to Little Water Street.

'Is the man you saw fleeing from the scene of the crime here in court this morning, Thomas?' Morton Anderson asked.

'Sure is, sir, that's him, sittin' right over there,' and Thomas pointed an accusing finger in the direction of Michael Crowley.

Turning to face the jury, Morton Anderson said, 'I think that is emphatic evidence placing the accused at the scene of the crime when Daniel Swain was set upon and killed.'

Addressing the Judge, he said, 'No more questions, Your Honour.'

'Mr Crowley, would you like to question this witness?' the Judge asked.

'I do that, Your Honour,' Michael Crowley replied.

'Well that does surprise me, carry on,' Judge Stansfield said, giving Crowley a quizzical look as he did so.

'I'd like to know how ye can be so sure it was me you saw, runnin' away from the scene of the crime.'

'It was you alright; I recognised your voice as well. As you turned into Cross Street, you said in yer Irish accent, "That's what you get for messin' with me wife, y' English..."' Thomas turned to the Judge and said, 'May I use the word he uttered, Your Honour?'

'You may indeed, as it may be vital to the case.'

Thomas continued, '"You English bastard." That's exactly what he said, Your Honour.'

Turning to Michael Crowley, he said, 'Had ye not been in such a rush; had ye looked to ye right instead of dashin' straight down Cross Street, you would have looked me straight in the eyes. Who knows, ye might have committed a double murder that mornin' and I wouldn't be here to tell the tale,' Thomas concluded.

At this point Judge Stansfield interjected again and said, 'I cannot allow the last comment to remain on the record, as it is pure conjecture.'

Thomas inadvertently had made a valid point that the jury would still take into consideration.

'Y' Honour, does the jury believe the word of this young ruffian from the Old Brewery, before a decent citizen like meself now? Sure, the place is teemin' with lyin' brats like yer man here.' Turning once more to Thomas Mays, Crowley posed the question, 'How do we know it's not you that should be here instead of me? Sure, those kids in there can kill like any man. Bred to it, they are. I have no more questions, Your Honour.'

'In that case you may stand down, boy,' Judge Stansfield said, thinking he was too young to warrant the title of Mr Mays and not deigning himself to be so familiar as to use a black boy's forename.

Morton Anderson rose to his feet slowly and announced, 'I call to the stand, Senior Officer Simon Pollock,' his head bowed, reading from his papers on the lectern in front of him as the Senior Officer responded and took the stand.

'Are you Senior Officer Simon Pollock of the Sixth Ward stationhouse?'

'I am, sir,' the officer replied.

'And could you tell the court where you live?'

'I am a single man and I have lodgings in the premises owned by Mrs Singleton, at 153, Mott Street.'

'Good, now could you tell the court your version of what happened after Thomas Mays arrived at the Sixth Ward stationhouse on the morning of Saturday 23rd February and reported there had been a murder?'

'May I read from my notebook, sir?'

'You may indeed, officer.' The officer wrestled to free his notebook from the breast pocket of his uniform and tried at a nervous apology to Judge Stansfield for the briefest of delays.

Judge Stansfield, never slow to maintain his reputation, chivvied the officer along, saying, 'Come now, officer, we haven't got all day,' and a semblance of a wry smile quivered at the corners of his mouth as the officer fumbled to find the page from which he wished to read.

Having regained his composure, the officer began his version of what happened after Thomas Mays reached the station.

'At first, the officer on the desk, had not believed the young black boy,' he eventually began. 'You have to act with caution at all times. It could possibly have been a deliberate ploy to lure a police officer into an attack. There are plenty people out there with a grievance against the police. When the officer at the desk recognised the boy as Daniel Swain's assistant, he raised the alarm.'

It was at this point that he began reading from his notebook.

'Realising what the boy was saying could be true, I decided to take action. Whereupon I despatched two of my officers to the scene of the crime as Thomas Mays had described, while myself and three other officers went to apartment 5B, at 38 Orange Street. We burst into the apartment and took the occupants, namely Michael Crowley, the accused, and his wife Mary Crowley, completely by surprise. At first, they never moved from the table where they sat. In those brief moments of surprise, Michael Crowley appeared to continue counting money from a pile in the centre of the table. The money consisted of dollar bills of various denominations. Michael Crowley, on realising who we were, resisted arrest with a fierce tenacity and it took all my men several minutes to overpower him. Once subdued, we searched him and found a blood-stained long-bladed knife in the waistband of his trousers. We collected the money up and placed it into a leather pouch, which was lying empty under the table. We confiscated the leather pouch and the money as evidence and took Michael Crowley and his wife to the Sixth Ward station. We placed Michael Crowley in a police cell. After further questioning of his wife Mary, I was convinced she had no prior knowledge of her husband's plans for that fateful morning and until his return home, she knew nothing of what he had been doing. She claimed she wondered where he had acquired such a large sum of money and up until my men and I charged into the room, he had given her no explanation. I was inclined to believe her. In due course, the two officers who I had despatched to the scene of the crime reported they had found the body of an Englishman, later identified as Dan Swain, lying dead in a pool of blood at the entrance to Little Water Street; stabbed through the chest and it would appear the weapon had pierced his heart. I formally arrested Michael Crowley for the murder of the said Daniel Swain and of robbing his victim of the sum of $339, which was the money we had found at the apartment; the same sum of money which he had withdrawn from the bank an hour or so earlier. May I say, throughout her husband's arrest, Mary Crowley co-operated with the police and it was obvious to us she had played no part in her husband's activities that morning. She was extremely upset on learning of the murder of Daniel Swain; so much so, she was almost in a state of collapse and it took one of my men several minutes to get her calmed. That concludes my account of what happened on the morning of Saturday 23rd February of this year, sir,' Senior Officer Pollock stated.

He struggled once more to return the difficult notebook to his breast pocket with the same frustration he had shown in extracting it earlier.

Unlike Judge Stansfield, Morton Anderson waited patiently until Senior Officer Pollock had buttoned down the flap on his breast pocket and was once more standing to attention.

'You have nothing more to add, officer?'

'No sir, that's exactly as it was.'

'Thank you, Officer Pollock, that will be all.' And turning to the Judge he said, 'There I rest my case, Your Honour.'

Judge Melville Stansfield looked down at the defendant, who by now was looking despondent and said, 'Michael Joseph Crowley, do you have anything to ask this witness?'

'No, Your Honour, I've nothin' more to add only to say again, that English maan had it comin' for what he did to me wife. As I said at the start of the proceedin's, these were the circumstances that drove me to do what I did. I would like the members of the jury to consider this before they make their decisions. I have nothin' more to add, Your Honour,' and he sunk to his seat between the two guarding officers.

These were Michael Crowley's last few feeble words in his defence as he slumped in his chair.

'So, Mr Crowley, am I right in thinking you are pleading there were mitigating circumstances that drove you to kill Dan Swain, his adultery with your wife? Moreover, you are putting this up as a reason why the jury should return the lesser verdict of murder in the second degree, which carries a life sentence and not one of murder in the first degree which carries a penalty of death,' Judge Stansfield reasoned.

'I do that, sir,' Crowley replied in a forlorn manner.

Judge Melville Stansfield began his summing up.

'I will not take long in my summing up of this case. Before us is a man whom the prosecuting counsel, who I might add, has put his case to you so clearly, it would be difficult for you not to believe that the man sat accused of this crime is indeed guilty. The prosecuting counsel has also put it to you clearly, that the accused was fully aware of his victim's movements on the morning of the crime and that it was premeditated murder. In addition, the fact he robbed his victim of a substantial sum of money – that he killed for gain – makes it murder in the first degree, which carries a sentence of death.

'On the other hand, the accused has chosen to defend himself, which is his prerogative. In doing so, I do not think he has done his case any good. What he has tried to prove to you is that there were mitigating circumstances, which were responsible for his actions. The defendant's wife has stated to this court, under oath, that she and the deceased had indeed committed adultery while her husband slept off a drunken stupor in the other bedroom. It is these mitigating circumstances that Michael Crowley would have you consider, thereby bringing a verdict of second-degree murder, a crime which carries a sentence of life imprisonment and not murder in the first degree, a crime that carries the sentence of death by hanging. That alone could be deemed an act where mitigating circumstance played a part and could lead you to return a verdict of murder in the second degree. Let me help you in your deliberations.

'The accused, knowing in advance, what Dan Swain's mission was that Saturday morning in February, and knowing the route he took each Saturday morning, to and from the Emigrants' Savings Bank in Chambers Street, the accused lay in wait for his victim's return. Whereupon he waylaid his victim and stabbed him to death through the heart. This is premeditated murder. An act of murder in the first degree, which carries a sentence of death. You have also been made aware of the evidence given by Thomas Mays who recognised the accused as he fled the scene of the crime. Thomas Mays has also said, under oath, he recognised the voice of the accused. Michael Crowley's wife Mary has said when giving evidence against her husband, that their marriage was breaking down because of his involvement with a nefarious gang known as the 'Dead Rabbits' and it was his behaviour that drove her into the arms of the deceased. Finally, you heard the evidence of Senior Officer, Simon Pollock of the Sixth Ward police force, who described to us that on entering the apartment of the accused that Saturday morning, amongst the things they found was the exact amount of money, which Daniel Swain had withdrawn from the bank barely an hour earlier. With all this overwhelming evidence set against the accused by the prosecution counsel, I can only recommend one verdict and that is guilty of murder in the first degree.

'Members of the jury, you must reach your verdict based on the evidence given in court today. It is your duty to retire and select a foreman and consider your verdict. Bailiff, would you please lead the jury outside the court to make their decision? The court stands adjourned while the jury considers its verdict. Take the prisoner away until the jury returns.'

The two officers led a dejected Michael Crowley away. The court stood while the judge left his courtroom, and the Bailiff led the jury to the jury room where he waited outside the door for their verdict.

After a comparatively short deliberation, the foreman eventually popped his head out of the door and informed the Bailiff they were ready. The Bailiff led them back into the courtroom and they took up their places once more on the jury benches.

'All rise,' the Bailiff announced as the Judge made his reappearance and everyone rose to their feet.

'Be seated; the accused will remain standing,' the Judge announced.

'Has the jury made their decision?' he asked.

The foreman of the jury rose to his feet, and said, 'Yes, Your Honour, we have.'

'And what is your verdict?'

'We, the jury, find Michael Joseph Crowley, guilty of murder in the first degree.'

Judge Stansfield paused for the briefest of moments, while the jury foreman took his seat and continuing, said, 'Thank you, members of the jury, I think your decision is the right one.'

The jury had been out for only thirty minutes and the trial was all over on the first day, thus maintaining Judge Stansfield's reputation for presiding over quick trials.

Judge Melville Stansfield addressed the court for the last time in the trial of Michael Crowley.

'Michael Joseph Crowley, the verdict of this jury is, they find you guilty of murder in the first degree and as such I sentence you to be taken back to the House of Detention, where on a date to be determined, you will be hanged by the neck, until dead. God rest your soul.'

*

In the Tombs Prison, there was a small row of cells known as *Death Row*. These cells set aside from the rest, were for the detention of prisoners awaiting execution and it was in one of these cells, that Michael Crowley lived out the last days of his life.

A courtyard separated the male prison from the female prison over which spanned a bridge named ironically *'The Bridge of Sighs'*, which connected the two wings. It was under this bridge that they erected the scaffold. At nine o'clock in the forenoon on Monday 1st April 1850, the Chaplain and Governor arrived at Michael Crowley's cell. They walked him sombrely from his cell to the gallows. The executioner placed a hood over his head and placed a strong rope noose round his neck. With the knot placed strategically under his left ear, the executioner quickly sprung the trap, despatching Michael Crowley to his maker, exactly two weeks after his sentence.

*

About five months after Michael Crowley's execution, Thomas Mays was at his work on the waterfront when one of the warehouse captains approached him and said a woman was enquiring after him.

'After *me*, you say?' Thomas asked with a puzzled look on his face.

'She sure is, and she appears to be with child. If y' get my drift. Whatever have you been up to, young Thomas?'

Whoever could that be and what does she want from me? Thomas thought.

He left the warehouse and once outside he saw the woman in question standing on the other side of his wagon and immediately recognised her as Mary Crowley.

'Can I help you?' he asked.

'I'm sorry to bother y', Mr Mays, but the truth is I've nobody else to turn to.'

'You're Michael Crowley's widow ain't y'?'

'That I am, sir, y' right enough there.'

Thomas studied the woman standing before him. Her appearance had deteriorated, in the time that had elapsed since he saw her last, in the dock at her husband's trial.

'What is it you want of me, Mrs Crowley?'

'It's like this, sir. Since the death of Michael, I now find myself destitute with nowhere to go. I have to leave my tenement because I can't pay the rent and I'm at me wits' end,' she revealed.

'Well, I can't do anything immediately to help you, I'm afraid, as I am in the middle of moving from the Old Brewery and the new place I'm moving to isn't vacant yet. I can give you money enough to pay y' for a week or so and to put food on your stomach until I move into my new place. After that, come to see me at my new address where you can work for me as housekeeper and companion for my ailing mother. Can you write, Mary?' he asked, not being able to write himself yet.

'Not much,' she replied.

'OK, well, remember this address, 69 Chambers Street, don't forget now and I will see you in two weeks,' Thomas Mays promised. 'By the way, Mary, get yourself cleaned up a bit. It's a bit different an area to the 'Five Points'. If you don't mind me askin', can't the father help y'?'

'Not very well, he's dead,' she stated confidently and without any hesitation. 'The father is Daniel Swain,' she blurted out.

Thomas, taken aback by Mary's revelation was flabbergasted to think, his benefactor, with all the qualities that Thomas admired, could be the father of Mary's unborn illegitimate child.

'You're sure you have your facts correct?' Thomas asked.

'Never been so sure of anythin' in my life before. Dan was the only man I had been with and I hadn't been with Michael for six months before the incident with Dan. That's what caused all the trouble between Michael and Dan. You were at the trial. You know what I said in the dock under oath and I was telling the truth,' Mary reminded him.

Thomas gave Mary enough money to buy her two weeks' lodgings and food in a cheap boarding house. The money also bought her some clean second-hand clothing, and he told her to come back in two weeks, by which time he would have moved into his new address.

Thomas Mays and his mother moved out of the Old Brewery and into accommodation in Chamber Street clear of the notorious Five Points as planned and accordingly Mary Crowley visited a couple of days after they had moved in. She was dressed in her *new* clothing.

'Have you considered my offer, Mary, of you movin' in with us as our housekeeper? I need someone to take care of my ma while I's down at the wharfs. The years spent living in the Old Brewery has crippled her. She now suffers badly from rheumatism and finds it difficult to walk these days; you would be company for each other. I'll pay you a wage and your keep and you can shop for our day-to-day needs. When your baby is due, we will arrange what will be necessary, nearer the time, Mary. Whatever happens, we will take good care of y' both.'

'Oh God bless you, Mr Mays. Ties a saint, that you are,' and she crossed herself.

PART 6

LIFE IN THE WORKHOUSE

Chapter 24

Norfolk, England

January 1850

In Durnham Union Workhouse, the day began at six a.m. when all the inmates were required to arise, carry out their ablutions and prayer. Seven a.m. to eight a.m. was breakfast time, after which, able-bodied inmates would take up their various tasks.

The authorities segregated the sexes for their daily tasks. Most of the women would be engaged in domestic work such as cleaning, washing and kitchen duties but those with specialist skills, were occupied in the workshop doing sewing, spinning, and weaving.

With Durnham being in an agricultural area, some men worked as labourers on the farms. Others worked inside doing more menial tasks such as crushing stones for road building, while some unpicked oakum for caulking ships and boats. Sack making and corn grinding kept the rest occupied. For the latter occupation, several men

"

operated a treadmill, which turned the grindstone.

Because of her condition and her ability to read and write, Frances helped in the administration office. Work duties would last until six p.m. with an hour break for dinner between noon and one p.m. Suppertime was between six p.m. and seven p.m. and after prayers, everybody would be in bed by eight p.m. The beds were primitive and only two feet wide. The regulation bedding consisted of a palliasse filled with straw. The authorities did not allow sheets and pillows, considering these items to be luxuries. Each dormitory contained twenty beds and bed sharing was common in the children's wards. Apart from your uniform, they allowed you only one other possession – your bed. Vagrants, known in the workhouse as casuals, slept on the floor.

The inmates ate in the large dining hall at one of many narrow tables, set in rows all facing in the same direction, so everyone looked at the backs of the heads of the people in front of them, thus denying any chance of conversation with the people opposite. The main constituent for all meals was bread, usually accompanied by gruel, but the diet generally consisted of vegetables and a daily allowance of meat, butter, cheese and three pints of watered-down beer. Sugar and fruit were a rarity and often, the authorities served diluted milk. The ringing of the workhouse bell summoned the inmates to their meals. Not a single word passed between them – by order.

The toilet facilities were primitive and consisted of a small daytime privy, which served one hundred other inmates. It was nothing more than a cesspit with a cover and having a hole in it over which to sit. There was a little more privacy at night-time as in each dormitory there were chamber pots. Washing of your hands and face was part of your daily routine but for Frances and the rest of the women inmates, bathing occurred once a week and under supervision.

Rules and regulations governed life in the workhouse and the many posters adorning the walls constantly reminded inmates of the fact. For those inmates who could not read or write and there were many, the rules were read out once per week.

Abusing a member of staff, assaulting another inmate, wilful damage, being drunk, or acting in an indecent manner, were all punishable by a reduction in diet and solitary confinement for up to twenty-four hours. The Justice of the Peace dealt with offences of a more serious nature.

Frances went into labour about midday of 23rd February and Dan Jr. was born later in the afternoon, in the delivery ward of the hospital wing, weighing seven pounds, eight ounces. She had decided in Dan's absence, to call him after her husband. As she cradled her new-born son in her arms, she had no way of knowing the horrendous crime, taking place on the streets of New York City. She was not to know, at the time she was bringing one new life into the world, a felon's blade had taken another cherished life from her.

Like all mothers, Frances quietly and secretly checked her new-born son for any imperfections. Slowly, she worked her way through his little fingers and toes, each in turn. As she checked the final perfect digit, a warm feeling of pride came over her. How she wished Dan could be with her to share this moment of joy at what their love for each other had created. Her ignorance of what was happening across the Atlantic Ocean kept this precious moment intact. The slow means of communication between England and America, kept the cold reality from her, allowing her the delight which the new-born child brought her. She had managed to get news of the birth of Dan Jr. to her other children via one of the inmates, a cleaner, whose duties took her into other areas of the workhouse. After her confinement, which lasted for ten days, Frances left the maternity ward and returned with her baby to the women's ward. She also returned to her clerical duties in the administration office with Dan Jr. by her side in a wickerwork bassinet.

She constantly wondered about her husband Dan and her three other children.

How she yearned to be out of here and reunited as a family once more. *Dan must have got my letter by now. Soon he will return and get us out of here,* she consoled herself.

Jemima, being the eldest, was quite resourceful and Frances knew she would cope. She had not seen her since they were admitted and being her only daughter, Frances missed her company. Jemima was a caring child and had always shown concern for her mother's well-being, and Frances knew she would be wondering how her mother was after the birth of her new baby brother.

The situation improved slightly one morning when the tall inmate who had attended at their induction, came into the administration office, and sought out Frances.

'Mrs Swain, I must inform you, your baby is to be baptised into the Christian faith after the morning service in the church next Sunday. You will be pleased to know, your other children will also attend as this is one of the few occasions when the Board of Guardians waive the segregation rules. Mind you, this is only for one hour, after which, you will all return to your places,' the tall woman said.

'Thank you,' was all Frances could say. She was so overwhelmed at the thought of a reunion with her children, even if for only one hour.

Sunday arrived and after breakfast, Frances dressed her baby in the baptism gown provided by the workhouse. It was obvious it had served numerous other such baptisms.

Once ready, she proceeded to the small church, which stood apart from the other gaunt structures, which made up the main workhouse complex. Although made of the same stone as the rest of the workhouse, the architecture of the little church made it more inviting.

In fact, on first seeing the little church, Frances wished she could attend each Sunday but only staff members enjoyed this facility; inmates being allowed to attend baptisms and funerals only.

As she approached the church, she could see her children waiting for her, looking somewhat unfamiliar to her, dressed in their regulation issue clothing and although she missed her husband, she was pleased he was not there to witness the ignominy of such a pathetic gathering. At the same time, she was not to know the poignancy of her thoughts.

She hurried to join the little group and the two boys broke away from the gathered group and ran to meet her.

'Ma, Ma,' they shouted, and Frances had to stop and brace herself for the impact of their bodies meeting hers.

Frances and her sons joined the group outside the church and the tall woman who had informed her of the baptism arrangements, said with unusual consideration, 'Hello Frances, let me take your baby.'

It was the first time she had shown any real concern for Frances or her children, which took Frances by surprise. Maybe the fact she was outside the confines of the main complex and in the precincts of the church, had an enlightening effect on her, Frances thought to herself. Handing her baby over, Frances cuddled the children to her, first the two boys and then Jemima.

'How are you, Ma? Are you well? I have been worried to death about you. I was over the moon when the cleaner told me you had had the baby,' Jemima said excitedly, hardly stopping for breath.

'I'm sure you want to see your baby brother,' the tall woman said, still surprising Frances with her newfound friendliness.

'Oh, he's gorgeous,' Jemima said. 'He's so like Da.'

'Do you think so?' said Frances. 'Good, because in the absence of your Da I've decided to call him Dan.'

'Da will be pleased about that, Ma – I'm sure he will. How I wish he could be here now, I miss him so much,' Jemima said. Frances knew what Jemima meant but Frances would have loved it, if instead of being here, she was standing outside All Saints in Renton, with all her family around her as it used to be.

The tall lady lowered the baby down and pulled aside the cowl of the shawl, which was keeping out the cold early March air, allowing the two smaller children to see the baby snuggled inside. The two boys in turn, peered inside and saw their baby brother for the first time. They both smiled but said nothing. Edward gently lifted the little chubby fingers of one hand, which had escaped from the shawl. Resting them on his own fingers, he compared them for size.

The chaplain moved across and introduced himself to Frances.

'Good morning Mrs Swain, I am Reverend David Naismith, and I am the acting curate at St Stephen's in Durnham Market and I am also chaplain, here at the Union Workhouse. I understand your husband is away in America on err...' He hesitated for a moment as he chose his words. '...Err, on business, I believe... I see,' he said sarcastically. He allowed himself time to consider the reality of the situation. *The father of the child is in America on business, while his wife is having their son baptised in the workhouse in his absence,* he thought. Like everyone else who learned of Frances's situation, he pondered briefly over the ethics of such a situation.

'That is correct,' Frances said, trying to maintain whatever vestige of credibility the truth contained. Once more, the burden of responsibility vested upon her while her husband was in America, rested upon her small shoulders.

'I see,' he said quizzically, adding, 'I think it is time we began.'

The chaplain led them to the front of the church and ushered them to their places, which had been set aside in the front pew. When they were all seated, the chaplain leaned over and said to Frances in quiet undertones, 'As you are aware from your experience at the baptism of your three other children, there is the necessity in the case of a boy child, for two godfathers and one godmother to witness your child's baptism. And under the present circumstances, I took the liberty to invite the sexton at St Stephen's, Mr Willis, and Mr Tomlinson, a respected member of the church council to act as godfathers, if you have no objection, Mrs Swain. Mrs Ramsey, whom you have met, is a trusted inmate at the workhouse and will stand as godmother.'

At last, the tall woman had a name. Until now, no one had bothered to make any introduction between her and Frances.

'Under my present circumstances I think I have little say in the matter, therefore the arrangements will be fine,' Frances replied.

'Well, we will get the morning service underway.'

After the last lesson at Morning Prayer, the Reverend Naismith led the godparents and the family members to the stone font, situated inside the entrance to the church. The font looked incredibly old, older than the church itself and Frances thought it must have come from some grander church, which had become derelict with time. It had intricate carvings of cherubs bearing garlands of flowers. The garlands draped over the bowl of the font and down the outside, making it altogether attractive. With everyone in his or her place the chaplain proceeded: *Dearly beloved, forasmuch as all men are conceived and born in sin: and that our Saviour Christ saith, none can enter into the kingdom of God, except he be regenerate and born anew of Water and of the Holy Ghost: I beseech you to call upon God the Father, through our Lord Jesus Christ, that of his bounteous mercy he will grant to this child that thing which by nature he cannot have; that he may be baptised with Water and the Holy Ghost, and received into Christ's holy Church, and be made a lively member of the same... Let us pray...'*

Addressing the godfathers and godmother the Reverend said, *Dost thou, in the name of this Child, renounce the Devil and all his works, the vain pomp and glory of this world, with all covetous desires of the same, and the carnal desires of the flesh, so that thou wilt not follow, nor be led by them?'*

The godparents answered together, *'I renounce them all...'*

The Reverend took the baby in his hands and said to the godparents, *'Name this child.'*

The godparents said together, *'Daniel.'*

The Reverend repeated the name as he poured water from the font over the baby's head, saying, *'I baptise thee in the Name of the Father, and of the son, and of the Holy Ghost. Amen.*

We receive this child into the congregation of Christ's flock...'

*

With the service over, there was little time left for Frances to spend with the children before they all returned to their normal day-to-day activities within the workhouse regime.

They said their goodbyes and with tears in their eyes, the tall Mrs Ramsey led them back to their various areas within the workhouse.

Chapter 25

Robert Hart had taken up his duties at Renton House Farm at the beginning of January with his wife Rachel who was heavily pregnant with their first child. Two weeks later, she went into labour, but it was not an easy birth. The baby had presented itself breech. A configuration that was dangerous for both mother and baby. After an extremely long labour and despite the efforts of the village midwife Nancy Urmston, assisted by Mrs Hayward and later by Dr. Thompson, the baby, a boy, was eventually stillborn with the umbilical cord wrapped tightly around its neck. In consequence, Rachel suffered a massive haemorrhage and she died in childbirth.

*

The following August, Martin Woods, the postman, knocked on the door of Renton House Cottage and Hannah Hayward answered.

'Good morning Martin, what have you got for me today?'

'This one is a bit difficult, Mrs Hayward, as I have a rather bulky letter here addressed to Frances but as the whole village knows she is in the workhouse. It must be important as it is from Barings' Bank in London, as is evident by the address on the back of the envelope.'

Looking at the large Manila envelope, she said, 'Maybe Dan has sent Frances the money for her and the children to join him at last, in America. He must be doing well if the letter has come from the bank and not just tickets from the shipping agent,' Hannah Hayward speculated.

'By rights, I am obliged; in fact, I am duty bounden, to return the letter to the Post Office in Durnham, from where it will be redirected to the workhouse. You can imagine what the authorities may make of it when they see the Barings' Bank stationary. She may never get to know of its existence let alone its contents,' Martin Woods suggested cynically.

At this point in the conversation, Robert Hart appeared from the direction of the farmhouse and the two, thinking he might be able to add some logic to the situation, sought his opinion as to what was in Frances's best interest.

'What you say regarding your duties, Martin, is absolutely correct. If you deliver the letter to me, under the circumstances, I will take full responsibility for its safe delivery to Mrs Swain and I will stand by you if there are any repercussions against your good self. Other than the three of us here, no one else need know,' Robert Hart said, conspiratorially. With great reluctance, and in fear of his job, Martin Woods released his charge of the letter into the hands of Robert Hart.

'Don't worry Martin, I am sure nothing will come of this,' he said reassuringly.

'I hope I'm doin' the right thing here,' the postman said nervously.

'You'll be all right, please believe me,' Robert Hart reassured the other two. 'Does either of you know which day is visiting day?'

'Wednesday,' they both replied almost in unison.

'Good, that is two days' time. It is then I shall deliver the letter to Mrs Swain personally,' Robert Hart declared.

'I hope you are right; if any of this gets out, I'll be looking for another job,' the worried postman replied and with Robert Hart's scheme in place, Martin Woods fretfully continued on his round.

*

The following Wednesday, as planned, Robert Hart visited Durnham Union Workhouse with the purpose of delivering the letter to Frances. Being instrumental in Frances's present plight, made him uncomfortable and he had no idea how Frances would react to him.

Frances appeared in the reception area and the attendant

introduced her to him. On first appearance, he bore no resemblance to the boy, with whom she had gone to school. This came as no surprise as eighteen years had passed since she last saw him. Of muscular build but a little taller, she thought he bore a slight resemblance to her husband.

Robert Hart introduced himself and waited for Frances's reaction. She shook his hand. Robert offered her a seat in one of two chairs, which Mrs Ramsey had put at their disposal, and he opened the conversation. Frances recognised Mrs Ramsey as one of the two women who carried out their induction to the Workhouse.

'About your eviction, I can understand if you despise me, Mrs Swain,' Robert said, tentatively, 'but what happened at Renton House Farm was all outside of my jurisdiction,' he added.

'I bear you no malice, Mr Hart, what happened was not of your doing. What has brought you to visit me, surely not an apology?'

Robert Hart hitched his chair closer to Frances and answered in a quiet undertone so as not to reveal their conversation to Mrs Ramsey.

'No Mrs Swain, a letter has arrived at Renton House Cottage addressed to you and I have taken it upon myself to deliver it to you personally. It is better this way as it is obvious by the stationery, the contents are important, and I wanted to be sure you received it intact.'

'That is most considerate of you, Mr Hart.'

'Please Mrs Swain, call me Robert; it is the least I could do under the circumstances,' he continued, still trying to create an amiable rapport with Frances.

Taking the envelope from the inside pocket of his jacket, he slowly and quietly slid it over to Frances's lap.

'Do I open it now?' Frances queried, trying hard to prevent Mrs Ramsey from hearing their conversation.

'I rather you did. This way, I will bear witness to its contents. I suggest this, not in an act of idle curiosity, but as a safeguard against any malpractice carried out by workhouse staff,' he said in a voice low enough to deny Mrs Ramsey being privy to the contents of the letter.

Frances slowly opened the envelope. Inside she found a letter and a further envelope. She began reading the letter…

Baring Brothers & Co,
8, Bishopsgate,
London.
Thursday 1ˢᵗ August 1850

Dear Mrs Swain,

First, may I offer to you and your family on behalf of my Company and myself, our humble condolences on the recent death of your husband.

Following recent correspondence between the New York City Police Department and Baring Bros. Bank in New York, it has fallen upon me to act as administrator of the effects of your late husband, Daniel Swain.

Frances read no further as she swooned and collapsed forward onto the lap of Robert Hart.

When Frances came around, she could almost make out the bleary image of Mrs Ramsey standing over her. As she strained to focus her gaze, she heard an insistent Mrs Ramsey saying, 'Here, drink this drop of sal volatile, it will help clear your head, my dear,' as she poured a few drops of colourless liquid from a small hexagonal bottle into a glass of water.

White clouds spread slowly towards the surface as the droplets mixed with the water. Mrs Ramsey swirled the glass completing the transformation. She continued her ministration by encouraging a semiconscious Frances to drink the cloudy concoction. 'Come on now, it'll do you good,' Mrs Ramsey prompted. Frances instinctively took the glass from Mrs Ramsey and cautiously sipped the draught. After a tentative initial sip, Frances drank the remaining liquid in one gulp.

Robert Hart, who had been massaging Frances's wrists stopped when he realised Frances was regaining full consciousness.

'Dunno what were in that letter, but it did give you a mighty shock,' Mrs Ramsey said, hoping to learn more of its content by alluding to it.

With Frances slowly recovering, she handed the glass back to the would-be nurse.

'Something dreadful has happened to my husband… he is dead,' she blurted out and burst into tears.

'There, there now, I know you've had an awful shock, but you'll make yourself worse,' Mrs Ramsey said, trying to console Frances.

'May I?' Robert Hart asked as he gently eased the envelopes from Frances's clenched fist. Frances was far too shocked to raise any objection…

Assuming Frances had no objection, Robert Hart read the letter.

Baring Brothers & Co.
8, Bishopsgate,
London,
Thursday 1ˢᵗ August 1850

Dear Mrs Swain,

First, may I offer you and your family, on behalf of my Company and myself, our humble condolences on the recent death of your husband.

Following recent correspondence between the New York City Police Department and Baring Bros. Bank in New York, it has fallen upon me to act as administrator of the effects of your late husband, Daniel Swain.

Please find enclosed a banker's draft made out to you for the sum of £78 and 15 shillings, this being the equivalent in pounds sterling of $339, the money stolen from your husband by his assailant.

In the second envelope, you will find an account, by The Chief of New York City Police, of the events leading to your husband's murder.

If I can be of further help to you on this matter, please do not hesitate to contact me at the above address.

I remain, Madam, your servant,
Signed
David Seabrook.
Secretary, American Business.

Robert Hart placed the first letter on his lap and opened the second envelope. He removed the second letter and commenced reading silently.

George A Ansell
Chief of Police,
New York City Police Headquarters,
8th April 1850

Dear Mrs Swain,

It is my painful duty to inform you that your husband Daniel Swain died from stab wounds inflicted by one Michael Joseph Crowley on 23rd February 1850.

I hope it is of some consolation to you, to know that the felon was apprehended, tried, and found guilty of your husband's murder in the first degree and as a consequence was executed at the New York House of Correction on Monday 1st April of this year.

Your husband was returning from the Emigrants' Savings Bank when Crowley waylaid him. He stabbed him and robbed him of his savings. The bankers' draft, which you will find enclosed, drawn up by Baring Brothers' Bank in London and made out in your name, is the sum of money, which your late husband was carrying when the attack took place. The sum of $339 is the amount he had withdrawn from his savings account that fateful morning. Also found on his person was a ticket to London aboard a ship sailing on the night of his demise, also the letter he had received from you telling him of your circumstances in England, together with his bank passbook to his account, which he had closed on the morning of the attack.

Following my officers' investigations and under questioning at the trial of the perpetrator of this heinous deed, witnesses revealed, that once back in England, your late husband did not intend to return to America. I submit this letter with my greatest respect to you and your family through Mr David Seabrook in his capacity as the New York representative of Baring Brothers & Co.

I am Madam, your servant,

George A Ansell

Also, inside the envelope from the New York City police chief, was a third envelope. Robert Hart carefully thumbed through the contents without fully removing them. Inside, he found Frances's letter-sheet to Dan, from which, he realised the police department had obtained her Renton House Cottage address. He also found the superfluous shipping-line ticket to England and the bank passbook. On all these articles, there were macabre stains, which Robert Hart realised were from the blood of Frances's late husband. He closed the envelope carefully so as not to draw attention and deciding these were of no further use to her; especially in this condition. Better to keep them from her rather than cause further upset. Therefore, he decided to secrete this envelope into his own pocket.

With the Barings' letter uppermost, the police letter on the bottom, and the banker's draft sandwiched between them, he passed the two letters back to Frances.

'Are you sure you are up to this?' Robert Hart asked thoughtfully.

'I have to find out exactly what has happened to my Dan,' she said bravely.

She nervously took the letters from him and once more began reading the Barings' letter. Her hands were trembling as she continued to read. When finished reading, she stared blankly at the letter and after a few moments, she placed it under the second letter and placing the banker's draft on the very bottom of the pile, she began to read the second letter. As she read, fretful sobbing interrupted her breathing. Her tears ran down her cheeks and stained the letter. On finishing, she aimlessly folded both letters and the banker's draft together and struggled to replace them into one envelope. Robert Hart taking the letters once more, replaced them for her into their respective envelopes, and handed them back to the bewildered Frances.

Mrs Ramsey once again showing her concern for Frances's shocked state, asked, 'Are you alright, my dear?' A somewhat facile question but well meant. Frances was too distressed to answer and stared aimlessly at the floor.

'I think you should take her to the hospital ward and let her rest a while,' Robert Hart suggested, adding, 'she will be shocked for some time after the dreadful news she has received.' Turning to Frances, he took her hands in his, saying, 'I will visit you again next week at the same time. Would you like me to take your letters for safekeeping?'

Mrs Ramsey said nothing, but a frown wrinkled her brow on hearing Robert Hart's suggestion.

'Next week we will discuss getting you and your children out of here,' he added and the frown on Mrs Ramsey's brow deepened.

'Thank you for your kind concern Mr Hart... er... Robert,' Frances said.

'Not at all; until next week,' he said.

He turned to Mrs Ramsey. 'Thank you for your assistance... sorry I didn't get your name.'

'Mrs Ramsey, sir.'

'Don't forget, Mrs Ramsey, Mrs Swain needs a few days of care and attention; she needs time to recover from the tragic ordeal that has befallen her.'

This said, he doubted whether she would receive such attention in a place like the workhouse. Robert Hart gave Frances a parting smile and left her in the 'care' of Mrs Ramsey.

*

The following week he returned as he had promised, and once more met Frances in the reception area.

'Is there somewhere Mrs Swain and I could talk? A stroll in the grounds, say?' he suggested to Mrs Ramsey, who had once again escorted Frances to the reception area.

'Of course, if you are back before visiting is over,' Mrs Ramsey said, condescendingly.

Robert Hart led Frances to the main door and out into the grounds. They strolled at a leisurely pace.

Frances was the first to speak. 'It is kind of you to come to see me again.'

'How are you feeling now?' he asked.

'I still can't come to terms with the fact Dan has gone from me forever. It never occurred to me until the next day, he died on the day I gave birth to Daniel Jr.,' she said as tears stung her eyes.

'I know how difficult these times are for you, and I would like to think I understand what you are going through. I too am grieving the loss of a loved one. Last January I lost my dear wife in childbirth. It was a difficult birth and our baby, a little boy, was stillborn; my wife suffered a massive haemorrhage from which she never recovered.'

'I am so sorry, Robert, and you doing all this for me, when you have your own cross to bear.'

'I am feeling a bit better about it now; it takes time and time heals slowly. Therefore, you see we are kindred spirits, and this is the basis of my plan for getting you out of here.'

'What do you mean, Robert?'

'Well, I am living in that big farmhouse on my own, you are in this dreadful place and you and your children are separated all the time you are in here. I know you have the money from your late husband, which will buy you a place of your own if you so wish but I thought if you came and lived at the farm as housekeeper you could have your children with you. They could go to school in the village as before. Renton is where you and the children belong, and I have no vested interest other than I need a housekeeper. Having done the job before, for the Haywards, you will be back in your old routine. Investing your banker's draft from America in a bank in Durnham, will give you compounded interest until such times as you need it. I can go along with you if you wish to set that up. You will not have to touch that money, as I will pay you a wage for housekeeping and your keep. There now, I seem to have done all the talking. Frances, I seem to have overwhelmed you with my plan. While we walk, give it your consideration.'

They continued their stroll and Frances turned Robert Hart's offer over in her mind and she found herself warming to the idea. In fact, the more she thought about it, the more Robert Hart's idea appealed to her. For a minute or so, neither said a word. Frances was the first to break the silence. Again, she had to justify to Robert Hart, why Dan had left her and the children and gone off to America, on his own to seek their fortune. She had to justify his actions to everyone, more so now, in the wake of what had happened.

'I would love to be back at Renton House Farm, we were all so happy there. So much so, I prayed, that Dan would change his mind on his big dream of going to America. Alas, he was convinced we would all have a better life there. I supported him fully when we talked of it, even before we were married. It was not to be, as each successive birth of our children jeopardised our original plans. Against my better judgement, I continued to be supportive of him. After all, he was not acting on a whim and we had discussed his plan repeatedly. When he left for America, he thought if he did not go ahead of us, we would never make the journey at all. In retrospect, I wish now I had been more assertive in my reassessment of the venture. I was not and now, alas, poor Dan is dead, and my four children are without their father. With that in mind, I have arrived at my decision readily. Weighed against another day of separation from my children, and your generosity, the balance comes down in favour of your offer, for which I thank you, Robert.'

Robert Hart pondered for a while, taking in Frances's account of how her present circumstance had evolved, and he took up the conversation.

'I am sure he did what he thought was in all your best interests. Now you have adopted my plan, I will carry it out with the utmost propriety; you and the children having your sleeping quarters, and I mine. In the meantime, the priority is to get you out of here and we can start that in motion as soon as we get back to the reception area. You can come back with me and stay at the farmhouse as my guests while you decide what is best for you and your children. Without wanting to put pressure on you, as I see it, you have two choices – either you buy your own place with the money you now have at your disposal or take up my offer. If you choose the former, you will still have to find work, as your money would not last forever. On the other hand, if you choose the latter, you would be earning your wages as a Renton House employee and I would provide you and your children's keep,' Robert Hart reasoned. Realising the time, he said, 'We must be getting back, we have important things to do.'

All the way back to reception, Frances considered the two options and she soon made up her mind that the offer of becoming housekeeper to Robert Hart was the more appealing of the two. She knew everyone at Renton House, and she would once more be close to Mrs Hayward, who since the death of Aunt Polly had become something of a mother figure to her. In addition, if she was not happy with the arrangement, she could always revert to the option of buying her own place. At least it would give her time to see how things were working out. On arriving back at reception, Robert Hart immediately set about arranging the discharge of Frances and her children from the workhouse.

Addressing Mrs Ramsey, Robert Hart said, 'Mrs Swain has decided to discharge herself and her four children from the care of this establishment. Would you please bring the children to her and make ready all their belongings, which the authorities confiscated on the day of their admittance?'

'She'll have to give three hours' notice,' Mrs Ramsey said, with an air of authority.

'Oh, come now, Mrs Ramsey, I do not think that will be necessary under the circumstances. I can see how this rule would benefit the authorities if an inmate took into their mind to leave of their own volition. I am sure, if you are perfectly honest with me, I am not creating a precedent here.'

Mrs Ramsey stood sheepishly in front of Robert Hart, knowing he had outmanoeuvred her deliberate attempt at obstruction.

'I'll do so, right away,' she said grudgingly.

'It's a pity they can't give us our hair back; I don't want to sound ungrateful but what they did to our hair was unforgivable,' Frances said as she remembered the ordeal at the time of their admission. Her hair had grown since that infamous day of frenetic shearing. It had not yet reached its former glory. Robert Hart glanced at Frances and tried to imagine her with longer hair. Even with her hair as it was, to him, she appeared as an extremely attractive woman. With her dark beauty and her fine features, she looked stunning. Her trim figure belied the fact she had borne four children.

A few minutes later – which seemed like an age to Frances – Mrs Ramsey returned with the children, accompanied by a short woman carrying their belongings. Frances realised it was the same woman who had assisted in the hair cropping on the day of their arrival.

The three older children once more rushed excitedly to her side and hugged her. Mrs Ramsey was carrying Dan Jr. whom she had collected from the nursery ward and she passed him over to Frances.

'You'll have to sign for these, and there's other paperwork to sign first,' said the short woman, taking on the role of authority recently relinquished by the now silent Mrs Ramsey who realised Robert Hart was not one to cross.

'I would suggest you get it ready forthwith,' said Robert Hart who was by now rapidly running out of patience with these obstructive little officious creatures who relished their tiny element of power.

Mrs Ramsey ushered them into the same side-room they used when they changed into the horrid regulation issue clothes and they changed into their own clothes once more.

With the all-important paperwork duly signed, they left the two women to their own company. Frances would never know the real name of the smaller of the two. She had decided, she would always remember her as Mrs Short and smiled at the notion of 'Mrs Tall' and 'Mrs Short'. They left the main building and crossed the cobbled yard.

Ahead was the ominous iron arch across the entrance leading out onto the street. As the little group approached the entrance, Frances thought, despite it being more difficult to read from this aspect, she could not help but think it read better walking in this direction than it did on entering and a feeling of well-being came over her, notwithstanding what had happened to her husband. This was the first time she had felt this way in a long, long time. They passed under the arch and walked out onto the street. With due respect to her late husband, she was at last free; free of the workhouse, free of America and free to make a new start in life. She was only thirty years old, she reminded herself, with four children and she promised herself there and then, whatever decisions she made in future affecting her and her children, would be of her own making.

As they walked away from the awful place that had been their 'home' for almost nine months, she turned to Robert Hart and thanked him for all he had done for her in effecting their release and said, 'I will be delighted to take up your offer of housekeeper,' she said and offered her hand as a token to the agreement.

'Splendid,' Robert Hart replied and shook her hand enthusiastically. 'You are sure you aren't acting in too much haste in reaching your decision?' he asked her cautiously.

'I am sure it is the best course to take for the immediate future. We will at least try it,' Frances said, happy at having made the first decision of her own and she liked the feeling of being in control of her own destiny.

'I think this calls for a celebratory lunch at the Market Cross Tearooms before we take the brake back to Renton,' Robert Hart suggested.

The children responded in a chorus of, 'Yes please,' and, 'Yippee!'

PART 7

A NEW BEGINNING

Chapter 26

Back at Renton House Farm, Frances and her children were happy. Once again, they were united as a family and free of the workhouse. Although they had been devastated at the news of the death of their father, in childlike innocence, they had quickly adapted to life without him; after all, it was virtually a continuation of the life they had come to know, once their father had left for America. On first moving in, they had been wary of Robert Hart; now six weeks into the arrangement, they realised he was not a threat.

Frances too was warming towards her new employer. She found him most charming in manner, more so in fact, than Dan had been. Then again, Dan had been a simple ploughman and lacking the refinement which Robert Hart had acquired from associating with his 'betters' at Holkham, plus his time spent at Cirencester had given him a certain polish. Indeed, Frances found these qualities quite attractive.

It was late December, and the winter winds were beginning to blow unchecked across the fens. Robert Hart and Frances sat reading, each in an armchair either side of the fireplace. The last embers of the peat fire settled in the grate; it was late, and they were letting the fire burn out before bedtime. It was the same room where Frances had undergone her interview with Mrs Hayward almost fifteen years previously. The children had gone to their beds about an hour earlier leaving Frances and Robert Hart alone together. *Much has happened since that March day in 1836,* she thought.

Putting his book down, Robert Hart spoke. 'It will soon be Christmas, Frances, what are your plans; do you have family still living hereabouts?'

'My parents live in Ditchington.'

'You will surely want to visit them at such a time,' he suggested.

'I would dearly, but I'm afraid that won't be possible.'

'Why ever not? I can spare you the time away if you so wish,' he replied.

'It is not as simple as that, Robert. This time last year, when faced with eviction from the cottage, I asked my mother for her support, but she made it quite clear she was not prepared to take us in, even on a temporary basis. Not even until my late husband had established himself in America. Sadly, I have not seen my parents since that day last December.'

'That *is* sad, Frances; we shall make the most of Christmas here together with the children and we shall invite Mrs Hayward round for her Christmas dinner. From what I understand, it is the custom for everyone employed at Renton House to receive a piece of beef taken from Tom Gibney's entry in the best Norfolk Red beef cattle Christmas competition and I see no reason to change what my predecessor began. Whether Tom wins again this year or not, we shall have a prime sirloin joint with all the trimmings, and we will buy sweetmeats and oranges for the children. I will put a new silver sixpence in their stockings, and we will make Christmas Day as festive as possible.'

'What a marvellous idea, Robert, such a pleasant contrast from last year,' Frances said.

'Without sounding selfish, I am pleased you and the children will be here to spend Christmas with me, as this is too big a place for me on my own. A home should ring with the voices of children at this time of year and having you and the children here will help me come to terms with what might have been,' his mind returning to his late departed wife and baby. 'I shall open a special bottle of port, which I have kept for such an occasion. Your good self and Mrs Hayward will join me in a glass of Christmas cheer,' he said emphatically.

'But I don't drink alcohol, Robert.'

'You must partake of only the one, as it will be Christmas,' he said excitedly.

Frances noticed an extra facet to Robert Hart's charm, which showed when he enthused over his plans for the forthcoming festive season, making her pleased inside at the prospect.

'Well maybe the one,' she relented. With that, she bid him goodnight and retired to her bed. As she lay on her pillow reflecting on Robert Hart's enthusiastic plans for the coming Christmas Day, she realised she was becoming increasingly attracted towards him. In her schooldays, she had noticed him for his academic ability. Now, in womanhood, a physical attraction drew her towards him. Surely not so soon after the death of Dan, she reproached herself. Sleep did not come easily. She was feeling the same inside as she had as a young girl. It was the very same feeling, which had kept her awake as an adolescent girl on first meeting Dan and she decided she must suppress these feelings for the time being.

The days leading up to Christmas were full of excitement, keeping Frances busy with all the preparation. She had already made the plum puddings some weeks ago, allowing time for the brandy to soak into the fruit. All the children in turn, had given the mix, *'a stir for luck'* and made a secret wish. Everyone was aware, to disclose the secret wish would break the magic and the wish with it. Now she was busy baking mince pies, which everyone would eat over the Twelve Days of Christmas. The tradition went: one pie eaten on each of the twelve days would bring good luck for each month of the coming year. Mince pies had been a savoury delicacy but now they had evolved into one containing no meat; filled instead with a sweet concoction of dried fruits, raisins, sultanas, candied peel, apples, spices, sugar, and suet. Here too, a dash of brandy would be added to the mixture and baked in a pastry case.

Frances loved this time of year. Although she had lost Dan, this year she did not have the threat of eviction hanging over her. Last year there had been no Christmas celebrations for her and the children although as in other years Frances had enjoyed attending the Christmas service, her prayers as she knelt in church that day had gone unanswered.

This year will be different, she thought, as she mixed the pastry. The children would have their stockings filled once again. The idea of spending Christmas with Robert Hart appealed to her. As she worked at her baking, she found herself once more musing over him. In her mind she was listing his virtues; trying to justify to herself why indeed she was giving him so much thought and why the thought of him made her feel so good inside. In the quiet of the kitchen, with the baby settled and the children at school, she analysed what it was about him that made her feel this way. Granted, she found him quite attractive physically and she had always admired him for his intellect. She would always be indebted to him for arranging her and the children's release from the workhouse. He had offered them a home here at Renton House and she knew these were not the only reasons why she found herself so attracted to him. Up until now he had been the perfect gentleman, maintaining the propriety he had promised her when offering her the post of housekeeper.

*

It was Christmas Eve night; the children's stockings hung from the mantle shelf. Edward had insisted they hang an extra one of his stockings for his baby brother. Frances and Robert Hart sat once more in the armchairs either side of the fireplace as they did most evenings after the children had gone to bed. A large turf of peat burned brightly in the grate giving a homely ambience to the room. Robert Hart was sipping a glass of sherry before he retired to his bed. Frances not being a drinker had declined his insistence of joining him in a nightcap. Robert unlike Dan was a smoker and was drawing on a long-stemmed clay pipe. Small wisps of aromatic smoke drifted slowly under Frances's nose before, drawn by the updraught, they quickly disappeared up the chimney.

The aromatic smell of the tobacco filled the air. 'Come sit by me,' Robert Hart invited.

It must be the sherry making him so bold, Frances thought as she responded immediately and sat on the floor at the side of his knee.

'I think this is going to be the best Christmas ever,' she said.

'Well I will do all I can to make it perfect for you and the children; do not forget we have to fill their stockings before we retire,' he reminded her.

'No, I haven't forgotten, we have the candy pigs and the oranges to put in and not forgetting your generous gift of a shiny new sixpence for each of them. They will be delighted in the morning. Thank you so much, Robert,' Frances said gratefully, and she placed her hand on his left knee. She had not meant the gesture to convey any suggestive message other than to show her appreciation for what he had done for her. Robert Hart placed his hand gently on top of hers; gentle enough to allow her to withdraw her hand if she so wished. Frances felt at ease and did not attempt to remove her hand. The gesture added to her feeling of wellbeing. She felt the warmth of his hand on hers. He looked down on her beautiful face, swathed in the jet-black hair, which free of the cruel workhouse discipline, was almost back to its former glory. With the back of his hand, he gently guided the hair on one side of her face and slowly lowered his mouth to hers and kissed her quickly on her lips.

Breaking away, Frances was the first to speak. 'I think it is time we filled those stockings before we retire to our beds,' she said.

'Does it have to be two beds?' Robert asked.

'I am afraid so, Robert, at this moment, I am not ready. It is too soon. I do have feelings for you but let us not act in haste,' she reasoned.

They completed the task of stocking filling and climbed the stairs. On reaching the landing, Frances turned towards her room. As she did so she stepped aside to let Robert pass her on the landing and as he did so, she kissed him gently on the cheek.

'Goodnight Robert, God bless and a merry Christmas.'

'Goodnight Frances and a merry Christmas to you.'

The following morning, the children emptied their stockings and were overjoyed with the contents. They each revealed excitedly how they planned to spend their shiny sixpences as they nibbled on their candy pigs.

'New ribbons for my hair,' said Jemima.

'A box of lead soldiers in hussar uniforms,' John said.

Young Edward said, 'I am saving mine until I make my mind up.'

After breakfast Frances and the children attended matins at All Saints in Renton accompanied by Robert Hart and Hannah Hayward. Later in the afternoon, they enjoyed a dinner of roast beef and all the trimmings. Having had their fill of the beef and vegetables and with the plum pudding eaten, the adults exchanged gifts.

Robert handed Mrs Hayward her gift. 'For you, Mrs Hayward,' he said as he handed a flat square-shaped package over to his neighbour.

'That is most kind of you, Robert,' she said as she removed the elegant-looking red satin bow and the brown outer wrapping.

'The ribbon was not my doing, but the lady in the shop offered to do it for me.'

Lifting the lid from the green inner box, she revealed a pair of handkerchiefs trimmed with the best Nottinghamshire lace.

'They are beautiful, Robert, thank you. I am afraid I do not have anything so grand for you, not that you would have any need for ladies' handkerchiefs,' she said apologetically and laughed as she passed a small soft parcel over to Robert. 'I hope it's the tobacco you use,' she said, not realising she had taken away the element of surprise in what the gift contained.

'Thank you, Mrs Hayward,' and he quickly removed the brown wrapping paper. 'It is Virginia tobacco, my favourite. Excellent choice, but you should not have bothered.'

The parcel Hannah Hayward handed to Frances notwithstanding the outer wrapping, did not conceal the contents. By the shape and weight, Frances immediately knew she was once more in receipt of a pot of Hannah's famous preserve.

Frances was genuinely pleased, as she did enjoy the preserves her former employer made each year from the produce of her garden, which she continued to tend.

'Thank you, Hannah, you know how much I love your preserve and gooseberry is a favourite of mine; I shall have a little each tea time.'

Again, it was Robert Hart's turn. 'For you, Frances,' he said as he handed her a small package. 'I hope you like them. These belonged to my late mother, God rest her soul, and I would like you to have them, Frances,' he added as Frances opened the box. Inside, she discovered a pair of tortoiseshell hair combs.

'Robert they are exquisite, are you sure there is no one else in your family more worthy of them than I?' Frances enquired.

'No, believe me, if there were, I would not still have them so long after she died. Being an only child there was no female relative to whom I wanted to pass them. It would give me much pleasure if you would receive them. I bought them for her in an antique shop in Cirencester while I was down there studying. It will be so nice to see them worn again, especially by someone with hair as beautiful as yours, Frances. My late wife was averse to tortoiseshell and showed no interest in them.' Frances pondered over Robert Hart's last statement and it made her uncomfortable to think her gift had belonged to a previous owner.

Hannah Hayward, who had been admiring her handkerchiefs during his conversation, looked up and gave Robert one of her wry smiles.

'I am honoured, Robert, and I shall treasure them always,' Frances said. 'Now it is time for my gifts to you,' she added, as she handed him his gift.

He opened it and was delighted at what it contained.

'David Copperfield,' he announced, 'the latest novel by Mr Charles Dickens, how thoughtful of you, Frances. I understand from the literary review in *The Times*, it is in part autobiographical,' he said excitedly.

'Now your present, Hannah,' Frances said as she passed her gift over.

Hannah Hayward opened her present to find a box of twelve of the mince pies, which Frances had baked two days previously.

'Thank you, Frances, I remember how good your mince pies were when you were living with me, before you and Dan were married.' She immediately realised how tactless she had been and tried to redress her remark. 'Oh, I am sorry, Frances, how thoughtless of me. Please forgive me.'

'Don't worry, Hannah, I know you meant well. I do forgive you and let us forget the matter. I understand what you mean, and the compliment is received in the way it was meant,' Frances said, generously. 'Don't forget you must eat one each day through the twelve days of Christmas,' Frances reminded everyone.

'In that case we will have our first now and I shall open a bottle of port with which to wash it down. The children will have to settle for non-alcoholic ginger wine, I'm afraid,' Robert Hart declared.

'Make that ginger wine for me too,' Frances reminded him.

'We are in luck, Mrs Hayward, it appears we have the bottle all to ourselves,' he said.

'I hope you aren't trying to get me drunk, Robert,' Hannah Hayward suggested.

'I wouldn't dream of such a thing, not a lady like your good self, Mrs Hayward,' Robert Hart replied, keeping the banter going.

'I don't rightly know where I will put it all,' Hannah Hayward said, by way of an apology for her overindulgence. Frances knew from Christmases past, she would have no trouble in seeing off the mince pie and port.

Halfway through his port, Robert Hart jumped up from his seat. 'I know, this calls for a sing song,' he declared, getting into the Christmas spirit, and he moved across to the foot-pumped harmonium standing in all its glory in the corner of the room.

'Now I am sure you all know, *The Twelve days of Christmas*, do you not?' he said as he made himself comfortable on the bench seat of the harmonium.

A resounding 'yes', came in reply from the rest of the company.

'So, it shall be,' he said, and immediately began to play the introduction to the melody.

'All together now, one, two, three,' he said as he counted them in.

'On the first day of Christmas…' they all sang in unison and managed to remain on key except for Mrs Hayward and young Edward much to the delight of Robert Hart.

The whole company sang with great gusto with Robert Hart leading the chorus and each of the others in turn singing each of the twelve days, with everyone joining in on the final day and almost raising the roof as they did so.

'Excellent, excellent,' Robert Hart enthused. 'We must continue in that vein, now we have found our singing voices; have we a volunteer for a solo from anyone?'

Jemima's hand shot into the air. 'I will, I will,' she shouted enthusiastically.

'Well Jemima, and what will you entertain us with at this festive time?'

'*I Saw Three Ships,*' she said.

'Splendid choice, Jemima, you lead, and I will follow,' he said, letting her start in her own key.

She began. *'I saw three ships go sailing in, on Christmas Day, on Christmas Day; I saw three ships go sailing in on Christmas Day in the morning...'* She ended her solo in perfect key and holding the final note beautifully; letting it fade away at the precise moment.

As the last note faded away, for a moment there was silence in the room as the little audience savoured the quality of what they had experienced. A round of enthusiastic applause eventually broke the silence. Robert Hart was the first to speak.

'What a splendid rendition, Jemima; where ever did you learn to sing so beautifully? I am most impressed. Has she attended singing lessons?' he asked of Frances.

'No, it is something she has always done, she is always singing,' Frances admitted.

'Maybe we should arrange for her to take lessons. A talent like hers needs nurturing. We must see what we can do as soon as possible. Most delightful, my dear,' Robert Hart enthused.

Jemima's face beamed at first, she dropped her head in coy embarrassment. Looking up she said, in a chatty manner, 'Ma has always sung to us and she was in the church choir at St Mary's up until her Aunt Polly died. Maybe that is where I get it. I don't remember Aunt Polly, I was only a baby at the time, but Ma has told us all about her, so in a way, I know her.'

'Now Frances, since it has been brought to our attention by your daughter that you too have a singing voice, could we tempt you to sing for us something of your own choosing?'

'Well I was hoping the choir at All Saints would have sung my favourite carol this morning, but they did not include it, so if you will bear with me, I would like to sing for you, *Adeste Fideles,* or to give it the more common name, *O Come all ye Faithful,* and please, everyone join in the last verse.'

As with Jemima, Robert let Frances make the opening and took the key from her.

They all joined her in the last verse with great enthusiasm.

'What a great time we are having. The old harmonium has not been played to a more receptive audience since the day it left my mother's home,' Robert Hart declared.

'Well I hate to be the one to break up the party,' Hannah Hayward said, 'but it is my way, to take a bit of a rest at this stage of the Christmas celebrations. What with the eatin' and the drinkin', I am always ready for a little snooze about now, so Robert, I will thank you for your kind hospitality. I have had a wonderful time and I shall see you in the morning, God willing. I will see myself out.'

'I am so pleased you have enjoyed yourself, Mrs Hayward. I'm sure I speak for everyone when I say how much we have enjoyed sharing Christmas with you.'

After Hannah Hayward had left, Frances got to her feet. 'Well I have more work to do, there is all the clearing and washing up to do in the kitchen. They won't do themselves and Sally Groves isn't here to help until Friday,' Frances said.

'I'll help you, Ma,' Jemima offered.

'Good girl, Jemima. Let us make a start. You, Robert, have a pipe full of Hannah Hayward's best Virginia and another glass of your port.'

'I might take you at your word, Frances,' and he poured himself another glass of port.

Chapter 27

March of 1851 had borne out the folklore adage; it came in like a lion and now it was going out like a lamb. Although still showery, the winds had subsided. Today, His Lordship had summoned Robert Hart to the 'Big Hall', to discuss future stock breeding.

The meeting over, Robert had got into conversation with Mrs Bethel, the housekeeper, and asked her casually if she knew of a music teacher in the area, explaining to her of Jemima's talent and how he would like to sponsor her.

'It is strange you should ask, but this evening, Professor Henri Colbert is to provide the musical diversion at a soirée being held to celebrate the Earl's birthday.'

'A professor you say, Mrs Bethel. Oh I wasn't aiming that high for young Jemima, I'm afraid.'

'Don't rule it out of hand, Mr Hart, I have it on good authority, he and his wife are refugees from France and find themselves on hard times. You know how the tittle-tattle gets around below stairs. I would at least try it. The story goes he is a teacher of music who fled with his wife from Paris almost three years ago, at the time of the revolution of 1848. His name is Henri Colbert, one-time professor of music at the Paris Conservatoire. At the time of the trouble, he and his wife had made their way to Calais. Once there, they had boarded the first boat available bound for England. The boat on which they travelled landed them in Lynn and they are now living in Durnham. Professor Colbert now made his living travelling around the grand houses of the landed gentry teaching their darling offspring the pianoforte and violin. He also takes engagements for soirées such as this evening. Therefore, you see it is quite possible he will be interested in your proposition. Indeed, there is the possibility, you may even meet him on the road this morning as he is coming to make the final arrangements for tonight's soirée,' Mrs Bethel explained.

'I can see me asking every fellow traveller I meet, if he is a Frenchman,' Robert Hart said jokingly.

'If the wind is in the right direction, you may even smell him coming, as I understand from Cook, they use plenty of garlic in their cuisine,' the housekeeper said.

'Well, good day to you Mrs Bethel, thank you for your information, you have been most helpful,'

Robert rode away from the Big Hall and headed down the long drive to the entrance to the grounds. The lodge-keeper let him through the large iron gates and out onto the open road. He had not travelled a mile down the road when he met a stranger on horseback coming towards him.

Could this be the professor? he thought, and steeled himself to ask.

'Excuse me sir, may I introduce myself? I am Robert Hart, farm bailiff at His Lordship's Renton House Farm in the village of Renton.'

'Good morning Monsieur Hart, it is my pleasure,' the professor said in his quiet French accent.

'Am I right in assuming you are Professor Henri Colbert? I hope you don't think me too forward in my approach, but my housekeeper's daughter has, in my humble opinion, a voice worthy of further development. I think she has a true natural talent. Although I would prefer you to be the judge of that with a view to you giving her singing lessons,' Robert explained.

'Will your protégé be at home tomorrow? I have some spare time,' the Frenchman asked.

'I'm sure it can be arranged,' Robert replied.

'Very well, but how will I find my way to Renton?' the music teacher enquired.

'It is pretty straightforward. I take it you will be travelling from the direction of Durnham.'

'That is correct, Monsieur Hart.'

'Well, at the Cromer crossroads, which you would have passed but a mile back, instead of taking a left-hand turn, as you did today, proceed straight ahead and follow the road until you reach Renton House Farm,' Robert explained.

'I shall look forward to meeting your protégé tomorrow, say five o'clock,' the professor suggested.

'That will be fine. I will see that Jemima will be available.'

'Until tomorrow,' he said and reached over and offered Robert his hand.

Robert shook the Professor's hand and said, 'Thank you for your time, Professor,' and they both carried on their separate ways.

*

Frances was so content to be back at Renton House and if anything, happier than she had been for almost two years, indeed not since Dan had gone off to America. Whenever she was alone with her thoughts, she found herself analysing the happy situation in which she now found herself and she wondered if she had come to terms with the death of her husband too readily. The time he had left her on her own, and the time she and the children had spent in the workhouse, albeit short as it was, had it hardened her? Notwithstanding all her efforts to the contrary, she was becoming more and more attracted to Robert Hart. He was constantly in her thoughts – last thing at night and first thing in the morning.

This evening, he was late back from the 'Big Hall'. She preferred it when they could all sit down together for dinner and exchange stories, but today she knew Robert would eat alone, by which time the children would be in bed. Frances was noticing, her new employer's visits to the 'Big Hall' were becoming more frequent and his return was becoming later in the evening. She would have liked to challenge him about the new demands on his time at home, but she decided it was none of her business and put it out of her mind.

She had waited all evening and eventually she heard his horse's hooves on the cobbles; her heart quickened as the door latch clicked and Robert walked in. She was so glad he was home; she realised she was in love with him. She found him extremely charming, not only with her, for she had watched how he was at ease in the company of any woman. Even in the way he treated Hannah Hayward; he could charm the birds out of the trees. He made such a fuss of the children and he was serious about Jemima having singing lessons.

As Robert sat eating his supper, Frances sat opposite him, listening intently, as he related the happenings of the day.

'I haven't forgotten about our plans for Jemima's voice training. Indeed, today I met a teacher of music and I have arranged for him to meet us here tomorrow to discuss the matter.'

Robert went on to explain to Frances of his chance meeting with the professor.

'Professor Henri Colbert is his name. He is providing the musical entertainment at the hall this evening.'

'How opportune of you, Robert,' Frances interjected. 'How did that come about?'

'It was Mrs Bethel, the housekeeper who told me of him. I met him when I was returning from the Hall. As he approached, I assumed by his dress, he may be the French music professor. Bidding him good day I introduced myself and indeed my assumption was correct.'

'What is he like, Robert? Is he grand? I should imagine he would be, being a professor of music and French to boot,' Frances said.

'No, on the contrary, he is a quietly spoken, unassuming man, who finds himself on hard times. He and his wife fled Paris three years ago to escape the political situation.

'I can't wait to meet him, Robert.'

*

The next day Professor Colbert arrived at Renton House Farm as planned, to assess Jemima's singing voice. Sally Groves answered the door to him and showed him into the living room where Robert Hart, Frances and Jemima were awaiting his arrival.

'Let me introduce you to Mrs Swain, my housekeeper,' Robert Hart said.

'It is my pleasure to meet you, madame,' and he took Frances's hand and shook it gently.

'And this, Professor, is Jemima, Mrs Swain's daughter, the little lady you have come to see and more importantly, to hear,' Robert Hart said.

'Hello, my dear, how nice to meet you.' The professor placed his well-worn music case by the side of the harmonium. 'What a fine parlour instrument, Monsieur Hart,' the professor declared as he raised the lid and pumped the bellows two-footed before playing two or three random chords. 'And in fine tune, I might add,' he said as he slowly let his fingers lightly caress the mahogany case as only a Frenchman would.

'What would you like to sing for me, Jemima?' the professor asked.

'I can sing for you *Sweet Lass of Richmond Hill*, if you like,' Jemima said.

'I would like that, my dear. Do you think you could sing for me *a cappella*? Sorry… unaccompanied,' the professor said rather patronisingly. 'In your own time,' he added.

Jemima went straight into her song and completed it note perfectly.

The professor thanked her, saying, 'Brava, my dear, most delightful.' And turning to Robert Hart and Frances, he said, 'I must say I share your opinion, it is indeed a voice of quality in one so young. How old did you say she was?'

'She is twelve years old, Professor Colbert,' Robert Hart replied.

'Now that is the reason why we must not rush her too soon. First,

I shall start her on her breathing and the solfège, or as you say, here in England, the Norwich Sol-fa, a training method of teaching singing, devised here in Norfolk by Miss Sarah Glover. We do not want to damage those little vocal cords before they have had time to develop. I will return next week at the same time, if these arrangements are favourable with Jemima and your good self, then we will begin the lessons.'

'Now there is the business of your fee,' Robert Hart said rather delicately.

'Well when I travel in the provinces and well out of earshot of the landed gentry and their grand abodes, I usually say sixpence, if you can afford it and three pence if you cannot.'

'Sixpence it shall be,' Robert Hart agreed.

'Until next week,' Professor Colbert said, and he bid his goodbyes.

Chapter 28

The marriage of Frances to Robert Hart had taken place privately by special license on the first Saturday in November 1851. Sally Groves and her fiancé George Binney stood as witnesses and the children had attended.

Jemima's singing lessons had continued for only twelve months. By 1852, the political situation in Paris had improved sufficiently to allow Professor Colbert and his wife to return to resume his duties at the Conservatoire of Music. Before he left, he told Frances he thought Jemima's slight frame would never support the rigours of a career in grand opera. Still, the time Jemima spent with the professor had proved invaluable. He had taught her voice and breathing control. He had also taught her musical phrasing and he agreed a career for Jemima, as a professional singer was still a strong possibility and it would be a mistake to dispel any such plans at this early stage. Indeed, news of her talent had spread throughout the local area and she was in great demand singing at weddings and funerals throughout the towns and villages.

*

Frances had been overjoyed when she married Robert. She had avoided sex with him prior to their marriage and she had looked forward to making love to him once she was his wife, but she found him disappointing in bed. While ever charming, he was not the lover Dan had been. He did not show her the same consideration Dan had; there was no tenderness. There was no caressing of each other's bodies. Right from day one he had took to using a rubber device, which he said would prevent her becoming pregnant. It was something he had learnt about from the rich sons of landowners attending Cirencester College of Agriculture at the same time as he.

'You must use a prophylactic, Robert; you do not want to get the local 'gals' pregnant, after all you do not know where they have been and indeed, with whom,' they had told him mockingly, knowing of his background. This he kept from Frances.

All this had an adverse effect on their lovemaking. It made it quite clinical, and by the time he prepared himself, the interest had left Frances. The sex act for her was one of total submission on her part, while Robert satisfied himself. It was all so dispassionate and over quickly, it was so one sided. He would leave her lying cold and alone in their bed while he dealt with the cleaning of the device. She had put it down to the effect the death of his first wife while giving birth had had on him; it was all too much for Frances.

One night, about two months into their marriage, on retiring to their bed, she had plucked up courage to ask outright the question of dispensing with this unnatural device. Robert became angry and immediately left the bedroom and he was missing for all of thirty minutes. On his return, he had lectured Frances on the prudency of avoiding a pregnancy, making it patently obvious to her, she had no say in the matter and he did not intend to have a family by her. It left her feeling used and inadequate and it was at this early point in their marriage she realised there was a side to her husband she was discovering for the first time. She put it down to what happened to his first wife, he did not want it to happen to *her* and she never asked him again to have unprotected sex.

*

One morning, about two years into their marriage, Robert Hart shocked Frances with a conversation, which he began between them.

'I have been thinking, Frances, the money you have invested, could be put to good use in buying our own place. With your money and my agricultural prowess, we could do well.'

As soon as he had uttered the phrase *'a place of our own'* thoughts of Dan came rushing back to her. 'I could never do that; the money is not solely mine. It is for the children also and I do not know at this stage of their lives, when they may need it,' Frances said emphatically.

'May I remind you, Frances, since our marriage, the money you have invested, on a point of law, now belongs to me?' By now, he spoke in a raised voice and there was anger in his eyes; anger Frances had not seen before.

'What ever do you mean by that remark?' Frances replied in a manner matching her husband's mood.

'I thought you would understand, under the present law of the land, when a woman marries a man, she and all her possessions become the property of her husband.'

'Aren't you forgetting the man who earned the money and died the day before he was about to return to me and our children?' She did not intend Robert Hart to reap the benefit of his labours. 'No, Robert, I could never agree to such a thing. I would deem it a dereliction of my duty, towards the children I bore Dan Swain, if I were to consider such a scheme. The answer to your suggestion, Robert, is an emphatic no!'

'Your first husband; some good he proved to be. Leaving you to your own devices, abandoned and penniless, while he sloped off across the world with you and your children dependant on the good nature of the parish,' Robert Hart yelled, bringing the back of his hard-knuckled hand violently across Frances's cheek, sending her reeling across the floor. Without any thought for Frances's condition, he quickly left the farmhouse slamming the door so heavily behind him it almost fell off its hinges.

'It wasn't like that at all, and you know it,' Frances yelled after him, but he was gone, and her final protestation went unheard. She could no longer hold back the stinging, salty tears, welling in her eyes. A shocked Frances was left sprawled and weeping, on the cold flagstones of the kitchen floor. Apart from the pain down the right side of her face, she was also suffering the pain of disappointment her new husband now instilled in her. The tears poured down her cheeks. How she wished Dan was with her now. How she missed him at this moment. The anger burned within her, more fiercely as the contemptuous words uttered by Robert Hart still rang in her ears. Left alone in the room, she broke down completely and sobbed uncontrollably into her apron. As she lay on the floor, recovering from her husband's violent attack, she was pleased Sally had not been around to witness what had taken place. Once more, Frances's world was collapsing around her. When would she ever find lasting happiness? The course her marriage was now taking made it clear to Frances her relationship with her new husband was becoming untenable. She could never love him now following his violent outburst and she ironically found consolation in the fact his prophylactic device had saved her from bearing the child she so much wanted by him. She found herself thanking God she had not become pregnant by him, one of the things, which attracted her to him in the first place. She knew she had to get free of this man who had shown her his true colours.

*

Following a run of ill health, Mrs Hayward left Renton House Cottage to live with her daughter in London. This allowed Sally Groves and George Binney, who had married in 1853, to move in.

PART 8

THE LARK RISING

Chapter 29

1855

It was late March and like her mother before her, Jemima, now sixteen, had found work as a housemaid. She was working at Red Barn Farm in the market town of Shinwell, which lay six miles to the south of Renton, and she was now 'living in' with Emma and Philip Miller who worked the farm's two hundred and fifty acres. While her engagements were lucrative, they were too infrequent to make a living from her singing.

'It will make her independent to be away from home and teach her to stand on her own two feet,' Robert Hart had argued when Frances had raised her objections to the idea, feeling at the time, she needed Jemima at home with her as an ally.

Because of the distance of six miles to Shinwell from Renton, Jemima got home once a month on the first Sunday and Robert Hart picked her up on his bay hunter Trojan.

Rachel Stebbings, Robert Hart's late wife, had been born and bred in the small market town of Shinwell and her mother still lived there.

One day Jemima was in town on an errand for Mrs Miller when an old woman stopped her as she left the post office.

'Excuse me, my dear; I believe you are working for the Millers at Red Barn Farm and your stepfather is Robert Hart.'

'Yes, how do you know so much about me and my family?' Jemima asked, surprised at the old woman's questioning.

'Word gets around in this small town. I am the mother of Rachel Stebbings, your stepfather's first wife who sadly died five years past, giving birth to their first child, something I have not come to terms with, even now.'

'I am so sorry, Mrs Stebbings, but what has it got to do with me?'

'I think it is more to do with your mother, and I think *she* needs to know your stepfather is a womaniser.'

This statement, made in such an abrupt manner, took Jemima aback and she challenged the old woman to explain what she meant.

'*You* do not have to believe me, young lady, but please warn your mother to be on her guard. It is more important for *her* to know of what is going on behind her back – believe me.'

'I appreciate your concern for my ma, Mrs Stebbings, but what you say cannot be true; he'd never do that to her.'

'Listen to what I say and tell your mother what I am telling you, for he is seeing a young widow in the town, namely Alice Denton, whom he met during his time in Cirencester. Rumour has it, she is still married, and her husband is still living down in Gloucestershire. Alice Denton has a child out of wedlock and the wagging tongues in the town say your stepfather is the father. I am of the opinion he only married my daughter to save face up at the Big Hall to get the bailiff's job. Your mother is my Rachel's replacement, if you catch my meaning. This would strengthen the view that Alice Denton's husband is still alive, and she and Hart are unable to marry.'

'I understand what you are getting at, Mrs Stebbings, but I dare not let my stepfather know what you say or you could find yourself in deep trouble, if he was to find out what you have told me today.'

'My dear, when you get to my age, trouble doesn't seem to be the threat it once was. Now honesty seems much more important to me when the actions of a man who I once thought I could trust and who now sullies the memory of my dear departed daughter. If he was to take umbrage with me, he would be taking on most of the township. On that thought, I'll bid you good day,'

'Good day, Mrs Stebbings,' Jemima said politely.

As Jemima walked back to Red Barn Farm, she pondered over what Mrs Stebbings had told her. What she had learned dismayed her, not so much for her own sake but for her mother's sake. She feared the news would completely shatter her mother's happiness, of which Jemima was ever mindful. Her mother had received too many cruel blows during her life. Being ignorant of her mother's present dilemma, to Jemima, her mother seemed happier than she had been since her father had left for America. If what Mrs Stebbings had said was true, her mother's new-found happiness would once more be in jeopardy. On reflection, she had noticed her mother had appeared a bit withdrawn of late and not as bubbly as she had become after first marrying Robert Hart. Had her mother heard already, gossip on the subject to which Mrs Stebbings had alluded?

*

The following Sunday was the first Sunday in April; the day for her monthly trip to Renton and as usual Robert Hart arrived at Red Barn Farm to collect Jemima. As usual, they made the return journey both sat on the back of Trojan with Jemima sitting behind Robert Hart with her arms clasped around his waist. This time she was uncomfortable with this arrangement, following what Mrs Stebbings had told her and throughout the journey back, Jemima was unusually quiet, and her stepfather drove what little conversation passed between them.

Bringing his hunter, Trojan, to a halt, he turned his head to one side to talk to his stepdaughter.

'What is wrong, Jemima? Are you going down with something? You seem unusually quiet today, not your usual bubbly self and not a single verse of *Sweet Polly Oliver* or anything else for that matter, to entertain us on the journey.'

Jemima was a bit sheepish and found it difficult to reply. Mrs Stebbings's exposure on her stepfather had made her uneasy in his company, with or without confirmation, for her allegiance lay with her mother. But for safety, she would have released her light hold on his waist, for even that, now made her feel uncomfortable.

'I'm fine,' was all she could bring herself to say and throughout the journey, her countenance was low, with Mrs Stebbings's voice running through her mind overriding any words uttered by her stepfather.

*

Later, while they were all taking a stroll, the boys had run ahead with their stepfather, giving her the chance to relate to her mother what Mrs Stebbings had told her concerning Robert Hart. Despite the way her husband had treated her, on hearing Jemima's account of what was happening in Shinwell, Frances decided to treat the rumour as nothing more than gossip until she had more proof of his behaviour with the 'widow' Alice Denton. 'Give him enough rope and he'll hang himself,' Frances claimed.

Chapter 30

A month later, Jemima was booked to sing for the guests at the wedding of Jeremy Bolton, the son of Bartholomew Bolton, a rich seed merchant who had his business based in Shinwell. After she had completed the first session of her engagement, she was taking refreshments when the young gentleman whom she recognised as the groom's best man, came up to her and congratulated her on her performance.

'May I say you have a most delightful voice, Jemima Swain? I may call you Jemima I hope?'

'Of course, sir,' Jemima said nervously.

'Come now, Jemima, not so formal; please call me Chris, short for Christian, a name I detest and such an imposition for anyone to even dream of aspiring to, I always think; I'm Chris Paxton.'

He bowed as he gently raised the back of her right hand to his lips. 'You can relax; I am but a lad from County Durham, who was fortunate to be born into money as they say and to gain a place at Cambridge, where I studied music. It was there I met Jeremy and we became good friends.'

'Pleased to make your acquaintance… er, em… Chris,' she said, uncomfortable with the familiarity. Calling such a fine young man by his Christian name on first meeting did not come easily to her.

'While I admire his enterprise and what he has achieved, I had no wish to follow in his footsteps. I will leave that side of things to my younger brother Peter, who has always shown an interest in all things mechanical. I believe my future lies in the arts: a legacy acquired through my Italian mother.'

'I am afraid my dad is dead; died five years back. I say died, but the fact is he was murdered, for that is the truth of it. Murdered in America for all his savings but it is a long story.'

'Oh! You poor thing. How dreadful this must have been for you. And your mother, is she getting over this tragedy?'

'Yes, she is, but it led to serious consequences for all of us.'

'Come now, let us take a seat and you can tell me all about it, only if you so wish, I might add.'

He led her to an alcove seat, which he thought offered a little more privacy.

'Now Jemima, in your own time, but first let me get you another drink, as I see your glass is empty, a sherry maybe?'

'Another barley water for me please would be lovely, thank you.'

'Of course, I should have known you need to nurse your delightful voice.'

'No, it isn't that. I don't care much for alcoholic drink, but I don't hold forth against those who do. My da was a total abstainer and my ma does not partake, but she has been known to have a single glass on special occasions,' Jemima naïvely confessed to the stranger.

'Splendid, in which case I will have a sherry,' he said as he beckoned a waiter.

With their glasses recharged, Jemima found herself relating virtually her life story to this pleasant young gentleman, deliberately omitting the part about their time in the Durnham Union Workhouse.

When she had finished, Chris Paxton was the first to speak.

'A sad, but most fascinating tale, Jemima, the like of which I have never heard. Look, I must leave you now, my friend and his bride are about to leave for their honeymoon in Tuscany and my duties decree I should be there to see them off. They are to spend their honeymoon in a villa owned by my mother's family. I am returning to Durham tomorrow but, if I may, I would like to meet you again. The first free time I have, I will return to Norfolk. With your permission, we could meet up again; where can I find you on my return? Perhaps you could show me around the town taking in some refreshment on our way. I shall mail you the details of my itinerary as and when I know them.'

'I have enjoyed your company today and I shall look forward to seeing you again,' Jemima said, trying hard not to appear too eager. 'Your letter will find me at Red Barn Farm on the outskirts of Shinwell, where I am maid to Mrs Emma Miller, the wife of Philip Miller who is the tenant farmer,' she revealed.

On her June trip to Renton, she had told her mother of her meeting with Chris Paxton and of his pending visit sometime in the coming weeks.

*

Barely three weeks had passed before the eagerly awaited letter was in Jemima's hands. She quickly opened it and rapidly scanned through the lines, not stopping until she read, *I will arrive Saturday the 9th June.* Her heart leapt at the prospect of seeing Chris Paxton again, for she had thought of little else since the wedding.

My stay will be for one week and I am booked into The Bear Hotel in the market place. I expect to arrive in Shinwell late Saturday evening, so I will call on you at Red Barn Farm on the Sunday at 10 in the forenoon.

That is perfect, she thought, realising it would not clash with her monthly trip to Renton.

*

On the morning of Sunday, 10th June, a knock came on the door of Red Barn Farm.

'Get the door, Jemima, no doubt it will be your visitor; bring him in so I can meet him,' Mrs Miller shouted through to her maid.

Jemima answered the door and Mrs Miller strained her ears as she listened for any conversation that might ensue between Jemima and whoever was calling. She heard the door catch click and the door creaked as Jemima opened it to the visitor.

'Good morning Miss Swain, what a pleasure it is to see you again,' Mrs Miller heard the visitor say in a cultured voice.

'Please come in, Mr Paxton, Mrs Miller would like to meet you.'

They smiled at each other at the mock formality, put on for Mrs Miller's benefit.

Jemima entered the room and introduced her visitor.

'Mrs Miller, may I introduce Mr Christian Paxton, he is visiting Shinwell from County Durham and will be staying at The Bear Hotel for one week.'

Chris Paxton chose not to offer Mrs Miller the shortened version of his name, thinking on this occasion, his full name being more appropriate.

'Mrs Miller, it is my pleasure to meet you. During my stay in Shinwell, I would like to spend time with Miss Swain as I find her company most agreeable, but only with your approval I might add. We met at my friend's wedding last month, where I had the pleasure both of acting as his best man and hearing Miss Swain sing so delightfully.'

'If Jemima so wishes, I have no objections, but the time spent with you must not interfere with her duties here at the farm. May I ask you Mr Paxton, do you have any sisters?'

'As a matter of fact, I have two; why do you ask Mrs Miller?'

'In that case, may I suggest you treat Jemima in the same manner as you would wish your sisters to be treated?'

'Fear not Mrs Miller, you have my assurance, Miss Swain will be treated with the greatest respect at all times.'

Jemima stood quietly listening to their conversation, thinking how fine her friend presented himself. 'Good, Mr Paxton; Jemima, you had better get your coat if this young gentleman has travelled all the way down from Durham to see you and take an umbrella as there are rain clouds gathering: there may be rain later. By the way, Mr Paxton, I too share your opinion of Jemima's fine voice. Mind you, don't let all this praise go to your head, Jemima.'

Jemima was pleased the way the introduction had gone, and it seemed, on first impressions, that Mrs Miller approved of her friend from County Durham.

*

The young couple strolled through Shinwell High Street, stopping to look in the shop windows whenever anything caught Jemima's eye, which was quite often. She, like all young women could not help admiring all the finery on display in the shop windows. Especially those of Madame Gray, who ran the ladies' outfitters. Jemima had heard from Mrs Miller that all the materials used in the production of the garments, came directly from Paris. This made the price way beyond the reach of a poor serving girl like herself, but it costs nothing to look and dream.

Who knows? One day I shall wear fine clothes like that, she thought.

They moved on at a leisurely pace. She wished Chris Paxton would offer his arm to link, but he, being ever the gentleman, made no such too familiar move and walked closely by her side.

'May I be so bold as to ask how old you are, Jemima?'

The question took Jemima somewhat by surprise and for a few seconds she remained silent. Chris Paxton noticing her reluctance to divulge such a personal detail to someone who was yet, a relative stranger and he quickly apologised.

'How thoughtless of me, Jemima, please forgive me if you can find it in your heart to do so.'

Jemima having had time to think the question over, realised there was no harm in her companion's curiosity. She decided to answer, what some people would deem to be an impertinent question.

'You are forgiven, sir,' she said coyly, adding, 'I had my sixteenth birthday last month.'

'Sweet sixteen,' Chris Paxton mouthed in a dreamy way, as if thinking aloud.

'What about you, Chris? How old are you?'

'How old do you think I am, Jemima?' he teased.

'Now, I know from what you told me on our first meeting, you have completed your studies at Cambridge, so I would guess you are at least twenty-one.'

'Not bad at all, I am twenty-two to be exact,' he admitted.

'Almost six years older,' Jemima calculated.

'Almost six years extra of life's experience, which if you would allow me, Jemima, to put at your disposal,' Chris Paxton offered rather presumptuously.

'Maybe we should get to know each other better first, Chris,' Jemima said cautiously.

'I admire your caution dear Jemima; but the offer still stands whenever you think the time is right,' Chris Paxton responded.

They arrived outside the Bear Hotel. 'They will be serving luncheon soon, let us go in and book a table where we can talk over our meal and get to know each other better.'

'That would be marvellous; I have never eaten in a hotel before, although I have had tea and cakes with my mother and stepfather and brothers once at the tea-rooms in Durnham on the day he took us out of the Durnham Union Workhouse.'

The moment she had blurted out that fact, a voice yelled in her head, *You fool!* and she wished she had not been so frank. 'I wish I hadn't told you that; I suppose you won't want to have anything more to do with me.'

'Nonsense, Jemima, you underestimate me. It is not like me to prejudge. I am sure there were circumstances beyond your control that brought about such a situation. Please tell me about it but only if you want to.'

'It is a long story so it will have to be a long luncheon,' Jemima replied.

'You can talk quickly, while we eat slowly and ignore the world of Shinwell as they pass by our window,' he teased. Chris Paxton ordered them both a selection from the cold platter. He listened intently as Jemima related the whole story of the events leading to their time in the workhouse and the happenings since her mother's marriage to Robert Hart. Without realising, she found herself being uncommonly open, even disclosing to him Mrs Stebbings's account of her stepfather's womanising. She finished her story, turned to her companion, and said, 'What about you, Chris? Tell me about yourself.'

'Well I told you my father was a successful businessman. Once he had established his business and to improve his standing, he embarked on a tour in Europe, which took him through France into Switzerland and on to Italy. While in Italy, he met a young Italian lady with the magnificent name of Gabriella Madonna Lucia Menotti, the daughter of a rich Italian merchant. She spoke perfect English and she showed him the famous landmarks and treasures of Florence, Venice, Naples, and Rome, before he returned to England. They continued to correspond after his return, and they were married a year later. He paid her father a handsome sum to gain her hand in marriage, which included a two-year-old thoroughbred colt. At least, he must have convinced Signore Menotti that he would provide for her 'in the manner to which she had become accustomed.' Two years after they were married, I came along and in successive years my two sisters, namely Lucia and Maria. Finally, two years after Maria's birth, my younger brother Peter arrived, whom I am pleased to say for my father's sake, is studying engineering and will probably carry on the family business.'

They were finishing their drinks when Chris Paxton came up with an idea he had been toying with since the first time he heard Jemima sing.

'Jemima, you have had a hard time of things so far in your young life, but I have an idea, which I have been turning over in my mind since I first heard you sing. You have a beautiful natural talent in your singing. Have you ever had lessons? The reason I ask, I notice how you breathe perfectly, and your phrasing is impeccable; have you ever considered using your talent professionally?'

'In answer to your original question, at the age of thirteen I received lessons from an eminent French professor of music, namely Professor Henri Colbert, who had fled from France at the time of the 1848 revolution. You could say my stepfather cashed in on the professor's misfortune. What do you mean by singing professionally?'

'Well, instead of working as a housemaid to Mrs Miller and singing occasionally at weddings and funerals, why not make a career of singing?'

'How could I do that? I know nothing of such things,' she said in a puzzled manner.

'How do you get your bookings for weddings et cetera?' he asked.

'Usually the people come to me; quite often when they hear me sing at a wedding and if they have a wedding in the offing, they book me in advance.'

'That is where I come in. Up until now, I have had no idea what to do with myself, not having any interest in the family business, which has provided me with full, and plenty. I do not want to sound ungrateful but unlike my father, I never wanted to get my hands dirty. Like my mother, I have always had an interest in finer things like art, books, music, and architecture. My father has already reduced my allowance since I told him I am not joining the family business. Now I have completed my studies, I need to make my mind up on which direction I am heading. I know his ultimatum will not make a ha'peth of difference as to my attitude towards casting machine parts for the industrial revolution. Therefore, with my having to make a life-changing decision, and you who, if I may take the liberty in saying so, need to make a life-changing decision also; I suggest I manage your singing career. I will also become your accompanist on the piano. I have studied the pianoforte and I can arrange your music to suit your voice. I will also be responsible for booking your engagements and negotiating your contracts. What do you say?'

'Well, to be honest, Chris, you have overwhelmed me with your idea. I had never had such high ambitions. I could not have imagined any such notion. I only sing because I love singing and the weddings get me a bit of extra pocket money and in the case of the Bolton wedding, the chance of sampling fine food. Not all the weddings come with a fee as handsome as I received that day, as I usually say, 'pay what you can', as most of the people getting married are no better off than I am.'

'What is your full repertoire, Jemima?'

'What do you mean… repertoire?'

'Oh, I am sorry; what else do you sing other than the ballads you sang at my friends' wedding?'

'I also sing Irish ballads when I am asked; it depends on the wedding. I memorised these ballads when I heard them sung at harvesting and threshing time parties. I learnt them from the travellers who would appear as casual workers at certain times of the year,' she explained.

'As fine as your ballads are, Jemima, I intend to teach you the arias from the operas of the great Italian composers. Works such as Lucia's aria. from *'Regnava nel Silenzio'* – Silence Reigned. Lucia's aria from *'Lucia di Lammermoor'*, by Donizetti. Alternatively, *'Tacea La Notte'* – The Night Is Still and Quiet, Leonora's aria from *'Il Travatore'* by Verdi. These are but two that spring to mind, to which, your fine soprano voice would do justice.'

'How could I sing such music? I don't even speak the language.'

'I speak fluent Italian and while I don't expect you to become fluent in Italian my dear Jemima, I know I can teach you to be fluent in the libretto of these fine arias. Have you heard of Jenny Lind?'

'No, I'm afraid I haven't,' Jemima admitted.

'Well let me explain. At present, she is sweeping all before her, and has sung for most of the royal households throughout Europe. They say she is a favourite of Queen Victoria no less. Well, I think, together we can make you as famous as the 'Swedish Nightingale'. This is what her public now call her, for this is how highly she is regarded. In fact, I would go as far as to say, it is a love affair. If you come with me, I mean to make you…' he thought for a moment '…the *'Norfolk Lark'*… Yes indeed. If Miss Lind can have a grand name, so can you. It will not happen overnight, but I know you can do it. We will start at the bottom and work our way right to the top. It will be all good experience for you… Oh I think I might be letting my enthusiasm carry me away. These are my plans for your future, however it will not happen overnight. Believe me, you can do this. I would not expect you to give me your answer immediately, not even before I leave for my return to Durham. All I ask at this stage is for you to give it serious consideration. I believe you have a great future ahead of you, Jemima, and I would deem it an honour if you were to allow me to be part of it.'

At this point, he paused to take in a deep breath, for his enthusiasm had left him breathless. 'In the meantime, let us enjoy the rest of our day in this delightful little town of Shinwell.'

They left the restaurant of the Bear Hotel and strolled along by the river. Mrs Miller's prediction on the weather was proving accurate as odd drops of rain began to fall. They decided to curtail their riverside walk and they hastily headed back to Red Barn Farm. As they re-joined the High Street, the rain began to quicken.

'Quick! Down this way, it is a shortcut back to the farm,' Jemima said as she took Chris Paxton's arm and steered him down an alleyway off the High Street. The swift manoeuvre took him by surprise and he almost hit the corner of the wall.

The diversion took them through Thetford Road. While not in the fashionable part of the town, the dwellings there were respectable and consisted of a mixture of detached and terraced cottages. Emerging from the alleyway Jemima noticed a man leaving one of the cottages, outside of which a bay hunter stood tethered to the fence. Jemima, seeing the shape of the white blaze down the horse's head, recognised it as Trojan, her stepfather's bay hunter.

'Stop for a moment, Chris, that is my stepfather leaving that cottage,' and she quickly steered him back into the alley. Peeping from the cover of the alleyway, they watched in secret as the scene further down the street enfolded.

Robert Hart and the woman embraced in what one could only describe, as a too familiar manner; not in the way a person would embrace a stranger, and more intense than someone would even embrace a close relative.

'It would appear Mrs Stebbings was correct in her opinion of Robert Hart,' Jemima whispered.

'That must be the infamous Alice Denton of Cirencester,' Chris Paxton replied in an equally quiet tone.

'Well I never,' Jemima said, somewhat bewildered by the revelation taking place before them. Despite Mrs Stebbings's forewarning, what she had witnessed had devastated her more than the old woman's disclosure had done.

Robert Hart mounted his horse and wheeling his mount round, he waved to the woman as he shouted, 'Goodbye, my darling,' as he made his departure down the street, leaving his clandestine lover waving in the doorway. Unbeknownst to him, his stepdaughter had witnessed his disloyalty towards her mother, confirming what Mrs Stebbings had said about his womanising.

Once Robert Hart's adulterous woman friend had closed the door behind her, Jemima and her companion emerged from the cover of the alleyway and continued their journey back to the farm. As they did so, they discussed what they had seen.

'From what we have witnessed, Jemima, it is obvious, your mother's marriage is under threat and she needs to know what is happening behind her back, but with caution. It is not my business; she should be reviewing the situation of her marriage to Robert Hart. If it *were* my business, I would suggest, your mother should leave him at the earliest convenient time, for her own well-being, for I see no future happiness for her while associated with this man. I suggest she should take the money your father left her, travel north to County Durham where she could buy a property large enough, whereby she could establish a boarding house, close to any of the big works that have sprung up in the county. This would be a natural progression. After all, she has been running households all her working life; it is something she has done before, and it would be a sound investment for her; far away from that adulterous husband of hers.'

'What you say, Chris, merits much thought especially on my mother's part. How far is it to Durham?'

'It is about two hundred miles,' Chris Paxton guessed.

'Two hundred or so miles, is nothing, compared to the journey we all would have undertaken if my da's dream had come true. The more I think about your idea, the more I think it makes sense for us all to make the journey together. I know it is a strange thing to say in the light of what happened to my da, but maybe there is someone up there somewhere, I know not where, who has sent you to us on behalf of my father to redeem the dream he had for us all.'

'Jemima, my dear Jemima, you burden me with the divine responsibility of carrying out God's work: a task for which I am not qualified. If that is how you see it, so be it. Who am I to shatter such a quaint view of the situation?'

*

They arrived back at the farm and Chris Paxton turned to Jemima and said, 'What an eventful day it has been, Jemima. The happenings of the day, plus all my plans for your future has left you with so much to ponder over. Do not despair; we will not do anything with haste. We have the rest of the week before I return to Durham and we can discuss it further as the week unfolds, or indeed, if you would rather, maybe not at all. With that, I will say goodbye to you and look forward to seeing you again tomorrow evening. I will give you time to complete your duties. I do not want to get on the wrong side of Mrs Miller at this stage. Let us get our plans in place first.'

He would dearly have loved to kiss her goodnight, but thought better of it in case anyone saw them so early in their relationship and bidding Jemima goodbye, he turned and set off back to his hotel.

As the difficult week evolved, they discussed further, the plans that Chris Paxton had devised and by the end of the week, they had a lucid view of what they wanted for themselves and Frances Hart. Before he left for Durham, he suggested to Jemima, she should discuss cautiously with her mother the plans they had drawn up. He also told her he would be in touch by mail of his own immediate plans, but warned Jemima, not to leave any correspondence between them, lying around and prudency was paramount. Any leakage of their subterfuge could be counterproductive if Mrs Miller thought Jemima had been scheming behind her back, and she may react adversely by exposing all their plans to Robert Hart.

Chapter 31

1856

It had been a quiet wedding for the son of a rich industrialist and although Chris Paxton's father had not condoned the wedding, all the same he had not hindered it and left them to wed of their own free will. He had learned some time ago, that when his son set his mind on something, nothing in the world would deter him and it was a waste of time trying to influence him otherwise.

So it was, Jemima and Chris married, and they honeymooned in Italy, in Milan. On the first night of their marriage, on retiring to bed, Chris Paxton had noticed the birthmark on the inside of her right thigh, and he commented on it. 'In some quarters they are regarded as beauty spots,' he declared.

'Mother always told me they were a good luck sign. Now you have confused me, Chris, by offering your meaning of such a mark,' Jemima said.

'Well, my darling, to back my claim, I would say that, like your beauty, the mark with which you were born, is unique to you. Therefore, and it is not like me to compromise, I am prepared to say, both your dear mother and I are correct, for you are the most beautiful woman I have ever seen.' He paused as he contemplated the beauty before him. As he gazed into her eyes, he continued, 'May your mother's prediction be fulfilled, for to have a successful career on the stage, you are certainly going to need a large helping of luck,' he continued.

They had chosen Milan for their honeymoon; first, Chris spoke the language fluently, and secondly, he wanted his wife and protégé to experience the thrill a visit to La Scala opera house would bring. La Scala, regarded worldwide as the home of Italian grand opera, was a difficult place in which to perform. Here, audiences were more critical of the performers on stage, than anywhere else in the world. The performance they had booked to see, was a new opera by the Italian composer, Giuseppe Verdi entitled *'Giovanna de Guzman'*.

*

After their visit to the opera, their views on its performance differed. While Jemima had thought the opera was wonderful and had marvelled at the performance of soprano Caterina Goldberg Strossi, in the role of Helena, Chris Paxton was more critical. He said, the performers overall, had *'given of their best'. He* thought the music was far superior to the libretto, which lacked polish. Later, as he scanned the Italian papers for the critics' comments on the performance, he came across an article claiming that, and he read aloud directly from the text for Jemima's benefit. *'Even the composer of the music, Giuseppe Verdi, was not enamoured with the performance of his opera, mainly due to the libretto. He felt that it had suffered in its translation from the original French, into Italian and felt it did not integrate the love and the history in the story and it needed further work before its next production.'* He folded his paper, slapped it down angrily on the table saying, 'I could not agree more.'

*

On returning from Italy, Jemima and Chris moved north to County Durham. Her singing career was blossoming under Chris's management. They had set up home in a Georgian townhouse in Durham City, situated on the opposite bank of the River Wear to the magnificent Norman cathedral.

Jemima was now singing at the supper rooms and Masonic Halls around the county under her new stage name of 'Mimi Martin'; a stage name her husband had conjured up for her. For at times, she would sing anything up to ten or more songs a performance when an audience was most demanding. These were difficult engagements where the eating and drinking came first and what was happening on the stage came secondary. Despite this, Jemima's beautiful voice never failed to silence the noisy ambience of these venues. Her silver cords quietening the clatter of cutlery on crockery and ale pot on table top. Chris had managed to get her booked into many of the Masonic Halls established in the area and her reputation was spreading throughout the region. These were much more civilised establishments, with more intellectual audiences, who listened with respect to 'Mimi Martin's' performances. She was pleased she had Chris to watch over her during these difficult early days of her career. Chris had pulled off his greatest achievement so far by negotiating a booking for Jemima to appear for one week at the Theatre Royal in Newcastle in four weeks' time, for which she would receive the magnificent fee of £50.

'Now is the time to introduce the operatic arias which we have rehearsed so intensively, into your public performances,' he said, adding, 'Jemima, this is where your real career begins. This is the music you were born to sing, as it does the greatest justice to your fine soprano voice,' he told her confidently.

'I hope you are right, Chris.'

'I know I am, and I want you to share my confidence,' he reminded her. 'But first we have some unfinished business down in Norfolk,' he added.

'Are you sure the time is right? After all we have waited over a year to get Mother and the boys up here to Durham with us. I would hate to think we acted in haste in the final stages,' Jemima said.

'Don't worry my dear Jemima, Jeremy Bolton has been organising everything in Norfolk like a military operation. He has checked and double-checked at each stage of the plan and everything is set for the first Sunday in July. That is to be the day we get your mother and brothers to Durham; away from Robert Hart.'

*

On learning of Robert Hart's transgression, Frances had challenged him about his affair with Alice Denton and he had reacted in a threatening manner.

'You have now stooped so low as to believe the tittle-tattle of a demented old crone. Have you no respect for me – your husband?' He raised his hand once more to strike her, but this time Frances was ready for him. Grabbing the large poker from the fire irons on the hearth, she raised it high above her head in defiance of his attack. 'If you lay another hand on me, I will go straight to the 'Big Hall' and tell them all about you and your double life. Half of Shinwell will back my story when Mrs Stebbings speaks of the way you are treating me,' Frances yelled in his face. This stopped him in his tracks. Fearing his whole career, at which he had worked so hard, and in which he had been so successful, would be under serious threat if the news of his double life reached the ears of his Lordship at the 'Big Hall'.

He brought his hand slowly down to his side as he contemplated the consequences of Frances's threat. Whatever happened to Robert Hart was of no concern of Frances now; after all, any love that had existed between them, diminished the moment she realised she would never bear his child. He would rather have her money than a family by her. Now, any remaining love for him had gone completely when she learned of his affair with Alice Denton. This latest revelation had made up her mind. She would remove herself and her sons to County Durham far enough away from the menaces of her husband. This, she decided, was the best way forward – make a fresh start to a new life, two hundred or more miles away from Norfolk and all the bad memories it evoked in her. Chris Paxton explained to Jemima the plan he and Jeremy Bolton had plotted to get her family away from her adulterous stepfather.

'Surreptitiously, Jeremy has recruited another resident of Thetford Road who has had Hart under surveillance for weeks and he has reported Hart is now visiting Shinwell each Sunday. He has become a creature of habit and leaves Renton House Farm at 8 o'clock each Sunday morning for his tryst in Shinwell. As a result, Jeremy has arranged for a coach and four to collect your mother and brothers from Renton House Farm next Sunday morning at 8.30 a.m. from where they will travel to Peterborough. From there they will travel on the Great Northern Railway to Durham, via Doncaster and York,' Chris Paxton explained.

Jemima was excited about her mother and brothers' defection to the Northeast but she was anxious about the journey they were about to embark upon, and she knew she would not rest until she was wrapping her arms round her mother's shoulders.

*

The following Sunday, Jeremy Bolton set the scheme in motion. As was his custom, Hart left Renton House at eight o'clock for Shinwell and at a quarter past, the coach and four pulled up outside to collect Frances and the boys to commence their journey north. Frances had quickly packed what few belongings were practically possible for the hazardous journey on which they were about to embark. Jeremy Bolton quickly had them on board the coach and with a hasty farewell to Sally Binney, they were off at speed for the journey westward to Peterborough, on the first leg of their journey out of Norfolk. Sally Binney watched with tear-filled eyes as the coach disappeared, the secret of her friend's defection, safe with her. She too had been instrumental in Frances's subterfuge in as much as she had been the go-between in Chris Paxton's plans for getting Frances and her sons to Durham.

*

The party reached Peterborough railway station without incident and with enough time to get their belongings and themselves on board the train for Durham. Although Frances knew she was doing the right thing by leaving Robert Hart, she was finding the whole experience rather daunting. She had never travelled on this modern mode of transportation and with all the secrecy and the urgency of the subterfuge involved in their exodus from Renton, her inside was turning like a butter churn. The three boys viewed it in an entirely different light. Edward, now sixteen, John, fourteen and Daniel now seven, regarded the happenings of the morning as one big adventure.

The dark green engine pulling its train of varnished teak carriages slowly drew into the station. Frances was amazed at this mechanical monster and she marvelled at how the wheels hugged the rails despite its size. The smells, the smoke and the steam were reminiscent of the traction engines that arrived at the farm at threshing time. They were not on the scale of the locomotive, which hissed and screeched, through clouds of billowing steam as it slowly came to a hesitant halt. Alongside, the excited passengers hurried and scurried this way and that as they sought their designated accommodation. The carriage doors bore markings in large figures of 1, 2, and 3, identifying the status of the fare-paying passengers. and ushering the boys to a carriage marked with a large figure 3, they boarded the train. She made herself and her sons as comfortable as they could be for the impending journey north. Once ensconced in the carriage, the churning in her stomach settled and a more relaxed feeling of pleasant excitement began to replace the angst, which she had endured throughout the journey thus far.

Unbeknownst to Frances, the train had a twenty-minute stay to allow passengers to take refreshment and her anxiety returned when she realised how long the train was stationary. She had visions of Robert Hart ripping the carriage door open at any moment and dragging her back to Renton. Frances, her imagination running rife with each delayed minute. She saw every male latecomer who hurried along the platform in the direction of their carriage, as a potential 'Robert Hart'. At ten minutes past eleven, after what seemed an eternity, the shrill note blown on a whistle and a waved green flag, finally signalled the train's departure, much to Frances's relief. The locomotive puffed a huge plume of thick, black smoke skywards, momentarily clouding the morning sunlight. This initial, powerful effort on the part of the large locomotive as it strained to overcome inertia, forced Frances back in her seat with alarming effect, for this was Frances's first experience of railway travel. Slowly and steadily, the locomotive and its train of carriages gathered speed as it huffed and puffed out of the station and continued its way northwards. As it built up speed, the noise from the engine and its train of carriages took on a more rhythmical sound, which conversely had a tranquilising effect on her. Frances breathed a huge sigh and quietly thanked God her and her boys were finally starting on their first railway journey that would quickly distance themselves from Robert Hart.

The train passed rapidly through fields of cows and sheep and horses, as it sped northwards. The three boys with faces flattened against the carriage windows, marvelled at the speed at which they were travelling. On the other hand, Frances's thoughts were on those big wheels staying in contact with the rails and she silently prayed they would do so throughout their journey.

*

The tired little party finally alighted at Durham railway station, situated in area of the city known as Gilesgate, where Jemima and Chris Paxton greeted them with great affection. The journey of one hundred and eighty or so miles had taken ten hours and ten minutes allowing for refreshment stops along the way. All that was left of their travelling was the two-mile journey by brake, into the city, where Jemima and her husband had set up home. Jemima was so pleased to have her mother and her brothers safely in Durham with her at last. She hugged them all in turn and taking her mother in her arms, she said, 'I am sure you have made the right decision to leave Norfolk, you will love it here, Mother,' she enthused. Frances noticed Jemima had chosen to call her 'Mother' and not her usual 'Ma' and detected a change in her daughter's accent. Since being married to Chris Paxton, she was picking up his cultured diction and choice of vocabulary and Frances approved of the refinement it brought to her daughter's speech.

'There is so much to see here, the city is steeped in history and such pretty walks by the river, are there not, Chris?'

'There are indeed my dear, and a marvellous view of the Norman castle and cathedral from our own window, which they will appreciate tomorrow morning since the light is now fading rapidly,' he replied.

'We have so much to tell you, Mother, these are indeed exciting times,' Jemima enthused.

'Indeed Jemima, but first let us get them home, the poor dears must be dead on their feet and starving to boot. Although the plan went off without incident, I would be telling lies if I said I was not afraid. All the time we were getting ourselves, and our belongings, onto the coach, I had visions of your stepfather returning and the whole plan would have blown up in our faces. I am pleased to say, it all went off according to plan and here we are to tell the tale. Mind you, I do not know what we would have done without the help of Jeremy Bolton; he was marvellous. I would not want to, nor need to do such a thing again. I am truly pleased we find ourselves, by the grace of God, here with you at last. The train journey although tiring, was a great experience,' Frances said, which prompted the boys to gabble out somewhat incoherently, their highlights of the journey.

The conversation during the short journey to Jemima and Chris's home was peppered with Frances and the boys' chatter about their first railway journey. They were impressed by the speed at which the locomotive had propelled them over the miles and they found it difficult to comprehend how far they had travelled at speed through rapidly changing scenery of fields and hedgerows, towns, and villages.

To Frances, the most impressive thing about her first railway journey, was the distance it had put between herself and her cheating husband and she felt contented.

*

After supper, Jemima was bursting to tell Frances of her latest engagement. 'I have some great news, Mother. In four weeks', time, I am to appear at the Theatre Royal in Newcastle for one week,' she blurted out.

'That is tremendous news, Jemima, I am so pleased for you,' her mother replied.

'But that is not all; you are all going to see the show.'

'Excellent, I can't wait to see you on stage,' her mother said excitedly.

'I am so proud of Chris; he is looking after my interests so well. I would never have got this far without him. He is working so hard to further my career; I am indebted to him.'

*

The following day in the bright sunshine of a perfect July morning, Frances and her sons saw the city of Durham's greatest gem in all its glory.

When they had taken breakfast, Jemima took her mother by the hand, led her, with her brothers in tow, into the front room of the house, and drew back the curtains.

'Have you ever seen a more magnificent view in your life, Mother?'

Before them, towering above the tree-clad riverbank opposite, perched high on the edge of a rocky crag, stood the Norman cathedral.

'Jemima, I do not know what to say, it is breathtakingly beautiful,' was all Frances could say, for the view had left her almost speechless.

The view before them was awe-inspiring. Taking a position in the bay of the window, the party had a panoramic view of the opposite riverbank. The twin west towers of the cathedral soared skyward above the river like twin sentinels, guarding against any waterborne raiding party. Notwithstanding these two impressive architectural masterpieces, the huge central tower of the cathedral thrust heavenward as if to defiantly outdo the lesser west towers, like some arrogant grey stone giant. The cathedral perched high on a rocky plateau, proudly dominating the city's skyline and further downstream, were the soaring ramparts of the castle.

That afternoon, the whole family went for a stroll along the banks of the River Wear. The walk began at Framwellgate Bridge and continued upstream along the riverbank opposite the cathedral. They reached Prebends Bridge from where the views continued to impress, especially from the bridge, looking back downstream to Framwellgate Bridge, from where they had begun their promenade. To the right of the bridge, the cathedral towered above the River Wear. Beneath the cathedral, at the bottom of the steep tree-clad riverbank and nestling in stark contrast to the giant above it was the Fulling Mill. A weir, constructed at an angle across the river at this point, directed the water towards the millrace that provided the power for the mill.

The party slowly crossed Prebends Bridge, but not without further stops to admire the views both upstream and downstream of the bridge before reaching the opposite riverbank. They proceeded, passing through a stone arch, leading to the South Bailey. Climbing steeply, the road continued to curve upwardly to the left until they reached a short street of quaint buildings named Dun Cow Lane, which joined at a right angle from the left. They proceeded up the lane and they entered an open area known as Palace Green. To the left, the full north side of the cathedral came into view. Standing facing the cathedral, to the left end and high in the building was a carving of two young girls with a cow. The dun cow, after which the short lane got its name. The story went, the monks carrying Saint Cuthbert's body on a cart to Chester-le-Street found the cart immovable. The monks from Lindisfarne overheard one of the girls ask the other if she had seen a lost dun cow thereabouts. The other girl said she had seen a dun cow on the road to Durham and the cowgirl set off in the direction of Durham. The monks overhearing this exchange between the two girls and noticing the cart was now moving freely in the direction in which the young girl had set off. Seeing this as a sign, they decided to follow the girl in the direction of Durham believing this to be where Saint Cuthbert had decided was to be the site for his remains.

Turning to the left, the aspect showed the cathedral at close quarters. It was huge, ranging in its full extent from east to west.

'We shall leave a tour of the interior for another day, Mother, for today we shall continue our walk in a circular direction,' Jemima said, enjoying each minute of showing her relatives around Durham City. 'Is it not the most delightful city, Mother?'

'You are right, Jemima, I have never seen any place like it,' her mother agreed.

They turned right and continued to walk along the side of Palace Green and yet another vista spread itself before them. The honey-coloured keep of the castle stood atop a green mound. The route continued down the North Bailey, another street of buildings of quaint architectural design, into Saddler Street, which in turn led them into the Market Place. There, a statue of Neptune atop a pump, which provided water, piped from a nearby well, greeted them. In the far corner was St. Nicholas's church with its square tower. Also, on the opposite side of the Market Place, stood the newly built Town Hall, with the ancient Guildhall to the left. Leaving the Market Place behind them, they descended Silver Street, which brought them back to their starting point at Framwellgate Bridge.

'A most enjoyable excursion, Jemima; a truly fascinating city,' Frances said.

'It is indeed,' Chris Paxton said. 'The industrial revolution seems to have passed Durham City by, thank goodness and hasn't the country's third university been established in the city in 1832. We must see the interior of the cathedral as soon as possible. I understand it is more spectacular on the inside,' he added.

They returned home and took tea in the room with the cathedral view. Over tea, Chris Paxton turned to his mother-in-law and announced, 'A property, which is close to my father's foundry in Standale has come on the market. In fact, it was the original farmhouse and since the establishment of the foundry, it has housed the engineering department and drawing office. Pleasantly situated and sufficiently distant from the daily activity of the busy factory, the house is of solid structure and was extended to five bedrooms, when first acquired by my father, making it ideal for a boarding house and well within your budget, Mrs Hart.'

He had always called Frances 'Mrs Hart' since first meeting her and even after his marriage to Jemima.

'Please, Chris, call me Frances for I am considering dropping Hart as my surname; I can't bear being called that anymore and how pleased I am we didn't have the boys' names changed to Hart,' she said.

'I take your point, Frances; I will make sure I do as you wish in future. Tomorrow we shall visit the solicitor and request a viewing of the property. What do you say? It is entirely up to you; I do not want to rush you, say if you would rather not.'

'I think it is a splendid idea and I can't wait to see the house; it sounds the ideal place for me and the boys,' Frances agreed.

'Tomorrow it is then. The sooner the better, as Jemima – or should I say Mimi – and I have some serious rehearsing to do in readiness for her debut in Newcastle,' Chris Paxton said. Frances smiled at the sound of her daughter's stage name. Frances glanced across at the grand piano close to the window and occupying the corner of the room.

'Don't remind me,' Jemima said.

'Don't worry, I have told you, you will be fine; the audience will love you,' her husband reassured her.

'I am looking forward to seeing 'Mimi Martin' win the hearts of the Newcastle people,' her mother said, reiterating her son-in-law's reference to Jemima's pseudonym.

'So am I, but first, we must see the house,' Chris Paxton stated.

Chapter 32

The following day, Frances went with her son-in-law to view the property at Standale, which lay twelve miles to the southwest of Durham City. They travelled to Standale by railway, which gave Frances her second experience of travelling on this modern mode of transport.

On arrival in Standale, they went to the office of Gridley & Simpkins, the solicitors acting on behalf of the vendors, Paxton's Foundry and Engineering Works. There, a young Joseph Simpkins, the son of one of the senior partners, accompanied them to the viewing. To reach the property, they passed the large gates to the foundry owned by Chris's father; a large establishment, both noisy and smelly, but as Chris had indicated, the property they had come to view was almost a mile beyond the foundry: far enough away to be free of most of the contaminated atmosphere.

During the walk to the property, young Simpkins took up the conversation, extolling its virtues with young enthusiasm, trying hard to secure the sale to impress his father and his father's partner.

'I suppose Mr Paxton has given you the history of the place we are going to see, Mrs Swain?' Simpkins queried.

'No, Mr Simpkins, I am sure you will do a good job,' Chris Paxton interjected, not wanting to dampen young Joseph's enthusiastic approach to the job in hand.

Frances realised her son-in-law had made the appointment in the name of Mrs Swain, of which she was pleased.

'Well,' Joseph continued, 'the property was the original farmhouse, built of stone and it stood alone before the industrialisation of the area. Mr Paxton's father bought the land belonging to the farmhouse as the site for his foundry. In the early days, the original farmhouse, served as the drawing office and engineers' department, providing both offices and sleeping accommodation for the engineering team. The successful expansion of Paxton's Foundry and Engineering Works has left the department somewhat divorced from the main site. Now a new, purpose-built Drawing Office and Engineering Department, has recently been added within the confines of the works, leaving the premises we are about to view, surplus to requirements,' the budding solicitor concluded as he ushered them down the main street that led to the property in question. They stopped outside an old stone-built farmhouse, of symmetrical design, with attractive mullioned windows either side of an impressive entrance. Protecting the blue front door to the property was a pair of columns supporting the porch, which Frances thought, was a more recent addition. On closer inspection, one could see where the extension to the front of the property, had been carried out, doubling it in size. Nonetheless, she approved of the addition.

On the front elevation, at the first level were three more windows all similar size and character giving a sense of balance to the whole structure. To the side of the property, there were three windows on each gable end.

*

At the end of the viewing of the property, Frances turned to her son-in-law and said, 'Mr Simpkins has been an exceptionally good guide today. Don't you agree Mr Paxton?'

'He has carried out his duties most admirably,' Chris Paxton replied.

'Please Mr Paxton, if you could somehow convey your sentiments to my father in that vein, it would stand me in good stead.'

'Have no fear, young sir; I will make sure it will be brought to his attention. As my father's legal affairs are in your father's capable hands, I am sure on their next meeting your prowess today could be the topic of their conversation.'

'I will be ever indebted to you, Mr Paxton.'

'Think nothing of it, sir; I too know how much store is placed on the shoulders of *'the sons of the fathers'*. Their expectations can place a crippling burden upon their young offspring.'

During this exchange, Frances smiled at young Simpkins's endeavour to please.

'This will be ideal for what I have in mind, Chris,' Frances said, thinking her enthusiasm for the premises would boost young Simpkins's confidence.

'I knew you would be impressed,' Chris Paxton replied.

'It is indeed a fine property and well preserved considering its age,' Joseph Simpkins enthused, not realising he did not have to sell this property as Chris Paxton had done all the convincing of Frances in advance. All that was now required of young Simpkins was to report to his father and get the legal wheels in motion.

'Thank you for your tour of the property, Joseph, you have been most informative both on the property itself and its history,' Chris Paxton said.

'I agree,' Frances added.

'All that is left is to agree the price with my father's company and we shall be in touch with your father in due course. I must add, time is of the essence in this matter,' Chris Paxton reminded their young guide.

'I am sure we will be as expeditious as possible in our task, sir,' the young clerk said.

'Of that I have no doubt, Joseph and now we must be getting back as we have a train to catch, which will take us back to Durham.'

Back at the offices of Gridley and Simpkins, Frances and Chris said their goodbyes to Joseph Simpkins.

'Convey our disappointment to your father for not seeing him today but we are in a tremendous hurry to get back as I am busy with my own business. As I said, Joseph, I will be purchasing the property on behalf of my mother-in-law and your father will be hearing from the Company soon. Thank you for all your splendid help today.' And with that, they set off back to the railway station.

*

On the journey back to Durham, Chris Paxton discussed the property. 'Do you realise, Frances, you have two options on the property? You can buy the freehold outright, or if you prefer you can rent the property; the choice is yours.'

'Well, I don't have to think too long on that question, Chris. As it was my first husband, Dan's desire to get our own farm, although for a different purpose, I think I have no other option but to buy the property outright and own the farmhouse for our family and myself. That way we will have indirectly, achieved Dan's dream and with the money for which he worked so hard, in his beloved America.'

'Well, I could not challenge you on the reason for your decision and having made that decision, I am sure I can persuade my father to use his influence to get the Company to let you have it at a price favourable to you. May I suggest, you take out a partial mortgage on the property to pay for the structural alterations required to convert the property to a domestic dwelling, thereby keeping a little in reserve for a rainy day, as they say.'

'I think that is sound advice, Chris; I will act upon what you suggest,' Frances concurred.

'Splendid, I will have a word with my father at first opportunity and set it all in motion with Gridley and Simpkins. With your approval, I will let my father know what your budget is, and I am sure he will make it well within your compass,' he said.

It was the opening night at the Theatre Royal, Newcastle. Chris Paxton had acquired two boxes, one for his father Miles Paxton and his party, and the other for Frances and her family.

On arrival at the theatre, the grandeur of the building impressed Frances. Built of sandstone, it had a magnificent portico supported by six huge Corinthian columns. It truly was a theatre royal in every sense of the word. A footman met the coaches on arrival and opened the doors and lowered the step for the occupants to alight. They were ushered inside the theatre where Jemima and Chris met them in the foyer.

After a short conversation, Jemima made her excuses as she had to prepare for her performance and she and Chris went back stage.

The theatre manager showed the party to their boxes by way of a magnificent staircase. Decorating the walls were sumptuous coverings and as she climbed the stairs, her feet sank into the deep pile of the carpet.

*

The orchestra settled into their places in the pit and with the random sound of the tuning of instruments fading away individually, the lights dimmed, and the curtain rose for the opening performance. A sole grand piano occupied the stage. Seated at the piano was a young Russian pianist who the master of ceremonies introduced as Vladimir Tomalin who for his opening number played the *Nocturne, in F sharp major,* by Frederick Chopin, which the audience received with rapturous applause. He closed his performance with an immaculate rendition of *Beethoven's Rondo in B flat major,* by which time the boys were getting restless and shuffled in their seats; not having heard of Beethoven let alone being familiar with his work. Much to the boys' annoyance and to the delight of the audience, he chose as an encore, another piece by Chopin, his *Mazurka, Opus 24, Nº 1.*

At the end of the young Russian's third solo piece for piano, the audience again gave him generous applause as he stepped forward gesturing his appreciation to the members of the orchestra who stood in the pit and received their own applause. With an exaggerated flourish of his right arm, high into the air and down across his midriff followed by an extended bow and drawing himself up once more to his full height, he turned and minced off the stage.

'When is Jemima coming on?' John asked which drew a discreet hush, from Frances as she gently pushed him back in his seat. The curtains closed behind him, and shuffling sounds emanated from behind the plush velvet scarlet curtain as they prepared the stage for the main act of the evening. The Master of Ceremonies again made his announcement introducing the star of the show as *'Mimi Martin',* the *'Norfolk Lark'.* The curtains parted, showing a stage decorated with a backdrop depicting an Italianesque garden. There, standing on a bridge reminiscent of Rome, was the star of the concert, *'Mimi Martin'.* She looked stunning in a long, white, classic-style, heavily pleated, sleeveless stola. Across the stola, she wore a crimson palla; a gold fibula fastened it to her left shoulder. The palla, drawn up onto the top of her head, partially covered her curly black hair.

Chris Paxton sat at the grand piano to the left of the stage as Mimi's accompanist for the performance. The lead violinist tapped his music stand twice and counted in the rest of the orchestra who struck up the introduction to a ballad entitled, *'I Dream of Jeannie with the Light Brown Hair',* by a contemporary American composer named Stephen Foster, who was presently taking New York by storm.

As she walked from the bridge to take her place, front of stage, she let slip the palla revealing her black curly hair piled in all its glory, atop of her head in Flavian style, completing the classic Roman effect.

Up in the box the boys, with renewed vigour focused their eyes on their sister now occupying centre stage. She completed the ballad and the audience applauded enthusiastically, rising to their feet with shouts of, 'More, more!' Chris Paxton left his stool and moved to the front of his piano.

'If you liked that, Mimi would like to sing another ballad this time by the Irish composer William Vincent Wallace, entitled '*Scenes that are the Brightest*', from his opera, *'Maritana.'*"

Jemima, alias Mimi, had the audience in the palm of her hand. They hung on her every note. She completed *Maritana's* aria and once more, the audience went wild with their appreciation of another musical treat.

Chris Paxton moved once more to the front of the piano. 'And now for the pièce de résistance, Mimi will now sing for your gratification, Lucia's aria, *'Regnava nel Silenzio'* – Silence Reigned in the Dark, Deep Night,' by Gaetano Donizetti, from his opera, *'Lucia di Lammermoor','* he announced.

Chris had rearranged the aria, shortening it by three minutes from its original duration, thus placing less demand on Jemima's voice. He had also rearranged the piece to suit her mezzo soprano range, Donizetti having composed the aria for a coloratura soprano. Jemima's dark and romantic voice lent itself to Donizetti's melodic music, and to complete the effect, Chris Paxton had arranged to have the lights dimmed to emulate the pallid glow of moonlight. Up in the box, the two eldest boys once more became restless before the end and again Frances had to reprimand them quietly. Meanwhile, little Dan had curled up in his seat and had gone to sleep. As the last note trailed away, enthusiastic cheers from the ecstatic audience led to a standing ovation, which did nothing to disturb him.

Jemima turned and looked at her husband, who smiled his approval. She reached out her left arm towards him and Chris joined his wife and together he bowed, and she curtsied repeatedly as they soaked up the applause. It was a moment in her life, Jemima would never forget; the moment when an artiste experiences for the first time, the power of an audience's adulation, which meant they had accepted her for her talent. She stood there in the centre of the stage holding Chris's hand and letting her head drop back, she looked up to the *gods* and for a few moments, she let the invigorating wave wash over her.

The noise of the crowd brought her back to reality with their cries of, 'More, more, encore, encore.'

Her husband, wanting to milk every drop of adulation, eventually gave the audience what they begged for and announced Mimi's encore as another aria from Wallace's Maritana, namely *'Tis the Harp in the Air'*, which was also received with the same rapturous applause. Finally, the audience allowed them to leave the stage. Once off stage, Jemima and Chris were showered with congratulations.

Frances was so proud of her daughter and her only regret was her father was not there to witness her success. The loud applause finally awakened Dan Jr. from his sleep. 'Is it time to go home?' he asked, rubbing both eyes with the knuckles of both index fingers.

Chapter 34

After her Newcastle success, Chris Paxton had booked Mimi Martin to appear at the Prince's Theatre, Glasgow. He had hired the theatre for the sum of £80 and the plan was to repeat the Newcastle programme, but it did not meet with the same success. It was obvious early in the first evening's proceedings that this Glasgow audience was not yet ready for a concert of music from the operas. While there was a ready and receptive following of grand opera developing in Queen Victoria's third city of her Empire, this audience was not part of that following. They had received Mimi's opening with the same enthusiasm as that which the audience had in Newcastle; but that is where the enthusiasm began to wane. The heckling began with a group in the balcony who were hell bent on disrupting Mimi's performance. They made it patently obvious, they were not prepared to tolerate any performance, no matter how good the performer's voice may be, or indeed, whoever the performer may be, if they were singing in a foreign language.

'Gi' us somethin' we ken,' yelled the main antagonist from up in the balcony, who appeared to be the worse for drink and determined to disrupt Mimi's performance for his own amusement.

That is rich coming from someone wanting a performance in English, thought Chris Paxton as he saw Mimi getting more and more agitated by the change in the reception she was receiving from a section of the crowd. The drunk's dissatisfaction spread rapidly through the audience like a candle flame to a sheet of tissue paper. At this point,

Mimi Martin could take no more of the crowd's barracking and she fled from the stage in tears followed by her husband, while the audience continued to barrack.

Off stage, Chris Paxton consoled his distressed wife. 'Do you think you could continue if I get them settled?' he asked her, hopefully.

'Only if I think they are prepared to listen to me,' she said, not convinced it was in the least bit possible.

'I can but try, but I make no promises. They are extremely irate,' he said, trying to gain time while he gathered his thoughts. This, Mimi thought was a gross understatement. Chris Paxton once more returned to the stage with his arms raised high above his head. With open palms and twisting his wrists to subdue the still complaining crowd as he took up his position downstage.

'Please! Please!' he yelled. The crowd totally ignored his appeal, which was hardly audible above the din. A man in evening dress seated in the front stalls jumped to his feet and turned to face the crowd.

'Quiet! Quiet!' he yelled, without immediate response. 'SILENCE!' he yelled, more emphatically. 'For goodness's sake, hear the man out and please, can't you see how distressed you are making Miss Martin? We have come out for a night at the theatre and to enjoy that experience, do not behave like a pack of hounds at the kill.'

This admonishment from a fellow member of the audience gave Chris the breathing space he required, and the crowd began to settle back to their seats.

With order restored, Chris Paxton addressed the auditorium once more. 'You appeared to enjoy the opening of the concert, did you not?' he asked.

'Aye, we did tha',' the drunk from the balcony yelled back.

'Well may I suggest, you allow Miss Martin to sing her full repertoire of Mr Stephen Foster's music for your delectation and I promise you, there will be nothing more in Italian.'

Slowly, after much muttering amongst themselves over the offer put to them by Chris Paxton, the audience quietened and as they settled back into their seats, Chris Paxton disappeared briefly from the stage and returned leading a red-eyed Mimi nervously back centre stage. The gentleman who had shown his support rose once more to his feet and began to applaud Mimi as she composed herself once again for the recommencement of her interrupted performance. Taking his lead, the rest of the audience clapped their support and the drunk slouched deeper in his seat, his moment of infamy over.

The rest of the concert went off without incident and at the end of her performance Mimi Martin left the stage to mixed applause; not a single encore was called for.

Back in her dressing room, Jemima Paxton sat at the dulled mirror which had seen better days; straining her eyes as she attempted to catch more reflected light from the glass with its silver backing creeping in from the edges. She talked to her husband's incongruous image as she attempted to remove her stage make-up. 'I shall never appear in Scotland again, not even if it is the only work I can get, I will give up the stage completely before I return to this place,' Jemima stated to her husband adamantly.

'Come now, my dear, you are bound to get an audience like tonight's some time or another. I know how harrowing the whole incident has been for you. In the end, I thought you handled the whole affair magnificently. There are bound to be other similar occasions throughout your career. Put it down to experience and out of your mind, my dearest. I take full responsibility for overestimating the type of audience you would have drawn in this area of Glasgow. The truth is, not all the audience were ready for Italian opera. Maybe, at some future date, we shall see,' he said finally.

'I shall leave that to someone else to prove as I have had my fill of the place. I am only pleased my family were not in the audience tonight to witness such humiliation,' Jemima said angrily. 'Had we not committed £80 to this week's run, I would suggest we closed after tonight and cut our losses.'

A sharp knock came on the door and the pageboy's voice announced, 'You have a visitor, Miss Martin.'

'One moment, please,' her husband replied.

Turning to Jemima, he asked in an undertone, 'Are you ready to receive anyone?'

'Not if it is that baying mob,' she said, her humour returning.

Chris Paxton slowly opened the door barely ajar and peeped out. On the other side of the door was a man in evening dress who he immediately recognised as he who had silenced the crowd during the fracas earlier in the evening.

The visitor held a business card in a white gloved hand, which he proffered through the partially opened door.

'Good evening, may I present my card? I would like a few moments of Miss Martin's precious time, if it is possible,' he requested politely.

Having already recognised the visitor, Chris Paxton invited him in.

'Please come in er… Colonel Mapson,' quickly reading the name from the business card as he opened the door to the stranger. He passed the card to Jemima before stepping aside and closing the door behind the visitor.

'It is so good of you to receive me unannounced like this. I had to see you before you left for your hotel. First, let me apologise for the unforgivable behaviour of that mob of an audience, which you had the misfortune to experience this evening. The behaviour of a certain minority was utterly despicable, and the rest were unforgivable for allowing themselves to be dragged to that level also.'

'On the contrary, Colonel Mapson, it is we who should be thanking you for the way you subdued the audience when they were at their intolerable worst, it was most chivalrous of you, and we shall be ever indebted to you,' Chris Paxton said.

'Put it down to my military training,' James Mapson replied.

Turning to Jemima, Chris Paxton said, 'May I introduce my wife, Miss Mimi Martin.'

'I am your servant, madam,' he said as he bowed and kissed Jemima's hand lightly. Jemima read the card:

Col. James H Mapson

Assistant Manager

Queen's Theatre

London.

'I am here tonight specially to hear you sing following a friend having attended your concert in Newcastle. He reported back to me and using his words, *she is a star in the making,* and I must admit I agree entirely. The reason I wanted to meet you both was to tell you I am putting on a production of *'The Bohemian Girl'* and I would like to offer you the part of *'Arline',* the daughter of the *'Count of Arnheim'.* I would not dream of holding you to an instant decision, as rehearsals for the production do not commence until the autumn in readiness for a December opening. You have my card and I await your reply, in your own time, of course. We can talk money when you have made your decision. Thank you, Miss Martin, for a most enjoyable evening of Stephen Foster. Good luck for the rest of the run here,' the Colonel said as he bid his goodbyes.

'Oh! One more thing before I go, I think you will be singing Italian opera to this lot before the week is out; believe me the word will get around now you have made them curious. Give it one more try.' He bowed once more and left the room.

'Well what do you think of that, Jemima?' Chris Paxton asked, after James Mapson had left.

'We shall certainly need his good luck wishes for the rest of the week here,' she replied.

'No, you know what I mean, darling, a season in London, at the Haymarket no less and so soon in your career. It's a wonderful offer and it fits in perfectly with my plans for the rest of your provincial tour,' Chris Paxton enthused.

His plans for Mimi Martin's provincial tour would take in, after Glasgow, the Royal Alhambra, Leeds, the Queen's Theatre, Manchester, culminating at the Royal Music Hall, Birmingham. 'Following Birmingham, we can have a short break back in Durham, before your debut season in the capital,' he said rather grandly as he quickly re-planned Mimi Martin's new itinerary following Colonel Mapson's offer. An offer of the female lead in his production of '*The Bohemian Girl*' appeared to be Heaven sent. This offer took the sting out of the unsavoury happenings earlier in the evening.

'This calls for a nightcap before we retire for the night, my dear,' Chris Paxton suggested and he kissed his wife on the top of her head as she continued to remove the rest of her make-up. James Mapson's prediction was correct and after the third night, Chris re-introduced the operatic arias, which the audience received with mild enthusiasm. A success by comparison.

Chapter 35

Frances Swain had reverted to her beloved Dan's name and settled into her boarding house in Standale; she loved the situation. Standing at her front door, she could look with an uninterrupted view north across to where the River Wear cut its way through the verdant valley, towered over by limestone escarpments. How she wished Dan was here, with her, to share the view. *He would have loved this place,* she thought.

Paxton's foundry, ideally situated with its links by railway to the coalfields of Northumberland and Durham to the north, the iron ore mines of Cleveland to the southeast and the Darlington railway works to the south of the county, placed it in the hub of the industrial revolution in the northeast of England. Business was good and her boarders were mostly long-term.

Towards the end of 1859 her sons Edward, now eighteen years old, and John, now sixteen, were both working as platelayers on the railway. They both liked the open air and neither of them fancied working inside a foundry; working at plate laying gave them the outdoors, which they preferred, something they must have inherited from their father. Dan Jr., now eight, was showing a great interest in all things mechanical and liked nothing more than going on a tour of the foundry with Miles Paxton who paid him much attention.

Frances was also thrilled at the direction in which Jemima's singing career was heading. She had no knowledge of the problem in Glasgow. Letters from Jemima had only revealed the provincial tour was now in Birmingham and audiences at all of Mimi Martin's appearances had received her with great enthusiasm, with the next stop a season at the Queen's Theatre, London, at the end of 1859. The latest letter from Jemima had indicated they would be returning to Durham at the end of the Birmingham run, for a short break before setting off for London for the beginning of rehearsals in September, in readiness for the opening in December.

'You have put on weight, Jemima, notwithstanding your gruelling schedule,' Frances said when her daughter and son-in-law visited her at the boarding house in Stanford.

'I think all mothers see what they want to see,' Jemima replied.

'Speaking of gruelling schedules, Frances, I hope you don't think I have been overworking her,' Chris Paxton quickly interjected.

'I hope not, or you will have to answer to me,' Frances replied, her mother hen protectiveness still strong even though Jemima was now a grown woman.

'Don't worry on that score, Mama, he has too much invested in me to allow any threat to his investment,' Jemima said. 'The truth of the matter is, I must keep up my stamina to cope with the long arias, despite Chris's clever re-arrangements to make them a little less demanding. Professor Colbert may not have been completely correct in saying I would not have the physique for grand opera, but he was correct in saying I would need to have lots of stamina to withstand long runs, plus the travelling,' she stated.

'You have worked wonders with this place; I think the changes you have made, make it much more fit for purpose,' Chris Paxton said approvingly.

'Do you think so, Chris? The alterations do allow me to use the house to its full potential without the boys and me losing our privacy. There are plenty of would-be occupants up at the works waiting to take a room here. Moreover, we are so happy here, Chris. Thanks to you and Jeremy Bolton, I never think of Robert Hart; this place keeps me too occupied to dwell on that part of my life. Although it is a time

I would rather forget, in doing so, let us not forget Robert Hart completely – even if he had ulterior motives – he *did* get the children and me out of the workhouse. There are times when I sit at the front door on a fine summer evening, looking out towards Weardale, I often think how much Dan would have loved being here in his own place before he was cruelly taken from us. Oh, how I still miss him,' Frances said with tears forming in her eyes as she remembered her first love. 'Please forgive me, I am being maudlin,' she added as she dabbed her eyes with her handkerchief.

'Not at all, Mama, I know how much you loved Father,' Jemima said as she placed a reassuring arm around her mother's shoulders.

Chapter 36

December 1859

'*The Bohemian Girl*' opened to a packed audience at the Queen's Theatre on Thursday 8th December 1859 and continued to draw the crowds throughout its run. Mimi Martin in the role of Arline was the talk of London. Over the years, her voice had matured to a well-rounded soprano. Moreover, contrary to what Professor Colbert had opined back in 1852 when Jemima was thirteen, it now had a rich quality in the lower register also. The show was such a success; they had decided to extend the original eight-week run to twelve. Mid-way through the run, Mimi Martin sat in the star's dressing room removing her make-up following yet another successful performance. Chris Paxton sat drinking a brandy as he waited patiently as his wife slowly metamorphosed from Arline – daughter of Count Arnheim – to Jemima Paxton, also known as Mimi Martin. 'You get better with each performance, darling,' he told her. A knock sounded on the dressing room door. Chris Paxton rose and opened it to find Colonel Mapson on the other side. 'Come in, Colonel,' Chris Paxton said, stepping aside as the Colonel breezed past him.

'Sorry to disturb you,' he said excitedly, 'but I have great news, which I'm bursting to reveal. In the audience tonight was no other than Reuben Goldstein, the American impresario, and he wants to take the show to New York at the end of the present London run.

Mimi, you are on your way; Broadway beckons you. I hope you have no objections but as tomorrow is Sunday and no performance, I have booked a table for the four of us at Rossetti's Supper Rooms for tomorrow evening. I do hope that's alright with you both.'

'Supper with Reuben Goldstein, how could we disapprove? That is fantastic, James,' Chris Paxton enthused. 'What do you say, Jemima?'

'My appearing on Broadway had never crossed my mind. Never in my wildest dreams did I think I would be going to America so soon in my career. When I first met you, Chris, on that fateful day I sang at your friends' wedding, I never thought I would have got this far, let alone America. It is all down to you.'

'Come now, my dear, it is your talent that Goldstein has recognised, and I am sure, Chris will agree with me. I must say Chris has done a great job in steering you in the right direction,' James Mapson declared. 'Tomorrow it is then. We shall look forward to it.'

*

Chris and Jemima entered Rossetti's Supper Rooms and were greeted by Mario the maître d'.

'Good evening Mr Paxton, Miss Martin. How delightful to see you both again. Colonel Mapson is expecting you. Please, this way.' He led them on a zigzag course between the tables. En route, several patrons congratulated Mimi on her performance in her current role. They reached the table, one of the better ones set in a private alcove on the periphery of the room. Colonel Mapson and the other gentleman rose from their seats as Jemima and Chris approached. Colonel Mapson held the chair for Jemima as she and Chris took their seats.

'Reuben, let me introduce you to Miss Mimi Martin known in this country as the Norfolk Lark; Mimi, this is the famous New York impresario Reuben Goldstein, who has come all the way across the Atlantic to hear you sing and from what he has told me, he is pleased he has made the journey,' James Mapson said enthusiastically.

'And soon, I hope to make you as famous in America; my pleasure Miss Martin,' Reuben Goldstein said as he offered Jemima his hand.

'And this Reuben is Mimi's husband and mentor, Chris Paxton. The man who, more than anyone is responsible for furthering Mimi's career,' Mapson said in generous praise of Chris.

'How so good it is to meet you Mr Goldstein,' Chris Paxton said, deliberately keeping his opening exchange to a minimum.

'Let me say here and now, it's mutual,' Goldstein said, being equally brief in return.

'In your absence, I took the liberty of ordering the fish which comes highly recommended by Mario. In the meantime, Reuben would like to run through his idea of taking the show to New York. Reuben, it's all yours,' Mapson said, subconsciously adopting the American expression.

'Thank you, James,' he said and settling his look in the direction of Jemima, he continued. 'My plan is to put the show on at Niblo's Garden a theatre on Broadway near Prince Street. It can seat 3,000 people at possibly $2 a time. We will confirm these figures later after we have discussed it further with the owners as to admission prices. This would give us a better idea of the financial potential.

'The way I see it, if the Broadway run proves as successful as here in London, we will take it on an all-American tour, culminating in Boston before your return to England. We will work out the full itinerary later but, meanwhile, think it over. One way or another, I think we are on to a winner starting with a grand opening in New York.'

During the supper, Reuben Bernstein set out his draft plans for taking *'The Bohemian Girl'* to Broadway.

'Your run here is due to close in mid-March and allowing a couple of months to get the show across to America, I foresee auditioning of support cast members taking us into June, with hopefully an opening in time for the summer season on Broadway. More realistic dates will be established once we have everything organised stateside,'

Bernstein concluded.

'Ah! The fish,' Mapson declared as the waiters arrived at the table carrying a fish kettle containing a whole wild salmon which one of the waiters proceeded to expertly fillet.

Chapter 37

New York

1890

Jemima and Chris made the journey across the Atlantic by steam ship, which unlike the journey her late father had experienced eleven years earlier was both quick and disease free.

In the company of her husband and impresario Reuben Bernstein, Jemima walked out onto the stage at the empty Niblo's Garden. She was impressed at the size and the construction of the theatre.

'In 1846, fire had destroyed the first theatre built on the site. Rebuilt in 1849, they introduced Italian opera in 1850 and tomorrow we start the production of an opera by Irishman, Michael William Balfe,' Reuben Bernstein declared and turning to his leading lady, Bernstein declared confidently, 'My dear, you are going to knock 'em dead.'

Looking out from the stage into the empty auditorium, beyond the extinguished footlights, and beyond the empty orchestra pit, the floor of the theatre was semi-circular in shape. Following the curve of the semi-circle were the private boxes. Above these and built on the same curve was the balcony; towering above this was the gods. As she stood there, Jemima gave forth with an impromptu few bars from one of Arline's arias and the sound resonated around the empty theatre for several seconds after she had released the final note. The acoustics were impressive. 'This will do nicely, I cannot believe I am here on Broadway, New York,' she said with awe.

With the auditioning for the American cast completed, tomorrow would see the commencement of rehearsals of the American production of *'The Bohemian Girl'* starring Mimi Martin in the female lead.

*

The show opened to great acclaim and after the first-night performance Reuben Bernstein sat in Jemima's dressing room with Chris Paxton and one or two other leading members of the cast.

'You were marvellous, Mimi,' Bernstein said, 'absolutely marvellous,' he reiterated, 'everyone was marvellous,' he continued enthusiastically. He swept his arm all about him and immediately went into generous applause. 'I know the show is going to be a huge success and I thank you all, but now I must take my leave of you, I have business to attend to. I have laid on champagne for you to celebrate a great opening night, enjoy yourselves,' and he immediately left the cramped dressing room.

After a couple of glasses of champagne Jemima caught her husband's eye and surreptitiously indicated to him, it was time for the rest to leave.

'Please may I have your attention for a moment? Thank you everyone,' he said, 'but I want Mimi to have an early night; it has been a tiring day for her and there is a busy time ahead of you all. Please, take the rest of the champagne with you if you so wish. See you all tomorrow, but for now – goodnight,' Chris announced.

'My dressing room is free, and you are all welcome to continue the party there; let's go,' declared Alistair Champion, Mimi's leading man. The other cast members slowly exited the dressing room and taking the champagne bottles and glasses with them, they chattered noisily as they made their way along the corridor to Champion's dressing room, leaving Jemima and Chris finally alone.

Chris Paxton took his wife in his arms and kissed her tenderly. 'Bernstein was right, you were marvellous, my darling, I do not think I have ever heard you sing so beautifully. The part could have been written especially for you; you made it your own tonight,' he said proudly and kissed her once more.

'Thank you. my darling,' Jemima said. 'I'm so glad it went so well. I had certain misgivings about how an American audience would receive me,' she admitted.

'You have nothing to worry about, you had them hanging on your every note. Now they know whom 'Mimi Martin', the 'Norfolk Lark' is, you are going to conquer America,' he predicted emphatically.

'Thank you for your confidence in me, kind sir,' she said in mock coyness.

'The reason I wanted rid of the rest, was to talk to you. I have been thinking, here we are in New York, the place where my dear father met his death, and I would like to attend church to say a silent prayer to his memory. There must be a church somewhere near, which we could attend this coming Sunday,' she suggested.

'Of course, my dear, it is understandable, you should want to remember your father especially now you are here in New York,' Chris Paxton agreed. There is Trinity Church on Broadway, we will find out the times of service and attend there.'

'Would you mind, Chris? It would mean so much to me, if we could.'

'We will try to attend this Sunday, Jemima,' Chris replied.

*

Sunday arrived and Jemima and Chris found themselves making their way to Trinity Church for morning service. On approach, they were impressed by the ornate spire, which Chris Paxton estimated, rose almost three hundred feet above the ground. 'This is a fine example of Gothic Revival architecture, I can't believe we failed to see that spire from the water as we steamed into our berth in New York harbour,' Chris Paxton declared. They entered and the beauty of the interior, which was both light and elegant, did not let down the magnificence of the exterior. A sense of peace and tranquillity exuded from the fabric of the place. Chris Paxton continued to extol the beauty in its design and the artistry in its construction. The light passing through the huge stained-glass window, which occupied most of the wall behind the altar, projected a myriad of coloured lights into the nave.

On entering, they chose seats at the rear of the church to the left of the huge bronze doors. To Jemima a sense of divine guidance had drawn her here and she soon slipped into silent prayer asking God to protect the soul of her departed father, murdered ten years previously.

They stayed in church throughout the service and on leaving, a young black man stepped from one of the little knots of people standing chatting outside the church. He was smartly dressed in a fine checked, brown tweed suit of expensive cut and politely doffing his brown derby hat, he introduced himself.

'Excuse me, Miss Martin. 'You too, sir,' turning to Chris Paxton. 'My name is Thomas Mays. I would like to say how much I enjoyed your portrayal of Arline in *The Bohemian Girl*, which I had the pleasure of attending on the opening night. If I may say so, your rendition of *I Dreamt I Dwelt in Marble Halls*, was sheer bliss.'

'How kind of you to say so; I am so pleased you enjoyed the show, Mr... I am sorry, your name again please?'

'Mays, Miss Martin... Thomas Mays,' the young black man replied. Jemima, taken by his smart dress and his articulation continued the conversation. 'How strange, my late father wrote of a young Thomas Mays, whom he had met on arriving in New York in 1849, you couldn't possibly be he, could you?'

'I may possibly be he, if only your name were Jemima Swain and not Mimi Martin,' the black man replied.

Jemima, taken aback by this chance meeting with this name from the past remained speechless as she gathered her thoughts. She recalled her father's letter from America ...*I have met this young black boy called Thomas Mays…* Her thoughts quickly returned to things of the present. 'What a strange quirk of fate this is turning out to be, Mr Mays, for my given name is indeed Jemima and this is my husband and manager Chris Paxton.' Chris Paxton shook hands with the young stranger.

'Pleased to meet you, sir, what an astonishing coincidence, it must be kismet,' Chris Paxton said.

'My maiden name was, indeed, Jemima Swain and my father was Dan Swain. Mimi Martin is my stage name,' Jemima revealed.

'I cannot believe I have the great pleasure of meeting the daughter of my benefactor Dan Swain. I owe everything to your late father, Miss Martin; he was truly a fine man. He gave me my start in life for which I will be eternally grateful. Had he not made the journey across the Atlantic, goodness only knows how I may have turned out. It would seem your father did not die in vain; for in the short time I knew him, he transformed my life. It was when we were returning from the Emigrants' Savings Bank on that fateful day in February of 1850, that he met his death. Oh! How insensitive of me, Miss Martin, you may not want me to bring the subject up right now.'

'No Thomas, on the contrary, I am eager to hear your account of how my father died, please continue.'

'We were returning from the bank where your father had been instrumental in opening the first bank account I ever had in my name. If only I had not left my passbook behind I would have been with him when his assailant struck. As it was, I had returned to the bank to retrieve it and on my return journey, on reaching the point where I had left Mr Dan, I found him lying on the pavement, fatally wounded and his lifeblood draining from him. Please tell me if you wish me to curtail my account of your father's murder, Miss Martin.'

'Please, carry on Thomas,' she replied.

'I alerted the police but when they returned your father lay dead. I can show you the spot and his grave if you so wish, Miss Martin, if you won't find it too distressing.'

'Not at all, Thomas, it would appear we were destined to meet. It was fortunate we decided to attend church this morning. It would seem it is what my father wanted me to do. At least I would like to think that was so.'

Chris Paxton spoke up. 'Are you sure you want to go through with this, darling?'

'I am certain, Chris, I have never been so certain of anything in my life,' she replied.

'In which case, lead on, sir,' Chris Paxton instructed the young black man.

The sombre party of three reached the junction of Little Water Street and Cross Street, the spot where Jemima's father had met his death. They remained with heads bowed, reverently contemplating the scene of the heinous crime ten years ago. No words passed between them for a few moments. Thomas was the first to break the silence.

'I don't come here if I can avoid it. It holds too many sad memories for me.' The other two continued staring at the ground. Even though it was summer, a chill caused the hairs to rise on the back of Jemima's neck. The sun's rays failed to reach into the street where her father had met his death, adding to the macabre atmosphere of the place. She continued to stare at the ground in pensive mood, visualising her late father's body lying on the cold cobbles at her feet. After a while, Jemima said, 'You can show us the grave now, Thomas, if it is no trouble to you.'

'Not at all, Miss Martin, I deem it my duty to guide you to these places that mean so much to you.'

They followed Thomas through the streets of New York as Dan Swain had done all those years ago. They reached an incongruous graveyard and Thomas led them to a grave with an understated headstone. Jemima read the inscription, 'Daniel Swain', then a space. 'Murdered 23rd February 1850', was all it stated. *Is this all that is left of my father's great American dream, a headstone with an incomplete inscription in some nondescript corner of New York?* she asked herself, noticing the graveyard bore no name, nor was it attached to a church.

'I had the headstone erected about a year after your father died, Miss Martin, but I couldn't put your father's year of birth or his age at the time of his death, on the inscription as I did not know it at the time; now I can complete the details.'

'1817, was the year he was born,' Jemima stated.

'I will have those details added as soon as I can arrange it with the stonemason. It is consecrated ground, as it was once part of an Episcopalian Church, which once stood here. Unfortunately, being constructed mainly of timber, it was destroyed by fire about three years ago now and that warehouse now stands where the church once stood,' Thomas Mays explained.

'That's kind of you, Thomas,' Jemima said.

'Think nothing of it, Miss Martin; thanks to your late father's generosity I am now rich. I developed the business and I invested many of my profits successfully in the New York Central Railroad, ironically, the railroad my late father was working on when he met his death. I visit your father's grave regularly to keep it tidy; your father meant so much to me.' Thomas led them back to Broadway where he left them a few blocks from their hotel.

'Please join us later for dinner at our hotel, the Metropolitan, next to the theatre; shall we say nine o'clock?' Jemima suggested.

'Until later then,' Chris Paxton said as he once more shook Thomas's hand.

'Thank you for everything, Thomas; your company has been our pleasure and we look forward to enjoying your company later,' Jemima said as they parted.

'How strange we should choose that particular church to attend, and to meet no other than Thomas Mays,' said Jemima.

'Strange indeed,' her husband replied.

'I am so pleased we came to New York; I have discovered so much tangible evidence of my father's achievement in the short time he was here. Moreover, by making the journey he had inadvertently changed the course of not only *my* life, but also that of Thomas Mays.'

Jemima stopped and suddenly looking skyward, said, 'Listen, Chris.' They both stood listening for a moment.

Chris Paxton was the first to break the brief silence. 'What are we listening for, my dear?'

'Is that the beautiful song of a lark I can hear?'

Chris Paxton listened, more intently this time, before stating, 'I am afraid, my dear, the only lark over New York this season is you… Mimi Martin… The Norfolk Lark.'

The End

ABOUT THE AUTHOR

I was born in County Durham but lived most of my life in Wiltshire. I got the idea for my book when I was researching my family tree. I reached an enigmatic phase, which despite my efforts I was unable to surmount. So, by embroidering the truth I hope I have created a good read. Much of the story is based on my great-grandfather who lived in Norfolk and married three times.